MATHS

DINOSAUR dig

Wendy Clemson and Frances Clemson

Tick Tock

An Hachette UK Company
www.hachette.co.uk
Copyright © Octopus Publishing Group Ltd 2013
First published in Great Britain in 2013 by TickTock, an imprint of
Octopus Publishing Group Ltd, Endeavour House, 189 Shaftesbury Avenue, London WC2H 8JY.
www.octopusbooks.co.uk

ISBN 978 1 84898 913 9

Printed and bound in China

10 9 8 7 6 5 4 3 2 1

Picture credits
t=top, b=bottom, c=center, l=left, r=right, f=far
1, 2, 3FR, 26B, 27T, 31T Lisa Alderson. 3FL, 3L, 3C, 3R, 6L, 6R, 17, 14BCL, 14BFR, 14BCR, 34T, 26T, 29B, 31B, 32 Simon Mendez.
5, 6C, 7B, 8L, 11B, 21, 23, 29T, 30 Luis Rey. 4TL, 4BL, 4TR, 8-9, 9T, 15B, 20, 27CL, 27C, 28T, 28L Shutterstock. 4BR BananaStock/Alamy.
14T David R. Frazier Photolibrary, Inc./Alamy. 19 Louie Psihoyos/Corbis. 15T Royalty-Free/Corbis. 24B, 25 The Natural History Museum, London.
27B Roger Harris/Science Photo Library. 18 Larry Miller/Science Photo Library. 13 Sinclair Stammers/Science Photo Library.
7T, 10, 11T, 12T, 12B, 14BFL 27CR, 28FL, 28R, 28FR Ticktock Media Archive.
Front cover: Shutterstock
Back cover: Ticktock Media Archive

Contents

MATHS SKILLS COVERED IN THIS BOOK:

Numbers and the number system
Comparing and ordering: p. 10
Comparing numbers: p. 6
Counting in tens: p. 15
Counting in twos: p. 7
Fractions: pp. 9–10, 23
Money: pp. 28–29
Number line: p. 24
Number order: p. 14
Odds and evens: p. 17

Mental calculations
Addition and subtraction: pp. 6, 8–9, 21–22, 29
Counting: pp. 6, 11, 20
Difference: p 22
Division: pp. 20, 26
Missing numbers: p. 24
Multiplication: pp. 9, 12, 15, 18, 20, 22

Shape, space, and measurements
Angles: p. 23
Comparing measures: pp. 12, 23–24, 26
Estimates: pp. 7, 13
Measures: pp. 8–12
Measuring equipment: p. 16
Measuring with a ruler: p. 11
Putting measures in order: p. 14
Scales and dials: p. 22
Solid shapes: p. 28
Units of measurement: pp. 7, 23
Using a ruler: p. 11

Organizing data
Block graph: p. 13
Charts: pp. 11, 16, 18, 20
Grid maps: p. 9
Sorting: pp. 17, 19

Problem solving
Finding the difference: p. 22
Length: p. 10
Predicting patterns: p. 16
Working out costs: p. 29

Supports the maths work taught at Key Stage 1/2

Let's Start Digging

You have an exciting job. You're a dinosaur expert! Dinosaurs lived millions of years ago. You try to find their bones, eggs and footprints. You use these clues to help you discover how dinosaurs lived. Then you tell everybody else what you have discovered!

What does a dinosaur expert do?

Look for bones that have been buried for millions of years.

Write about your finds and read what other scientists have written.

Show your dinosaur discoveries in a museum.

Sometimes you talk to children about your job.

But did you know that dinosaur experts sometimes have to use maths?

In this book you will find lots of number puzzles that dinosaur experts have to solve every day. You will also get the chance to answer lots of number questions about bones and fossils and find out a lot about dinosaurs, too.

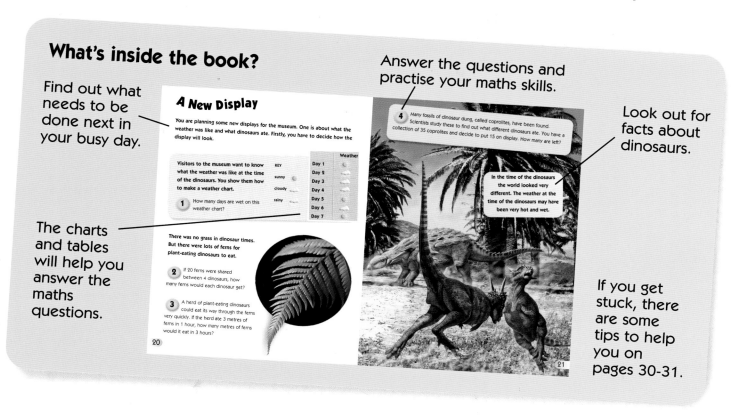

What's inside the book?

Find out what needs to be done next in your busy day.

The charts and tables will help you answer the maths questions.

Answer the questions and practise your maths skills.

Look out for facts about dinosaurs.

If you get stuck, there are some tips to help you on pages 30-31.

Are you ready to be a dinosaur hunter for the day?

You will need paper, a pencil, a ruler and don't forget to bring your shovel! Let's go...

Walking with Dinosaurs

Hunting dinosaurs is not as difficult as you might think. Dinosaurs roamed the Earth millions of years ago. They have left a lot behind them, including footprints, eggs and bones. Today you are going on a journey to search for dinosaur bones in North America.

The time when dinosaurs lived is divided into three different periods.

- **Cretaceous Period**
- **Jurassic Period**
- **Triassic Period**

This map shows some places where dinosaur fossils have been found.

Map of Canada and the United States

1 How many Triassic sites are there?

2 Which period has the most sites?

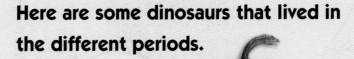

Here are some dinosaurs that lived in the different periods.

Diplodocus
lived 150 million years ago

Liliensternus
lived 220 million years ago

Triceratops
lived 70 million years ago

3 Which dinosaur lived longest ago?

You have arrived at a site in the desert where the ground is dry and rocky. You know dinosaurs used to live here. Suddenly you see a giant footprint.

4 Look at this dinosaur footprint next to a hand. How many hands do you think might fit across this footprint?

1   2 to 3   more than 3

Some dinosaurs went around in groups called herds. This helped to protect them from enemies. A herd may have been very large. Fossil hunters have found up to 30 dinosaur skeletons in one place.

5 Try making 30 by adding the same number many times. 30 is
30 ones   3 tens   how many twos?

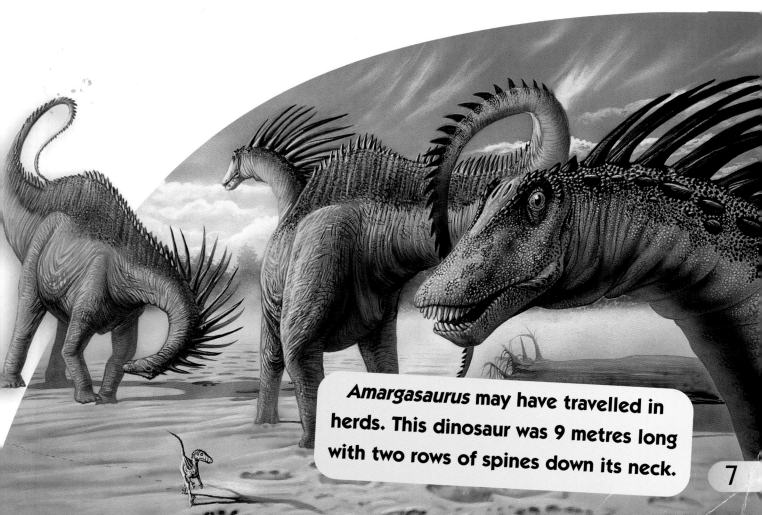

Amargasaurus may have travelled in herds. This dinosaur was 9 metres long with two rows of spines down its neck.

Whose Footprint?

You have to find out which dinosaur made this footprint. You look it up in a book. It looks like the footprint of *Iguanodon*. This dinosaur usually moved on all four feet but it could also stand on just its back feet. This made *Iguanodon* different from other dinosaurs.

1 *Iguanodon* had three toes on each of its feet. Its front feet also had a thumb and a spike for holding plants. How many toes did *Iguanodon* have all together?

2 *Iguanodon* was 10 metres long from the tip of its nose to the end of its tail. If its tail was 3 metres long, how long would the rest of it be?

A dinosaur footprint, showing the three toes of the back foot.

You find three more footprints, and you decide to make some plaster casts to take back to the museum.

Instructions

1. Mix the plaster with some water.
   Use 1 litre of water for 1 pack of plaster.
2. Pour the mixture into the footprint.
3. Wait 5 minutes for the plaster to dry.
4. Ease out the plaster cast.

3 It takes you 15 minutes to make each plaster cast. How much of this time is spent waiting for the plaster to dry?

1/2 **1/4** **1/3**

4 How many litres of water do you need if you use 3 packs of plaster?

5 If you make 8 plaster casts of each of the front feet and 3 of each of the back feet, how many casts will you have in total?

6 Now you draw a plan to show where you found each footprint. Starting from the back left footprint, which footprint did you find 2 squares up and 2 squares right?

Bony Clues

You collect other bits of bone that you find. Then you spot something half buried in the sand. You hurry towards it, careful not to tread on any other fossils. It looks as if it might be part of the leg of the dinosaur *Stegosaurus*.

Stegosaurus was 9 metres long. It had two lines of plates along its back. At the end of its tail it had 4 long, sharp spikes which it could swing at attackers.

1 One of the bits of bone you find is 50 centimetres long. If this is half of the bone, how long was the bone?

LENGTH OF BONES

You collect three dinosaur bones. You draw a sketch of them and write the length of the bone underneath.

Front leg bone
1 metre

Hip bone
2 metres

Back leg bone
20 centimetres

2 Put the bones in order from longest to shortest.

Now you have found a tooth – this is very exciting. We know what dinosaurs ate by what their teeth look like. Plant-eaters' teeth were not very sharp. Meat-eaters had very sharp teeth. They were pointed and of different sizes.

3 Measure this dinosaur tooth with a ruler. What is its length?

You check a chart which tells you which kinds of dinosaurs were meat-eaters and which were plant-eaters.

4 How many dinosaurs in this chart are plant-eaters?

Plant-eaters	Meat-eaters
Diplodocus	Tyrannosaurus
Stegosaurus	Oviraptor
Triceratops	Velociraptor
Iguanodon	

5 How many dinosaurs are there all together?

Tyrannosaurus weighed 6 tonnes. That's the same as over 200 children!

Fossil Finds

Next, you visit some cliffs. This is a good place to find some fossils of sea creatures. You are looking for ammonites, which were alive at the same time as the dinosaurs, and trilobites, which lived millions of years before them.

There were over 10,000 different types of trilobites. They varied in size from 2 cm to 50 cm.

1 Which of the numbers below mean 50 cm?

Half a metre

½ metre

A quarter of a metre

One metre

Fifty centimetres

Trilobites were one of the first animals on Earth.

2 You find three ammonite fossils like this. Each one is 20 cm across. You pack them side by side into a box. How long does your box have to be?

3 You pack another box. This has three rows of fossils with four fossils in each row. How many fossils are in the box?

4 Look at this picture of a
rock. How many ammonite fossils do you think are in this picture?

A. about 5

B. about 10

C. about 25

COUNTING YOUR FINDS

5 You find 4 plant fossils,
9 ammonites and
6 trilobites. You draw a block
graph to show what you have
found. But wait, you have made
a mistake. Look at the graph.
Can you spot the mistake?

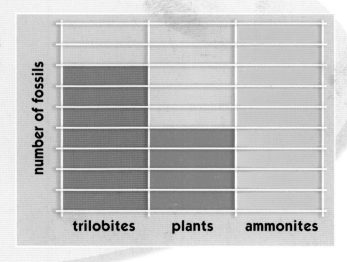

number of fossils

trilobites   plants   ammonites

To the Museum

You now have to take your fossils back to the museum. Because you are on a site in the middle of the desert, you are picked up by helicopter and flown back to the museum.

The first thing you see at the museum is the awesome skeleton of the mighty *Tyrannosaurus*. This dinosaur moved around on its hind legs. It had between 50 and 60 teeth. It could easily crush the bones of other dinosaurs.

Tyrannosaurus had a huge head. Its skull was over 1 metre long.

1 Which of these numbers are between 50 and 60?

53   62   75   57   65   49

Tyrannosaurus was big, but it was not the heaviest dinosaur. Many plant-eating dinosaurs weighed much more.

Apatosaurus
30 to 38 tonnes

Triceratops
6 to 12 tonnes

Tyrannosaurus
5 to 7 tonnes

Brachiosaurus
33 to 48 tonnes

2 Put these in order from the lightest dinosaur to the heaviest dinosaur. Use the greatest weight for each kind of dinosaur.

One of your favourite exhibits at the museum is *Apatosaurus*. It took about 10 years for *Apatosaurus* to become fully grown. It may have lived for 100 years in total.

3 How many tens in 100?

Apatosaurus had a huge neck. It could easily reach the tops of trees to eat.

Triceratops was a plant-eater. Its name means "three-horned face." Its 3 horns helped it to defend itself against meat-eaters like Tyrannosaurus.

4 There are 5 *Triceratops* on display, how many horns is that in total?

Triceratops lived in North America. It ate bushes and trees.

Labelling Finds

You take your finds to the museum storeroom. Here you have to label each one. Each bone, tooth, fossil, or footprint is given a label with a code on it.

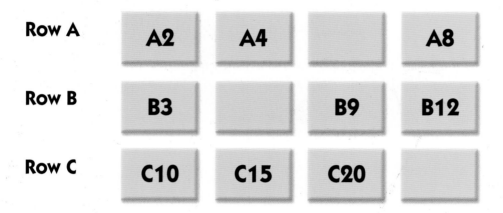

Row A   A2   A4   [ ]   A8

Row B   B3   [ ]   B9   B12

Row C   C10   C15   C20   [ ]

1 Choose the correct labels below to fill in the gaps in each set above.

A1   C26   B8   B6   A6   C25

You also have to measure each of your finds. Here are some of the measuring tools you use.

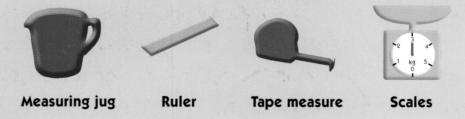

Measuring jug   Ruler   Tape measure   Scales

2 Which tool would you use to measure:
A the length of a bone about the size of your hand?
B the weight of a fossil?
C the length of a hole dug to find fossils?
D water for making a plaster cast?

Stegosaurus might have used its plates to keep warm. It could have stood so that the sun shone on its plates.

You are now putting together a model of *Stegosaurus* for display.
The plates to go on the model's back have been labelled. Each plate has been numbered so that it goes in the right place. One row is going to be odd numbers and one row even numbers.

3 Can you sort the plates into the two rows?

7 3 10 2 9 8 1 6 13 11 5 4 12 14

Checking the Fossil Footprint

You unpack the plaster casts you made of the dinosaur footprints. Can you use them to work out more about the dinosaur that made them? You would like to know how tall it was and how fast it was moving.

1 You can work out a dinosaur's height up to its hip, using its footprint. You take the length of the dinosaur footprint and multiply it by 4. The footprints you found are 50 cm long. How high is your dinosaur, up to its hips?

2 You now look at your dinosaur's stride length. This is the distance a dinosaur travels in two steps. Your dinosaur has steps that are 2½ metres long. What is its stride length?

3 With your dinosaur's hip height and stride length you can work out how fast it was moving. Divide the length of stride by its hip height. This gives you a number. Look at this chart. Is your dinosaur running, trotting or walking?

DINOSAUR SPEED

	stride length divided by hip height
walking	under 2
trotting	between 2 and 3
running	over 3

You now have to see if you can make a whole skeleton out of the bone fossils that you found.

4 Put these bones in order, from the head of the dinosaur to its tail.

ribs neck bone front leg bones

skull tail bones

Experts use dinosaur tracks to learn about behaviour. One set of tracks means the dinosaur travelled alone. Sets of tracks that are side by side means the dinosaurs travelled in groups.

A New Display

You are planning some new displays for the museum. One is about what the weather was like and what dinosaurs ate. Firstly, you have to decide how the display will look.

	Weather
Day 1	☀
Day 2	🌧
Day 3	🌧
Day 4	🌧
Day 5	☀
Day 6	☁
Day 7	☀

Visitors to the museum want to know what the weather was like at the time of the dinosaurs. You show them how to make a weather chart.

KEY

sunny ☀

cloudy ☁

rainy 🌧

1 How many days are wet on this weather chart?

There was no grass in dinosaur times. But there were lots of ferns for plant-eating dinosaurs to eat.

2 If 20 ferns were shared between 4 dinosaurs, how many ferns would each dinosaur get?

3 A herd of plant-eating dinosaurs could eat its way through the ferns very quickly. If the herd ate 3 metres of ferns in 1 hour, how many metres of ferns would it eat in 3 hours?

4 Many fossils of dinosaur dung, called coprolites, have been found. Scientists study these to find out what different dinosaurs ate. You have a collection of 35 coprolites and decide to put 15 on display. How many are left?

In the time of the dinosaurs the world looked very different. The weather at the time of the dinosaurs may have been very hot and wet.

Flying Visit

One of your favourite subjects is creatures that could fly. *Archaeopteryx* is the oldest known bird. It had feathers and it could fly, although not very well. It was a very fierce hunter.

1 What is the difference between *Archaeopteryx's* length and wingspan?

2 *Archaeopteryx* had three claws on each wing. It used its claws to grasp onto branches. How many wing claws did it have in total?

Here is a chart showing what *Archaeopteryx* measured.

ARCHAEOPTERYX	
Length	30 centimetres
Wingspan	50 centimetres

3 *Archaeopteryx* ate small animals and insects. How many insects are here?

4 *Archaeopteryx* weighed between 300 and 500 grams. If we put *Archaeopteryx* on a scale which of these balances would be correct?

A

B

The biggest pterosaur had a wingspan of about 12 metres.

During dinosaur times there were some reptiles that could fly. They were called pterosaurs.

5 This pterosaur has made a quarter turn in a clockwise direction. Which picture is correct?

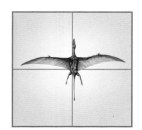

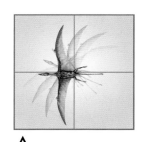

A

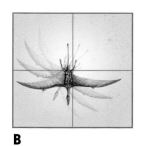

B

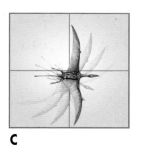

C

6 Your star fossil is now going on display. It is a *Pterodactylus*. This flying reptile had a wingspan of 2 metres. Its body was half as long as its wingspan. Which is the correct display label?

PTERODACTYLUS
Habitat: rivers and seas
Wingspan: 20 cm
Body length: 10 cm

Label A

PTERODACTYLUS
Habitat: rivers and seas
Wingspan: 200 cm
Body length: 50 cm

Label B

PTERODACTYLUS
Habitat: rivers and seas
Wingspan: 200 cm
Body length: 100 cm

Label C

Dinosaur Parents

Dinosaurs laid eggs. You decide to put on a display showing a dinosaur nest with some eggs.

The eggs of *Hypselosaurus* were laid in a line as the dinosaur walked along. These eggs are not in order. One is not there.

1 Which one is missing?

2 8 12 4 6 10 9 13 1 3 7 5

Some dinosaur eggs were very big indeed. The eggs of *Hypselosaurus* were like footballs, at least 30 centimetres across.

2 If you filled a *Hypselosaurus* egg with water it could hold about two litres. How many millilitres is that?

Maiasaura lived in groups. The group stayed near the eggs until the babies hatched. Each mother laid between 15 and 20 eggs.

3 Which of these numbers are between 15 and 20?

17 12 25 52 10 16 19

Some dinosaurs made nests and sat on their eggs to keep them warm, just like birds today. *Oviraptor* **was one of these.**

4 Look at these hatched dinosaur eggs.
Find the pieces that fit together to make whole eggs.

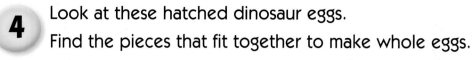

A   B   C   D   E   F   G   H

Oviraptor was about
2 metres long and
walked on two legs.

Is this a Record?

You have been asked to make a list of dinosaur record breakers. New dinosaur fossils are being found all the time so records have to be kept up-to-date.

LONGEST

The longest dinosaurs were gigantic. They ate plants and they moved slowly. *Seismosaurus* was among the longest.

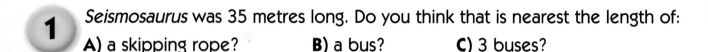

1 *Seismosaurus* was 35 metres long. Do you think that is nearest the length of:
A) a skipping rope?   **B)** a bus?   **C)** 3 buses?

2 Meat-eating dinosaurs were not so long, but one of the longest was *Tyrannosaurus*. It was 12 metres long. Do you think that is nearest the length of:
A) a skipping rope?   **B)** a bus?   **C)** 3 buses?

TALLEST

The tallest dinosaurs, like *Brachiosaurus*, had long necks. They could reach up to eat the leaves at the top of tall trees.

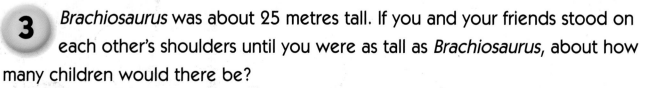

3 *Brachiosaurus* was about 25 metres tall. If you and your friends stood on each other's shoulders until you were as tall as *Brachiosaurus*, about how many children would there be?
5,   25,   or 100?

SMALLEST

One of the smallest dinosaurs was *Bambiraptor*.
This dinosaur was only 1 metre long and
weighed about 3 kilograms.

4 Which of these may weigh the same as *Bambiraptor*?

an egg   a shoe   a bag of potatoes

Some meat-eating dinosaurs
were quite small. *Velociraptor*
was about 2 metres long – and
half of this length was its tail.

In the Shop

All your displays are now ready for the Grand Opening tomorrow. On your way out you go into the museum gift shop. You like the model insects inside see-through blocks.

The museum has some real insects from dinosaur times. The insects got trapped in sticky stuff from trees called resin. The resin became hard and turned into amber.

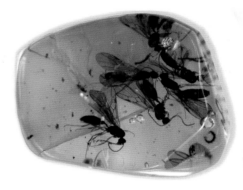

A piece of amber showing insects which were trapped millions of years ago.

A　　　　**B**　　　　**C**

1 Here are some plastic models of the amber. What are the names of these shapes?

2 A plastic model costs £1.50. You give the cashier £2. How much change will you get?

3 Which of these fossils is the most expensive?

A　　　　**B**　　　　**C**　　　　**D**

£3　　　　75p　　　　£2.50　　　　£3.75

> **Brachiosaurus** was 12 metres tall, about the height of a 4-storey building.

4 Look at the poster on the right. How much money do you save if you go on the Grand Opening day?

5 You bring two friends to the Grand Opening. How much will the entrance fee cost all together?

6 You love the exhibition! You go once for the Grand Opening and twice later. How much do you pay all together?

Meet *Allosaurus*
and other dinosaurs!

Entrance fee........................... £4

Entrance fee on
Grand Opening day............. £3

Tips and Help

PAGES 6-7

Putting numbers in order – To put these numbers of years in order, try looking at the 'hundreds' first, so 150 has one hundred, 220 has two hundreds and 70 has no (zero) hundreds. In order the longest ago is 220 million years, then 150 million years, and 70 million years is the most recent.

PAGES 8-9

Subtraction – If we take away the length of *Iguanodon*'s tail from its total body length we are doing a subtraction.

Fractions – A fraction is part of a whole. When we share or cut something into two equal parts each part is the fraction ½ (half). If it is cut into three equal parts each is the fraction ⅓ (a third) and in four equal parts each would be ¼ (a quarter).

PAGES 10-11

Putting measures in order – Check that the measures are all made in the same unit of measurement. Here you can change them all to centimetres. Remember there are 100 centimetres in one metre.

Measuring length – When you use a ruler, place the '0' (zero) on one end of the line you are measuring. Then you can 'read off' what it measures at the other end of the line.

PAGES 12-13

Metres and centimetres – There are 100 centimetres in one metre and 50 centimetres in half a metre.

Rows and columns – 3 rows, each of 4 fossils, gives the same total as 4 rows, each of 3 fossils.

Estimates – When you say how many ammonites you think there are in the picture, this is an estimate. Careful estimates are useful when doing maths.

PAGES 14-15

Numbers between – To work out where numbers fit, think of a number line, order the numbers along it. Then you will see where they fit. Here your number line looks like this:

So only two numbers fit along your number line.

50	51	52	53	54	55	56	57	58	59	60

Lots of three – This is the same as counting in threes or the products in the three times table. It is good to remember them:
0 3 6 9 12 15 18 21 24 27 30 33 36

PAGES 16-17

Measuring tools – It is important to choose the right measuring tool for a job. Remember that a jug is used to measure liquids, and scales are used to measure weight. A ruler and a tape measure are tools for measuring height, width and length.

Odds and evens – Even numbers are the numbers in the counting pattern of twos: 2 4 6 8 10 12 14 16 18 20…. and so on. Odd numbers are the numbers not in this pattern; that is 1 3 5 7 9 11 13 15 17 19…. and so on.

PAGES 18-19

Multiplying and dividing – We can see how these are connected:
$2 \times 2\frac{1}{2} = 5$ and $5 \div 2 = 2\frac{1}{2}$

PAGES 20-21

Sharing – Sharing is the same as doing division. We can find out either how many are to have a share, or the size of each share. Here it is the number of ferns for each dinosaur (that is how many in each share).

PAGES 22-23

Kilograms and grams – 1 kilogram is 1000 grams.

A ¼ turn – There are four quarter turns in one complete turn.

Clockwise – The direction in which the hands of a clock move.

clockwise

anti clockwise

PAGES 24-25

Litres and millilitres – 1 litre is 1000 millilitres.

PAGES 26-27

Longest, smallest, tallest – Remember we say 'longer', 'smaller', or 'taller' when we compare two things, and 'longest', 'smallest' and 'tallest' when we compare three or more than three things. Here we are comparing lots of dinosaurs.

PAGES 28-29

Money – One pound is 100 pence.

Answers

PAGES 6-7

1 6
2 Cretaceous
3 *Liliensternus*
4 2 to 3
5 15 twos

PAGES 8-9

1 12
2 7 metres
3 ⅓
4 3 litres
5 22 plaster casts
6 back right footprint

PAGES 10-11

1 1 metre
2 hip bone, front leg bone, back leg bone
3 6 centimetres
4 4
5 7

PAGES 12-13

1 half a metre, ½ metre and fifty centimetres
2 60 centimetres
3 12
4 about 10 trilobites
5 graph shows 7 trilobites

PAGES 14-15

1 53 and 57
2 *Tyrannosaurus, Triceratops, Apatosaurus* and *Brachiosaurus*
3 10
4 15 horns

PAGES 16-17

1 Row A - A6
   Row B - B6
   Row C - C25
2 A - ruler
   B - scales
   C - tape measure
   D - measuring jug
3 2, 4, 6, 8, 10, 12 and 14
   1, 3, 5, 7, 9, 11 and 13

PAGES 18-19

1 2 metres
2 5 metres
3 trotting
4 skull, neck bone, front leg bone, ribs, tail bone

PAGES 20-21

1 2 days
2 5 ferns
3 9 metres
4 20 coprolites

PAGES 22-23

1 20 centimetres
2 6 claws
3 16 insects
4 B
5 C
6 Label C

PAGES 24-25

1 11
2 2000 ml
3 16, 17 and 19
4 A and D
   B and E
   C and H
   F and G

PAGES 26-27

1 C - 3 buses
2 B - 1 bus
3 25 children
4 bag of potatoes

PAGES 28-29

1 A - sphere
   B - cube
   C - pyramid
2 50 pence
3 D
4 £1
5 £9
6 £11

ARCHITECTURE an INSPIRATION

Ivor Smith

This book could not have come to fruition without the support of three people. Constance Barrett has devoted an enormous amount of time at every stage of the project, giving constructive criticism with meticulous attention to detail. Her enthusiasm and enjoyment has been a continuous encouragement. Nick Pawlik has designed the book with great care, and put it all together, making this part of the process exciting. Audrey has read the book several times and often suggested a pithy phrase; she has also patiently tolerated a husband living in a different world.

Picture editor Nick Wheldon has been exceptionally helpful and a delight to work with. Many architects and friends have generously provided photographs of their work.

Matador
9 Priory Business Park
Kibworth Beauchamp
Leicestershire LE8 0RX, UK
Tel: (+44) 116 279 2299
Fax: (+44) 116 279 2277
Email: books@troubador.co.uk
Web: www.troubador.co.uk/matador <http://www.troubador.co.uk/matador>

ISBN 978 178462 0691

British Library Cataloguing in Publication Data.
A catalogue record for this book is available from the British Library.

Printed and bound by Gutenberg Press

Matador is an imprint of Troubador Publishing Ltd

Contents

This book is a tribute to **Charles Rennie Mackintosh.**
On 23rd May 2014, shortly after the chapter on the
Glasgow School of Art was written, a fire broke out
in the western end of the building. Although much
of the building was saved, the magnificent Library,
Mackintosh's masterpiece, was devastated.

INTRODUCTION

This book is addressed to all those who enjoy buildings, cities and landscapes, and would like to have a deeper appreciation and a basis for their likes and dislikes. It is also addressed to students of architecture to help with the daunting task of designing.

Architecture is part of everyday experience; it impinges on peoples' lives in many ways; it affects the way people relate to one another whether at home, at work or in the street. It can provide a feeling of identity, a sense of belonging to a particular place. The quality of space and light, form and facade can give great pleasure and make life more worthwhile.

It is not surprising that the architecture of different times and places has such a strong appeal. This is evident from the popularity of visits to famous cities, the fascination of buildings of the past, and a certain curiosity (and sometimes suspicion) about what is new. Guidebooks everywhere help people to discover what to see, and set every detail in the context of its time, but only rarely is there any guidance on what gives a place its particular quality.

This book then is about appreciation; it is an attempt to explain what architecture essentially is, rather than merely what it looks like. A full appreciation demands careful observation rather than a quick glance through a camera lens. It requires walking around, outside and inside, up and down, and enjoying the quality of detail. In the pages that follow we will make many explorations of this sort.

Architectural design, as we will discover, is the reconciliation of a whole range of often conflicting issues and their resolution into a human and poetic synthesis. For students this is difficult because there is no 'right' way of designing, there is no prescribed way of moving forward. Architectural education is centred on the studio where students learn by designing and by critical reviews of what they have done, but students often miss the importance of what is said. The same issues occur again and again, and some of these are so simple that their significance is not at first realised. As D'Arcy Thompson, the author of the seminal book on design in nature 'On Growth and Form' commented, *"It behoves us always to remember that in physics it has taken great men to discover simple things"*;[0.1] the same could also be said of design. In the architectural studio these simple things are seldom written down, and this book is an attempt to do just that and for the benefit of a wider audience.

Critical appreciation and designing are complementary. By appreciating the qualities of great architecture students may become clearer about their own objectives, and, by understanding more of the way architects think, laymen may be able to be more perceptive and gain more enjoyment from what they see and experience; they may even be helped to overcome certain prejudices and be more receptive to the architecture of today.

I have opted to structure the text around different themes, each with a particular emphasis and illustrated by a detailed description of a selection of buildings. The themes are all interconnected; an example that illustrates one theme might equally be used to illustrate another, although in some programmes one particular aspect may predominate. It might have been easier to follow a chronological sequence, but I have been keen to focus on those aspects of architecture that are relevant to any time or place.

The book is divided into two parts.

The first part is about the nature of architecture; it describes what is necessary. The chapter headings describe the basic requirements which to varying degrees must always be met: facilitating activity, moderating climate, relating to context, respecting material and structure, and conveying meaning and delight. They may be regarded as an elaboration of *'utilitas, firmitas, venustas'* as set out by the ancient architect and writer Vitruvius.

The second part of the book is about the nature of designing; it focuses on what the designer brings to the task. The chapter headings were suggested by Alvar Aalto's essay 'The Trout and the Mountain Stream', where he hints at some of the different ways of thinking that designers use. These are elusive and not necessarily conscious; they include the use of reason and intuition, the value of experience and precedent, the role of metaphor and the search for harmony. For students this is not a prescription; it simply attempts to make designing manageable, to point towards important issues, to help clarify intentions, and to assist in the making of choices.

A.1 - The Abbey at Einsiedeln

A.2 - The Abbey of Le Thoronet

I had several reasons for writing at this particular time. Firstly, from the evidence around we can see that some of the basic requirements of architecture are either not understood or ignored (for example, the response to climate or context), and secondly, there has emerged an obsession with style that is revealed in different ways; on the one hand there is the artificial conflict between 'traditional' and 'modern', and on the other there is the fashion that every building should be an icon. Architects from Sir Christopher Wren to Le Corbusier have forcefully expressed their opposition to style and fashion.

So much of what is written about the architecture of today is negative that it seemed opportune to take a positive approach and point to the great body of work that is good, now and in the past, and to reiterate some of those qualities that are timeless. This does not set out to be comprehensive; the examples are chosen from the work of a few selected architects. They represent a personal journey to buildings and cities that I have enjoyed and found particularly inspiring; the majority are in Europe and especially in Britain where I have lived and worked.

Inevitably there is a bias; the simplicity of the Abbey at Le Thoronet, for instance, is clearly preferred to the lavishness of the Abbey at Einsiedeln. I make no apologies for this; it simply shows that different people have their own preferences because they see the world in different ways.

Part One

1.1 - Glasgow School of Art view from north-west

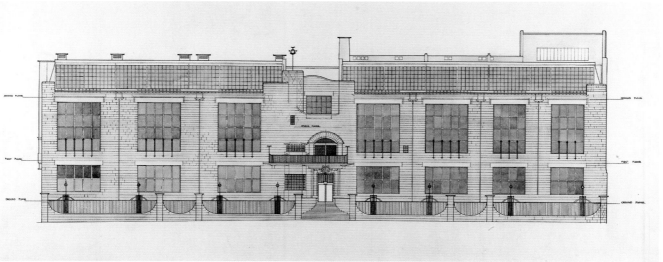

1.2 - Glasgow School of Art north elevation

1 The NATURE of ARCHITECTURE

THE GLASGOW SCHOOL OF ART

I chose the Glasgow School of Art for the prelude to my inquiry into the nature of architecture for a number of reasons. Firstly, it is not a building that immediately hits you in the eye, it does not have the 'wow' factor of, say, King's College Chapel in Cambridge or the Sydney Opera House or the Piazza San Marco in Venice. It is a building you have to carefully observe rather than casually look at. I got to know the Glasgow School of Art over the years when I was an examiner at the School of Architecture, and as I delved more and more deeply I discovered new, intriguing and poetic aspects. Secondly, it is a unique building and is rightly regarded not only as the high point of Art Nouveau in Britain but also as the genesis of modern architecture. I am interested to consider it not in terms of style or history, but to discover the way the Glasgow School of Art embodies aspects that are fundamental to architecture as a whole and the way they relate together.

1.3 - Glasgow School of Art entrance

1.4 - Glasgow School of Art studio window

1.5 - Glasgow School of Art studio interior

The competition for the new Glasgow School of Art was held in 1896. The site chosen was a strip of land about 75 metres long running east-west on the south side of Renfrew Street with the main frontage facing due north; it is about 25 metres deep and slopes very steeply down (about 10 metres) to the south towards the back of the buildings in Sauchiehall Street.

The competition conditions were very precise and detailed. The number and size of every room was given as well as the way they should relate to one another; the main studios should face north, the entrance should be in the middle, with the room for the Headmaster (as he was then called) close by at an upper level, and it was suggested that the Museum might be on the landing next to the main staircase. As is usual with architectural briefs, the requirements concentrated on use, and this was summarised towards the end of the conditions; "*What is required is a building with class rooms conveniently arranged and well lighted.*". [1.1]

The winning scheme was submitted in the firm's name of Honeyman and Keppie, but it was later acknowledged that Charles Rennie Mackintosh was the designer. His plan precisely followed the conditions laid down in the competition. From the outset it became clear that the building would need to occupy the whole of the site. The footprint is essentially very simple;

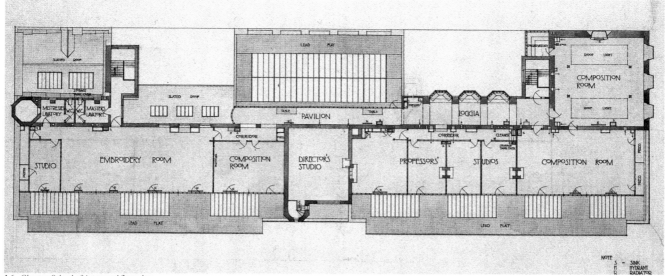

1.6 - Glasgow School of Art second floor plan

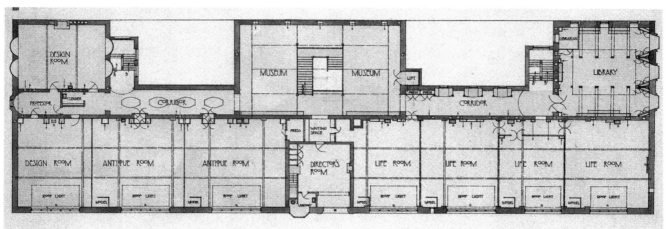

1.7 - Glasgow School of Art first floor plan

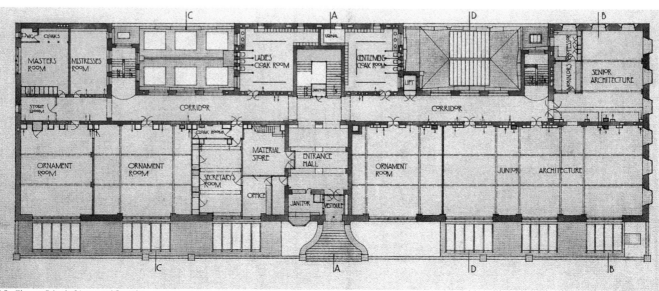

1.8 - Glasgow School of Art ground floor plan

the E-shaped plan exploits the street frontages to the north, east and west, providing appropriate light to the rooms within, whilst the spaces between the wings at the south and behind the railings along the front allow rooflights to illuminate the workshops in the basement. The disposition of rooms within the plan has a look of inevitability. All the painting studios on all the floors face north; on the ground floor the entrance is in the middle with stairs and cloakrooms in the wing behind; the east wing contains staff rooms, and the west wing contains the original architecture studio. In the basement, in addition to the workshops, there is the lecture room together with the boiler room (providing a heating system ahead of its time); the first floor has the Director's room in the centre at the front with the stairs and Museum behind, the Board Room to the east and the Library to the west; on the second floor the Director's studio is in the middle with studios on either side joined by an external corridor known as the 'Hen Run', and the flower painting studio is in the west wing with a cantilevered greenhouse.

It is interesting to speculate how this plan might have been realised in, say, the mid-20th century. One can envisage a curtain wall covering the whole of the north façade relieved only by its central doorway; a functional solution to satisfy the competition criteria! This was not to be Mackintosh's approach; from his straightforward plan he created a richness of place inside as well as out.

Because of a shortage of funds the School of Art was built in two phases; the first phase, built between 1897 and 1899, consisted of the east end including the central entrance; the second phase, built between 1907 and 1909, saw the completion of the building including the addition of a third floor of studios, escape stairs, and the 'Hen Run' on the south side. This delay was propitious because in the intervening years Mackintosh had designed and completed a number of exciting commissions including the Tea Rooms for Miss Cranston. In that time he had become a more mature and innovative architect.

The School of Art is essentially a Glasgow building; like much of the city built at that time it is made of stone, a strong building that befits a great industrial city. Its simple form acknowledges and contributes to the grain of the streets nearby.

The north façade is dominated by huge industrial-like windows lighting the studios which are in contrast to the solid central feature. At the pavement, the entrance is in the exact centre and the railings on either side are identical, yet on the elevation above there are three studio windows on one side and four on the other. How does this come about? The front door is modest, made grand by a tapering flight of steps with a curved balustrade. It is on the axis of the stairs going up, a

1.9 - Glasgow School of Art Library

1.10 - Glasgow School of Art Library gallery

direct approach to the Museum on the first floor. At this point the axis shifts to the centre of the stairwell, the centre of the Museum, and the entrance to the Director's room. It is this shift of axis which causes the asymmetry of the studios in plan and elevation as well as the asymmetry of the central wall element in relation to the front door. The asymmetry of this façade is then ingeniously brought into balance by the positioning of the different elements; the domestic bay windows, the balcony, the wide arch of the Director's room with his studio above, and the connecting staircase in a tower. This composition owes much to the vernacular buildings that Mackintosh had drawn in his early travels and which had become ingrained in his memory.

1.11 - Glasgow School of Art main staircase

The studios are everyday working spaces, with unwrought timber on the walls, bare floorboards, and bold timber mullions and transoms in the windows. The studios are places for creativity, for making a mess with paint or clay - even for making a noise. These contrast with a series of rooms that display varying degrees of specialness - the entrance hall, the staircase and corridors, the Museum, the Director's room, the Board Room, and the magnificent Library.

The entrance hall is low with a barrel-vault, heavy columns, and subdued light; this leads to the lofty staircase which has slender extended newel posts and light flooding down from above. Arriving up into the Museum is to experience ingenious timber construction and the dramatic manipulation of light and shade. Four massive trusses, with their members subtly shaped, divide the space into three bays; the central half is pitched and glazed whilst the edges are flat. The stairwell occupies the central bay and is defined by four timber posts that extend up to the trusses; they are gently tapered and have a square plate near the top giving the hint of a capital. The brightness of light from the roof contrasts with the darkness of the wood. Originally the walls were dark and panelled which further exaggerated the contrast, and also set off the white sculptures to advantage; painting the walls white has reduced the drama.

1.12 - Glasgow School of Art Museum

The corridors running east and west are each lit in a different way; they are places not only for display but also for conversation, with seating bays set into the wall.

The Director's room has a character all of its own. It is a white panelled room, domestic in scale, with a fireplace. Its most notable feature is the coved ceiling above the arched window that has leaded lights, some as small as 150mm x 50mm. It is a measure of Mackintosh's genius that on one elevation he managed to bring into harmony such an audacious range of different windows, each appropriate to the space inside.

1.13 - Glasgow School of Art corridor

The Board Room forms the end of the east wing on the ground floor. It also is domestic in scale, partly panelled and painted

1.14 - Glasgow School of Art Library window outside

12

white with a splendid fireplace. Two tall gently bowed windows on both the east and west sides have Georgian-like panes giving the quality of light as in a drawing room. When escape stairs were added in the second phase of building, the windows on the west were fitted with obscured glass. This room forms part of the carefully balanced composition of the east façade, which, as part of the first phase, embodies a number of vernacular references.

The Library is unique not only in the Glasgow School of Art but also within architecture as a whole. It is a square room that occupies the whole of one floor of the west wing. Its total height is similar to that of the first floor studios, and it is divided vertically into three levels with a balcony at the first level and a store at the top. The main part of the Library is below the store and only rises to its full height by the windows. The Library combines an ingenious unadorned timber structure with delicately crafted detail. Two rows of four tall wooden posts run east to west resting on steel beams in the floor; they are wider at the base to support double beams running north to south to carry the balcony which is set well back from the posts. It is in the enrichment of the balcony that the verticality of the room is emphasised: firstly, by the three chamfered and brightly painted balusters that are intricately carved to sparkle in the light, and secondly, by the alternate panels of the balcony fronts that are gently bowed and project below the floor. The many different planes of timber reflect the light in different ways making it appear in places dark brown, in others grey. Above all, it is the uniqueness of the three great west windows that gives the room its specialness, its verticality, and its splendid quality of light. They are bay windows exaggerated internally by cupboards extending from the jambs. It is their height that is so dramatic; they extend beyond the library ceiling to the top of the store, forming, as you look up, a remarkable lofty hexagon. The height and the sparkle of light is further exaggerated by the smallness of the panes of glass (only about 225mm square) set in metal frames.

In the Library, Mackintosh was equally concerned with the quality of artificial light. In the centre of the ceiling, sixteen square coffers define a square with lights suspended from them, some at ceiling level, some lower down. The lights are complex vertical constructions made of metal, and pierced with small slits and squares to give out a sparkling light that contributes to the theme of the whole room.

1.17 - Glasgow School of Art Library bay window

1.18 - Glasgow School of Art Library lights

The Library is small but grand, calm yet lively, and subtly enriched by small intricate details. Above all it is a room that imparts a sense of quiet for study and reflection.

Externally the impact of the Library marks one of the most dramatic elevations in the history of architecture. It is interesting to note the changes that were made from the original competition scheme. At that time, the third storey of studios was not included, and the top of the west side of the building stepped down the hill; this façade was pierced by quite ordinary holes in the wall, and the only feature was the central windows of the library that were in a projecting bay extended vertically. With the addition of the extra storey Mackintosh seized the opportunity of dramatising the height just where the ground level was lowest. The three great bays of the Library are extended up to the top of the building and down to the floor level of the architectural studio. As in the interior the small windowpanes reflect the light in different ways. This masterly expression of verticality is further exaggerated by three clever devices: firstly, by tall cylinders of stone intended for sculpture on either side of the Library windows; secondly, by the addition of three further bay windows to the architectural studio so that these six windows together form a horizontal band in contrast to the vertical; and thirdly, by the use of dressed stone around the windows (subtly curved upwards where the horizontal meets the vertical). Intriguingly, a tiny window is cut out of the rough stone on the upper studio wall and serves to emphasise its thickness.

A notable characteristic of the Glasgow School is that all four elevations are different. The south elevation has no street frontage and is therefore the back, and unlike the other three stone facades it is made of brick, covered with roughcast rendering; it is reticent, and only the south side of the west wing, the loggia and the 'Hen Run' have individual expression.

From the outset the clients were concerned about the cost, and called for a plain building. It is not surprising that Mackintosh could not resist discreet embellishments; he was a beautiful draughtsman and painted semi-abstract watercolours containing mystical symbolic scenes, often within a circle. He was also married to his gifted fellow student Margaret MacDonald with whom he often collaborated. In the stonework of the building Mackintosh occasionally used subtle curves, and inside he used several types of roof truss. He enjoyed designing constructions in wrought iron which we see in the railings to the street, the brackets that brace the mullions of the studio windows (designed partly to support planks for window cleaners), as well as the finials on each of the towers. He designed a round carving over the front door, and a range of lovely small stained-glass inserts in many of the interior doors, all with symbolic images. He

1.19 - Glasgow School of Art west elevation of Library

1.20 - Glasgow School of Art south-west corner

1.21 - Glasgow School of Art south-east corner

delighted in geometry; he used both the square and the circle in the design of a clock, and he used the square divided by many small squares for the layout of the coloured tiles in the staircases denoting different levels. All of this was in addition to the design of fireplaces, light fittings and furniture.

The Glasgow School of Art encapsulates the essence of architecture in its many parts. At the most basic level it is *fit for its purpose*, it works, but in a way far beyond what was required in the brief. As Denys Lasdun has said "*It is not the job of the architect to give people what they want, rather it is to give people what they never dreamed they could have*".[1.2]

The Art School *addresses climate*, it manipulates light magically in different ways for different purposes, it plays with the contrast between light and dark. The Art School *exploits materials*; the massiveness of stone for walls, the range of simple but ingenious roof trusses and the special qualities of timber for posts and cladding. It *relates to its urban context* and forms edges to the city block. The Art School is *full of meaning*; nowhere else in one building is the difference between the everyday and the special so clearly expressed. The Art School is full of delight, and as he worked over each part again and again, one can imagine Mackintosh chuckling to himself with sheer delight - a delight for all to share.

1.22 - Glasgow School of Art Director's room

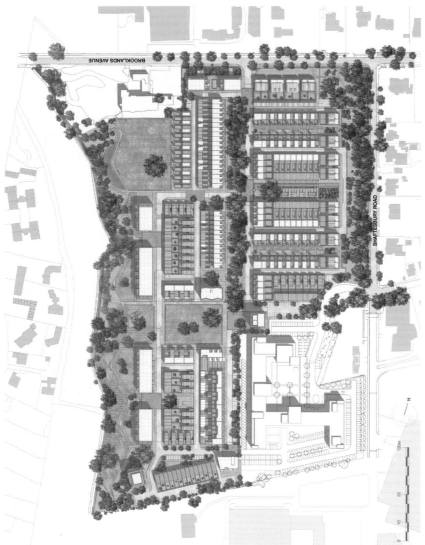

2.1 - Accordia site plan

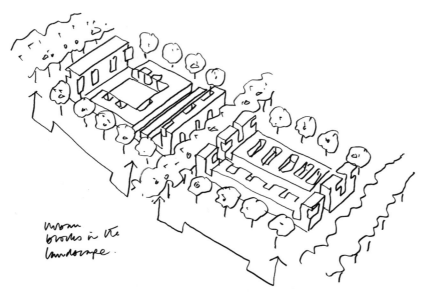

2.2 - Accordia sketch:urban blocks in landscape

16

2 FACILITATING ACTIVITY

Architecture begins with a need. In this way it differs from the arts of painting and sculpture which, though they may celebrate a particular person or event, or mark a special place, seldom originate from the same sort of programmatic requirements. We have noted that the brief for the Glasgow School of Art simply emphasised the use; "*What is required is a building with classrooms conveniently arranged and well lighted*". Many briefs define the task in this way, and it is obviously necessary for a building to function properly, to be fit for its purpose, or as often described 'to work'. But is practicality enough? Aldo van Eyck referred to "*seeking the mute requirements that are not in the brief but are still there before you start* ".[2.1] These are issues that lie behind the task as set, and form the basis of what the architect brings to the task. They are not added on; the programme is interpreted and reframed by different architects in various ways according to their particular insight and experience. To exemplify this we will consider a range of very different activities: the dwelling, the work place, an underground station, an opera house, and a national library.

THE DWELLING

Apart from those things that are practically necessary, what makes a house a home? Essentially a house is a place to feel secure, sheltered emotionally as well as physically, a private place apart from the world outside. It is also a place to belong, to feel a sense of identity. A house is a place to come together, it is also a place to be alone; sometimes it is a place for peace and quiet, at other times a place to party. People are different and enjoy different amounts of contact and privacy, some are gregarious, others are reclusive. These differences may be cultural, for example, in the way noise between neighbours is acceptable in some societies but not in others. A house needs to be flexible; peoples' needs vary at different times in their lives, from being single, then a couple, having young children who become teenagers and move away leaving an empty nest. Later perhaps a grandparent needs looking after, or part of the house becomes a place of work. These differences in lifestyle may require different sorts of space, where at some time noisy play and quiet study are kept apart in separate rooms, whilst at other times different activities can coexist and a more open plan is appropriate. On both the outside and the inside of a house every detail is seen close-to, and consequently the colour, texture and

2.3 - Accordia side street

2.4 - Accordia landscaped garden

2.5 - Cambridge Backs

2.6 - Accordia mews of Brooklands Avenue villas

2.7 - Accordia four-storey houses

touch of materials has a strong impact on its character and the feeling of homeliness. A house relates to its surroundings, to its own open space, its terrace, courtyard or garden; it relates also to a wider world, to the city, the street and the neighbours nearby, or to the open countryside.

The housing known as **Accordia** in **Cambridge** is best appreciated against the background of many of those housing estates that have been built throughout Britain on the outskirts of cities, towns and villages; anonymous developments that are unrelated to their locality and could be anywhere. Yet the need for identity is clearly demonstrated; people attempt to make the house their own by changing little details of their doors and windows, by colour and by planting; developers add a variety of different materials and decorative features to counteract sameness. Sometimes, as at the Duchy of Cornwall's village at Poundbury, pastiche images from the past are intended to foster familiarity. But these are all superficial gestures.

Accordia, in contrast, is a distinctive place. It was designed and built between 2002 and 2006 by **Feilden Clegg Bradley Studios, Maccreanor Lavington,** and **Alison Brooks Architects** with **Grant Associates** in charge of the landscape. The site lies between the railway station and the Botanic Gardens and is about fifteen minutes walk from the Market Place. It is a development of nearly 400 dwellings and it relates not only to the city and the University of Cambridge as a whole, but also to the distinguished 19th- century house and garden on the site.

The centre of the city enjoys an exceptional number of open parks planted with avenues of trees, whilst most of the colleges are enclosed around courtyards with gardens beyond. The architects therefore set out to design 'a city in a garden', and this led to three overarching and innovative ideas: firstly, to make defined built forms clearly differentiated from the streets, the gardens and lawns; secondly, to replace private gardens on the ground with generous outdoor terraces on each level related to the rooms within; and thirdly, to provide a mix of dwelling types and sizes. In this way each group of similar dwellings creates a small 'city block' with clear edges that separate the private from the public domain, defines a particular area, and serves to foster a sense of identity.

The site is deep with a short frontage to Brooklands Avenue, a street that contains a series of substantial detached and semi-detached villas. The site is divided into two by an existing avenue of splendid trees and a new access road running north to south. Along Brooklands Avenue to the east there are four pairs of semi-detached houses designed to respect their neighbours. They have garages at the back with studios or granny flats

2.8 - Accordia private terrace

2.9 - Accordia affordable houses

2.10 - Trinity Lane in Cambridge

above. Beyond these are a series of terraces at right angles to the access road each with its particular house type. One side of the house faces the street whilst the other side faces into a carefully landscaped area. Both the street and the garden are places to gather. The street is primarily for residents on foot as well as for children to play, and has just enough room for cars to turn into the garages that are tucked in beside the front door. The street façades tend to be quite sheer whilst the other façade steps down towards the communal garden. In both form and elevation, each side reconciles the private requirements within the house to the differing public domains outside. In some places these façades celebrate their chimneys in homage to Trinity Lane, one of the most striking streets in Cambridge. The ends of these streets are cleverly modified to present a formal three or four-storey façade towards the access road rather than just a gable end.

On the western side of the site two four-storey blocks of apartments face Brooklands Avenue and contribute to its scale. Set behind the splendid trees along the access road are two long terraces of narrow four-storey houses with deep plans that recall those in a Georgian square in London. Behind these at the north end is a row of luxurious courtyard houses with terraces stepping down towards the lawn of Brooklands House; these have dramatic chimneys that denote each separate house. Further south are terraces of affordable housing, each house elegantly defined by a simple monopitch roof. Along the west of the site are four blocks of four-storey apartments with generous balconies. The houses are planned to provide a close contact between inside and out, with the terraces serving as an outside room that is often enclosed by columns and beams around the edge.

Accordia offers great diversity within an overarching unity. This is achieved by a consistent use of a limited palette of materials, and most predominantly by the present-day equivalent of the traditional Cambridgeshire gault brick. This subtle tension between diversity and conformity gives to each part a strong sense of place within the context of the whole.

2.11 - Accordia courtyard houses

2.12 - Accordia courtyard houses showing private terraces

2.13 - Apeldoorn view from above

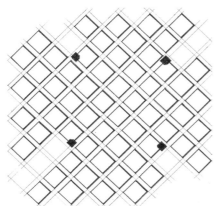
2.14 - Apeldoorn plan

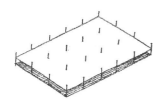

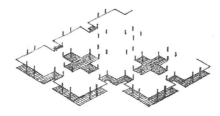
2.15 - Apeldoorn diagramatic organisation

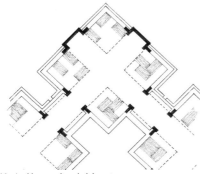
2.16 - Apeldoorn various desk layouts

THE WORKPLACE

Herman Hertzberger has always been concerned with the way that people relate to one another, and this was the prime issue in his design for **The Centraal Beheer Insurance Offices** at **Apeldoorn in Holland** which employs around a thousand people. It was built between 1970 and 1972 when it was current thinking that communication in an office was best achieved by a large open plan (known as *bürolandschaft*), with sound absorbent furnishings to cut down the noise, and with plants in pots to make it homely. Hertzberger challenged this impersonal environment where so many people are thrown together in such an anonymous space. His view was that this gives them too much freedom and makes it difficult for them to choose an arrangement that is most appropriate for their needs. He used an apt analogy: "*It is like the sort of menu that offers such an endless array of dishes that instead of making you hungry, dulls your appetite*".[2.2]

Hertzberger's interpretation of the programme was to make distinct places where a small group of people could work together as they wished, and yet be in contact with a network of other groups. For this he devised a particular structural system which is based on a tartan grid of units nine metres square separated from one another by three metres. Each unit is supported by a pair of columns placed centrally on each side with a circulation route between them. The corners of the unit are therefore cantilevered and each provides a working place for four or five people, giving a total group nearby of between sixteen and twenty on the four corners. However, another looser grouping occurs, as each corner looks across at three others on the same level and down to others below, cleverly creating different degrees of contact. The arrangements within the units are very flexible and have proved able to accommodate the changes that inevitably occur. The formal geometry of the concrete structure is very strong, and everyone is encouraged to make their workplace home with all manner of posters and plants. The result is more like a studio in a school of architecture than an insurance office!

The whole complex is divided into four by two primary routes that cross the central area where there are cafes, restaurants, shops and a bank. The whole of this communal area is open to the public and fulfills Hertzberger's intention to break down the barrier between work and home. It has been compared to a Mediterranean village with narrow streets leading to a market square.

Centraal Beheer is constructed in fair-face concrete and concrete blocks left exposed, and with all the junctions detailed with great care; it is beautifully put together. With a skill that looks

2.17 - Apeldoorn typical corner workspace

2.18 - Apeldoorn exterior

effortless but was clearly the result of meticulous reworking, all the services are carefully integrated and both support and enhance the overall architectural intention.

Certain questions about place and identity arise from the use of the same formal structural grid throughout the whole scheme. Consistency can be a weakness as well as a strength, and here it has to some degree diminished the contrast between the everyday world of the offices and the special world that is communal. In the analogy of the Mediterranean village the grain of the built form is cut through by streets arriving at a clearly identified square. Similarly, whilst appreciating that the architect wished to avoid formality, a clearer celebration of entry might help to give more visible identity to the company. Nevertheless, Centraal Beheer has been shown to satisfy the needs of the client in an exceptional way, and over the years it has acted as an important polemic about the relationship between people at work.

2.19 - Apeldoorn group of workspaces

2.20 - Apeldoorn workspace

2.21 - Canary Wharf entrance

2.22 - Canary Wharf escalators

2.23 - Canary Wharf booking hall

AN UNDERGROUND STATION

The design of an underground station poses extreme practical problems, with the need to cope with vast crowds of people, especially in the rush hour. At street level it must be easy to find, if only, as in London, by a well-understood striking logo or, as in Paris, by an Art Nouveau canopy. Often, the entrance then leads to a dreary ticket hall with crowded turnstiles, and from there down stairs or escalators on a long walk in a tunnel to the train - the daily rat race has begun. In some cities decorative devices have been used to alleviate this oppressive experience. In Moscow the long yet spacious tunnels are made to emulate a gallery in a luxurious palace with elaborately framed pictures, decorative lamps, and the occasional sculpture. Elsewhere, advertisements are used as a distraction, and sometimes, more successfully, the platforms are decorated with images of what is above ground; a literal attempt to establish some sense of place.

Canary Wharf Underground Station designed by **Foster and Partners** is the most dramatic of a number of new stations that were built on the Jubilee Line in East London Docklands to coincide with the millennium in 2000. Each station was designed by a different architect commissioned by London Transport's enlightened chief architect Roland Paoletti, and each exploits a new and refreshing use of space and light.

2.24 - view of Canary Wharf development

Canary Wharf station is situated at the base of the highest tower of the Canary Wharf office development designed by Cesar Pelli. The three entrances are at the ends and the middle of a new park, and each consists of a discreet bow-like arch with a glazed elliptical roof that emerges out of the grass; it is almost as if the ground has been gently lifted up for you to enter below it. The main entrance towards the Canary Wharf tower gives onto a large paved square opposite the dock, with other towers at the sides, and cafes, restaurants and bars all around. The glazed roof illuminates the escalators and penetrates deep down into the space below. As you descend, you experience the carefully formed geometry of a vast concrete structure leading to an overwhelming spacious world below ground; the level of the turnstiles, ticket office and administration. Another series of escalators takes you further down to another hall of equal grandeur at platform level. There is a rather special delight in going down and looking up. As at Stansted Airport, Foster has addressed the problem of vast crowds of people moving about and waiting that is so often the cause of stress and claustrophobia. The essential idea was to create an awesome height like that of a cathedral above the crowds below. We may note the precedent of great roofs at major railways around the world, such as King's Cross or Paddington in London, where vast height and wide spans serve at one move to dissipate smoke

2.25 - Canary Wharf view from park

2.26 - Canary Wharf entrance inside

2.27 - Canary Wharf side view of entrance

and steam, cope with the arrival and departure of trains as well as hordes of passengers, and also act as a gateway to the city.

Canary Wharf underground station is beautifully made. The entrance canopy is formed by a simple system of tapered steel ribs that support equally simple glazing bars. The columns in the central row are oval in section and support the gently curved ribbed and vaulted roof, all in immaculate fair-face concrete. The geometry of junctions is most elegant as in that between the glazed entrance and the roof. A carefully designed expansion joint forms the hint of a capital at the head of the columns, so that all the details together reinforce the clarity of the whole.

Air conditioning ducts are discreetly hidden by louvres incorporated into the vaulted roof. Artificial light from downlighters in the entrance canopy and lights in the side of the escalators give a welcoming sparkle to the way up and down, and uplighting the concrete vault emphasises its height.

The bases of the columns and the trim of the escalators and turnstiles are clad in stainless steel to ensure cleanliness and avoid graffiti. The ticket offices and the glazed screens between the platforms and the track are made of anodised aluminium and detailed at an intimate human scale. Signs (which because of the clarity of circulation are kept to a minimum) are discreetly suspended from above. On the platforms the traditional logo for the station name is combined with a simple seat.

Canary Wharf underground station is efficient; it works! More essentially, passengers can move on their way in a calm and peaceful place that helps to ameliorate the stress of travelling.

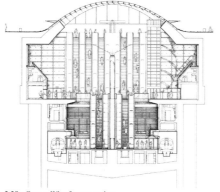
2.28 - Canary Wharf cross section

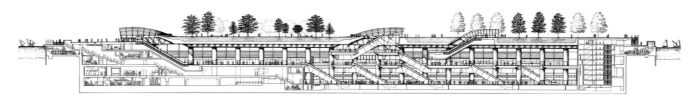
2.29 - Canary Wharf long section

AN OPERA HOUSE

The programmatic requirements for an opera house are extremely complex. The production of an opera involves the singers and the orchestra together with their dressing rooms and rehearsal rooms; it requires costume and wig makers, lighting specialists and scene makers, all requiring a canteen and services. In addition, the Royal Opera House includes the Royal Ballet with its own rehearsal studios. As different performances take place during the week, it is necessary to accommodate many different sets and allow for many rehearsals to take place simultaneously.

All of this activity must be kept separate from members of the audience. They are likely to arrive and leave around the same time and need to be able to find their way easily. Above all they need to enjoy a great occasion. A night at the opera is more than just seeing and hearing what takes place on stage, important though that is. From the moment of arrival the sense of theatre begins, with the audience moving around and enjoying the buzz of the crowd, stopping for a drink, seeing others and being seen, dressed up for something special, and taking in the spectacle from many angles.

The site for the new **Royal Opera House** at **Covent Garden in London**, designed by **Dixon Jones,** is confined and occupies a whole city block. It is further constrained as it includes the existing Opera House and portico designed by E.M. Barry in 1858. It also includes the Floral Hall which was part of the market, and in addition it forms half of one side of the Covent Garden piazza that was designed by Inigo Jones.

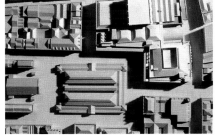

2.30 - Royal Opera House site plan

Three strategic moves determined the design: to renovate Barry's much-loved auditorium, to raise the Floral Hall to the level of the half-landing of the grand stairs, and to make a pedestrian link between the piazza and Bow Street. Two entrances are provided, one in the classical portico and another in the new pedestrian link, with the two sharing the ticket desks and cloakrooms. Both entrances lead up to the Floral Hall, a magnificent glass and cast iron structure, that has become the main foyer with a central bar and restaurant on galleries around. It was originally eight bays long but it had to be reduced by half to allow scenery to travel behind to reach the stage; a new end wall of mirrors cleverly gives the illusion of the original, and every detail is made to sparkle with light. Access to the auditorium is either directly from the foyer or by travelling up an escalator to higher levels, a route that gives fascinating views down into the Floral Hall. The escalator arrives in the amphitheatre bar where a huge window projects out, giving an intriguing view down into the foyer. From below, set within the mirrored wall, this appears as an elevated platform uncannily

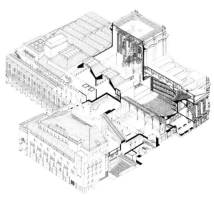

2.31 - Royal Opera House axonometric

2.32 - Royal Opera House exterior of Floral Hall

2.33 - Royal Opera House interior of Floral Hall

2.34 - Royal Opera House link between the piazza and Bow Street

2.35 - Royal Opera House escalator outside the Floral Hall

suspended in space. On one side of the amphitheatre bar is a restaurant, and behind it a rooftop loggia with views down to the piazza and out over London beyond. From this loggia there are windows into the costume workshops giving a glimpse of a part of the inner workings of the house whilst enjoying the panorama outside. The other side of the amphitheatre bar leads to the upper seats of the auditorium - the cheaper seats (the gods) - that in the old house were approached by a dreary staircase from a side door. In this way the whole of the new house is open for everyone to enjoy.

The magnificent horse-shoe shaped auditorium with its three golden galleries and its delicately domed ceiling has been restored and renovated even beyond its former glory; it has better sight-lines and acoustics, more comfortable seating, and all its original colours and gilding.

An intricate network of minor routes, out of the public eye, enables the backstage activities to operate smoothly. In the Royal Opera House, coping with the arrival, construction and moving of scenery is especially difficult because it has to take place at the side rather than at the back of the stage. It requires a vast industrial area higher than that of the stage and with floors that are moveable in different directions threaded behind the Floral Hall. The scenery 'get in' has to cope with huge pantechnicons requiring massive doors on the same street frontage as the entrances that welcome the public.

Internally the new areas of the Opera House enjoy the spaciousness, the dramatic use of light, the sensitive use of materials and the quality of detail that is typical of the work of Dixon Jones. Where new meets old as in the Floral Hall the transition is discreet yet uncompromising. The new pedestrian way from the piazza to Bow Street is usually open to the public, and is therefore both an inside and outside place; it is generous and airy rising high under the escalators, and glazed to give glimpses of the Floral Hall. It is reminiscent of the pedestrian route through the Carpenter Centre by Le Corbusier or that through the Neue Staatsgalerie in Stuttgart by James Stirling. Externally the design of the Opera House responds both to the internal requirements of each part and the external demands of the urban context. It presents a different face on each side. The original portico by Barry is made of painted stucco, the new façades to the streets are Jura limestone, and those to the piazza are Portland stone. Within the city block the most celebrated façades are those to the piazza and to the portico and Floral Hall in Bow Street connected by the pedestrian link. A colonnade of classical columns forms a frontage to the piazza behind which is a wide and high barrel vault with lunettes cut into it to illuminate the luxurious shopfronts. The wall above has two

2.36 - Royal Opera House view from the piazza

2.37 - Royal Opera House roof terrace

rows of windows between flat pilasters, a simplified version of a classical façade. The pitched roof of the loggia along the top has a simple directness appropriate to its use and position. Both Barry's portico and the Floral Hall give a majestic grandeur to the points of entry, whilst the rest of that façade and that in Russell Street accept their more workaday role.

The design of the Royal Opera House is not determined by any single architectural system but rather by the different parts being allowed to become what they want to be. The mixture of different architectural languages as a collage in different parts of the building inside and out is a masterly innovation. It reflects an attitude akin to Charles Rennie Mackintosh at the Art School rather than that of Herman Hertzberger at Apeldoorn. It enables the building to accommodate many different uses, but essentially it provides a place for people to enjoy. In future this diversity is likely to increase as architects Stanton Williams propose further sympathetic interventions.

2.38 - Royal Opera House view accross Floral Hall

2.39 - British Library 1962 proposal

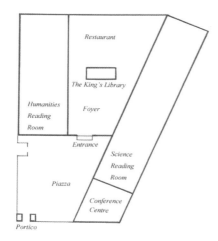
2.40 - British Library plan

A NATIONAL LIBRARY

The **British Library** in London has many different uses. It is an educational resource aimed to encourage a wide range of enquiry as well as the love of books; it is a centre of research where scholars spend many hours extended over many weeks in quiet individual study; it is full of ancient treasures available for the public to view either physically or digitally. As the Cambridge scholar Stefan Collini has commented *"We are merely custodians for the present generation of a complex inheritance which we did not create - and which is not ours to destroy"*.[2.3] The building therefore requires a special ambience that celebrates the essence of history, science and culture, yet on a scale where an individual scholar feels at home.

The Library had formerly been housed in the British Museum with its great circular Reading Room designed by Sydney Smirke in 1857. This was a room that was held in deep affection by its readers but it was not nearly large enough. In 1962 **Leslie Martin** and **Colin St John Wilson** were appointed to design a new library south of the Museum. The first proposal opened up an impressive piazza all the way down to the church of St George Bloomsbury by Nicholas Hawksmoor. The new Library was to be to the east and the Prints and Drawings Collection to the west, with housing and shops behind. Changes to the brief and to the boundaries of the site resulted in a second project in 1972, but this also proved to be too cramped to allow for the inevitable expansion that a library requires.

A new site was then acquired in Euston Road west of the splendid St Pancras Station designed in 1867 by George Gilbert Scott with its complex and overpowering roofline. The closeness of such an impressive neighbour in itself presented an enormous challenge. To the west is an interesting residential development named Levita House designed in the mid-twenties and loosely based on the Karl Marx Hof in Vienna.

Colin St John Wilson and Partners were deeply involved in formulating a very complex brief. This required storage for twelve million books and other documents, different requirements for science and humanities, access for the public to view treasures such as the Magna Carta, sophisticated computer facilities that are likely to change over time, and the magnificent King's Library. The architects and clients worked together to define these diverse elements of use.

The four parts of the Library are located in response to the site. The piazza to the south pushes the entrance back away from the noise of Euston Road; the Science Reading Rooms lie to the east towards St Pancras, and the Humanities and their associated specialist reading rooms lie to the west, with the great communal concourse between. The Science wing presents a higher mass

2.41 - British Library entrance from piazza

2.42 - British Library gateway from Euston Road

2.43 - British Library King's Library

2.44 - British Library Science reading room

towards the station whilst the Humanities wing is kept lower to preserve light to the flats beyond.

The piazza is entered from Euston Road under a bold portico with a view straight ahead to Eduardo Paolozzo's sculpture of Isaac Newton. The ground surface of the piazza is defined by a square grid of stone with a brick infill, reminiscent of those in many Italian cities but, unlike them, divided up by a raised terrace and a circular amphitheatre for possible informal activities. In the angle between the Science and Humanities wings an impressive slate roof cascades down towards the front doors marking a welcoming entrance.

After entering under this low canopy, the space opens up rising dramatically to a height of five storeys; it has a wave-like ceiling illuminated by clerestory windows and rooflights. The floor pattern echoes that of the piazza outside with the terrazzo continuing up the stairs and with the handrails bound in leather. The side walls are brick in contrast to the whiteness of the columns, beams and ceiling. A huge and magnificent tapestry designed by R.B. Kitaj adorns one of the brick walls. This rich array of natural materials serves to humanise a vast space.

In a prime position beyond the concourse stands the King's Library, a great collection of beautiful volumes left to the nation by George III on condition that it should be kept together and on show to the public and not just to scholars. This is housed in a 'jewel case', a six-storey tower made of bronze and glass; grand materials not used elsewhere in the building. To add to its symbolic role it stands on a polished marble base that acts like a mirror reflecting the books downwards as if into the enormous store of books below.

The Science Reading Rooms have open access to the stacks which are used for comparatively short periods of time, and consequently there are only a few reading desks. In contrast, the Humanities Rooms have closed access to the stacks, they are almost totally given over to desks, and readers stay much longer. A sophisticated electronic retrieval system collects required books from the basements. Because of their different uses, the two sets of reading rooms are very different in their spatial arrangement and in the way they are lit. In the Science Rooms three floors of stacks with low ceilings could feel oppressive, and therefore the two upper floors are stepped back giving a three-storey space leading from the entrance, and lit from the sides. The Humanities Rooms step back more generously forming terraces over the main part of the room that becomes an expansive volume lit from above. These different lighting and spatial arrangements give each discipline its own special identity. Each of the Reading Rooms is enriched by a rhythmic repetition of ventilators, balustrade uprights, and uplighters set against the wider spacing of the columns.

2.45 - British Library entrance foyer

2.46 - British Library Humanities reading room

2.47 - British Library stairs in the foyer

The unique collection of historical books and documents in the British Library can be seen by members of the public, by parties of schoolchildren and by students. They are housed at ground level off the main concourse, without natural light and in a carefully controlled environment.

We have noted the way each part of the Library has its particular characteristics, the splendour of the main concourse, the magnificence of the King's Library, the subdued light of the exhibition rooms, and the difference between the two types of room for the different disciplines; each has an identity within the whole. Individual readers have a strong sense of their own place; they come to the library to do their personal research, to concentrate intensely, to think and reflect, working alone but within a building for several hundred other people. Even those scholars who originally regretted the move from their much loved Reading Room in the British Museum have enthusiastically recorded their satisfaction.

The design of the British Library had been frustrated by changes to the brief, to the area of the site, the phasing of building, as well as funding. Colin St John Wilson had spent twenty three years on this building in addition to the many years on the earlier designs. Asked how he had managed to survive such a long ordeal, his response was that *"he had been saved by his sense of history"*;[2.4] did he perhaps have in mind the eighteen years that Brunelleschi spent on the Dome in Florence?

3.1 - Colonial house

3.2 - Pleached limes in France

3.3 - Farmhouse, Arisaig in Scotland

3 MODIFYING CLIMATE

Differences in climate affect lifestyles, personalities and cultures. In a hot climate with constant sunshine people can live outside, eat and drink on the terrace, and sit in a café on the street. They try to keep out of the sun, and often enjoy a siesta in the middle of the day. They find it hard to imagine how people can tolerate fighting the cold, revel in putting on extra clothes or huddling by the fire, constantly being uncertain of the weather, and welcoming, if not worshipping, the sun.

The brightness of the south in contrast to the long dark winter nights of the north contributes both to a different outlook on life and to differences of personality, caricatured as the cheerful outgoing extrovert against the more dour and sombre introvert. Of course this is a generalisation and an exaggeration, but it is given expression in literature, music and painting. It is hard to imagine Ibsen coming from Cannes, or Louis Armstrong from Oslo, and Edward Munch could hardly have sprung from Trinidad nor Picasso from Finland.

Living in the south of France is different from living in Norway, and different again from the tropics where daylight begins and ends at a regular time and the seasons hardly show. Life in a village high up in the mountains is different from that on the plains below. Life by the ocean is fiercer than the more sheltered world inland. Climate therefore helps to establish where we are and gives a sense of place and identity.

Buildings modify climate; they provide shelter and protect against the elements. For those fleeing from oppression, famine or disaster, the dwelling may consist of nothing but a tent; for others in squatter settlements or ghettos, it may be a shack made of discarded materials, cardboard, timber or corrugated iron. More substantially, it may be a little house made of local materials, with water and sewage disposal provided some distance away. This is the lot of many in the developing world and still for many in industrial cities around the world. Paul Oliver's book 'Dwellings: the House Across the World'[3.1] charts the story of unsophisticated structures that provide basic shelter in a resourceful and elegant way. Different climates have generated different architectures and these in turn have added to the distinctiveness of place.

Response to climate has a major impact on human settlements. Their *raison d'être* may be defence, trade, manufacture,

3.4 - Five Foot Way, Singapore

3.5 - Five Foot Way exterior, Singapore

transport, administration, authority or a combination of these, but their location is often determined by issues of climatic exposure and protection. A hill-top position may be good for defence and in some hot climates attract a welcome breeze, but in other regions the cold and gales can make life unbearable. Coastal towns may be located for trade and transport, but they need to be sheltered in the lee of the wind and protected by strongly engineered harbours. Traditionally rivers have powered mills, and gradually they have generated settlements around them that need protection from floods. These are issues that have been addressed not necessarily by architects but by those who have inherited a close understanding of the locality.

ARCHITECTURE IN HOT CLIMATES

Protection from the sun, rain and wind influences the form of the city. When **Sir Stamford Raffles** founded Singapore he passed an ordinance that every building should have a 'five-foot way', a covered arcade along the street. It was an edict that was so transparently reasonable that it was willingly accepted, and it created a city that was both climatically friendly and very special. In sad contrast to this, in the modern high-rise city of Singapore the streets are hot, and the shops are enclosed in air-conditioned malls. Although it is a city full of trees, these have been planted as a landscape feature rather than to provide shade.

In Italy, the city is cooler than the countryside; in Bologna, the streets have colonnades as in old Singapore, and in Siena, the narrow streets between high buildings are in deep shadow for most of the day. In a typical Italian piazza, a loggia often makes a welcome shaded place, whilst the terrace of a particular café might be patronised more in the morning or the evening according to the position of the sun. Often, up at roof level, a private loggia or gazebo can be seen to enjoy both the breeze and view.

In France, nearly every town and city has a park or square where avenues of pleached limes form a canopy for sitting under, playing boules or, more prosaically but usefully, for parking cars.

The typical **colonial bungalow,** built by the British around the world and designed by government engineers, copes well with the extreme climate of the tropics. Its large roof, hipped or gabled, protects against the searing sun and torrential rains, and oversails a wide verandah where most of living takes place. The edges of the roof are adorned with fretwork, a simple and clever device to alleviate the glare between the brightness outside and the comparative darkness within. The house is kept cool by cross-ventilation under the floor and through louvres in the doors and windows. It is usually single-storey though a more affluent version may have two floors with a balcony around the

3.6 - Bali pavilions

3.7 - Geoffrey Bawa's office internal view

Patel House 1st floor

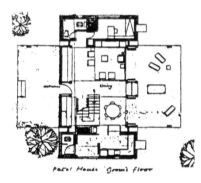
Patel House Ground floor

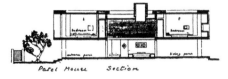
Patel House Section

3.8 - Hasmuck Patel house

upper level. It tends to be made of timber with the roof covered in shingles or more cheaply with corrugated iron. The colonial bungalow fulfils the two most essential requirements for living in the tropics, shade and ventilation, albeit that its fretwork has tended to become a somewhat stylistic feature.

Geoffrey Bawa, the Sri Lankan architect, has used the great roof to protect buildings in a hot climate. He has worked in Bali where interestingly there is a tradition for the same plan form to be used for a wide range of building types, whether for a school, a temple or a house; this consists of a group of separate pavilions within an enclosing wall. Bawa was asked to design a small gallery for a painter together with twelve houses each on a plot of around an acre. The various requirements for each house - living, sleeping and guest rooms - occupy separate pavilions, some have one floor, others two. The pavilions have shingle roofs with wide overhanging eaves; bedrooms and guest rooms are enclosed but some living pavilions are quite open under the roof. The art gallery is on two storeys with an enclosed space below and a completely open area above. As in the British colonial house, the roof acts as an umbrella or parasol. A house split up into parts like this provides opportunity for splendid landscaping with shading trees and cooling pools.

Geoffrey Bawa's gift in transforming the landscape of a garden is to be seen in all his work since his magical garden at **Lununanga,** started in 1949, with its variously composed vistas, its carefully formed steps and paving, and its specially positioned pieces of sculpture. This care continues in the many courtyards in his **own house in Colombo** which allow it to open up and breathe in the hot sun. It is evident also in his office where an atrium is at the centre with a long formal pool on the main axis. Here is revealed another quality of Bawa's work - a calm restful grandeur. This is due not only to the manipulation of space but also to the sensitive use of natural materials, stone and tiled floors, timber posts, and exposed rafters set against white plastered walls. This simplicity characterises all his work which is in some ways traditional yet at the same time innovative and timeless.

The Indian architect **Hasmukh Patel** is among those who have devised ways of achieving shade and ventilation other than with a pitched roof and a large overhang. He lives and works in the hot dry city of Ahmedabad, and was greatly influenced by Le Corbusier with whom he had worked. His aim was to design a naturally ventilated house for his family that would not need air-conditioning; this he managed to achieve except during two or three weeks in the year just before the monsoons. It is a two-storey house where the first floor is cantilevered about four metres over the ground floor on the north and south sides. This provides a shaded porch and a verandah whilst allowing a

3.9 - Ligornetto house

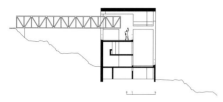
3.10 - Riva San Vitale section

3.11 - Riva San Vitale entrance bridge

3.12 - Riva San Vitale view from south

breeze to flow underneath into the central double-height living room and out through the roof. The bedrooms that face north and south on the first floor have deeply recessed and shaded windows formed by a wall of cupboards. Patel's architecture could not be more different from that of a colonial bungalow but the same principles of shading and ventilation still obtain.

Mario Botta similarly used deeply recessed openings to provide shade. This can be seen in a number of houses in the Ticino in the south of Switzerland where the climate is very hot in summer but cold in winter. He also had worked for a short time in the office of Le Corbusier as well as that of Louis Kahn. Following their influence, his architecture consisted of pure platonic forms without any disturbing projections.

The house at **Ligornetto** is a rectangle on plan. The north façade is blank except for a vertical opening in the centre; the south façade has openings grouped together and carved out of the simple form. On the first floor, a deep balcony pushes the living room windows back into the shade, and on the second floor the void is doubled in size with a further balcony to the main bedroom, thus similarly shading the windows on this floor. The stark simplicity of the house is relieved by bold bands of different coloured concrete blocks that are reminiscent of some Romanesque churches.

The house at **Riva San Vitale** is a square tower on a steep hillside overlooking Lake Lugano. It is a severely simple form standing alone in the landscape; its pure geometry is defined by solid corners right up to the roof, and its sides are precisely and deeply cut out to reveal the volumes within. The house is entered on the top floor along a steel footbridge designed as a box girder; this leaves the form of the tower intact and accentuates the mass of its concrete block construction. The bridge arrives at the upper level of a double-height space, and the visitor is immediately aware of the variety of open volumes and terraces that make up the building. The plan of the building and its openings are arranged diagonally, and each floor is different. This gives a rich variety of spaces overlooking voids of different heights, so that the various rooms and terraces enjoy ever-changing views of lake, mountain and sky. As at Ligornetto, shade is provided in summer, not by a projecting canopy but by bold recesses behind the overall envelope. In winter this gives a protective zone away from the snowy outside.

Charles Correa regarded climate as a prime generator not only of architecture but also of every aspect of the culture of a country. Working mainly in India, he coined the phrase *"open to sky space"* [3.2] to emphasise the need and enjoyment of living out of doors in that climate.

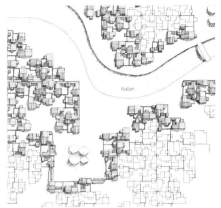

3.13 - Belapur housing plan

3.14 - Belapur house courtyard

3.15 - Kanchanjunga apartments

Early in his career he designed the **Memorial Museum to Mahatma Gandhi** on the site of his ashram in Ahmedabad. It consists of some sixty square aedicules with pyramidal roofs that form a loose informal grid. Some are used for exhibitions and are enclosed with louvred windows; others are open and provide cool and shaded places that attract the breeze. In the centre is a square water court which adds to the sense of calm. The construction of these simple forms is very basic; tiled roofs are supported on bare concrete beams which form wide gutters resting on robust brick columns; it is all lovingly detailed. Appropriately for a building in memory of Gandhi, it is a place for quiet contemplation.

In all his housing, whether for the poor or the rich, Correa sought to provide individual terraces or gardens. This is most clearly demonstrated in two particular and very different schemes: the Belapur housing in New Mumbai, and the Kanchanjunga apartments in the centre of Mumbai.

The **Belapur** housing, built between 1983 and 1986, is one of a number of low-rise and high-density schemes where each house has its own square plot of land and its own 'open to sky space' designed to be airy and open. The layout is based on a hierarchy of groupings; six or seven houses form a cluster around a small courtyard, and three or four clusters are grouped around a larger 'local' courtyard, and in turn three localities form a neighbourhood sharing some communal facilities. This simple configuration is human in scale, it is built of everyday materials, and it allows for whatever interaction between neighbours that they might choose. Initially some of the houses have just one room and a W.C. but because none of the houses share a party wall, change and expansion is easy.

The **Kanchanjunga** apartment block in Mumbai, completed in 1983, is an unusual work by Charles Correa; it is a high tower of twenty-seven storeys designed for high-income families. Its response to climate embodies similar principles to those used in housing on the ground, and aims to achieve as much 'open to sky space' as possible.

The building is square on plan and orientated east-west to exploit the best views and sea breezes. To mitigate against the low morning and evening sunlight the living room windows are set back behind deep double-height balconies; they are like terrace gardens, and are planted with trees to provide shade. The cross-section of the building consists of two interlocking apartments which have their living rooms and terraces alternately on opposite facades, rather like those in the Unité d'Habitation by Le Corbusier. On the outside the cut-out of the terraces serves to reduce the scale of a high tower.

3.16 - Neue Vahr south side

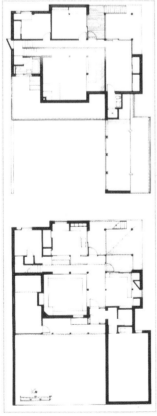

3.17 - Neue Vahr east side

3.18 - Cornford house plans

ARCHITECTURE IN COLD CLIMATES

Latitude has a strong effect on climate. Travelling south from the north of Europe is to experience a gradual transformation of traditional roof forms. The heavy winter snows of Scandinavia and Switzerland require houses and farms to have steep roofs and wide projecting eaves, whereas towards the south roof pitches change down to the low pantiled roofs of the Mediterranean. This creates a strong regional variation and a clear and rewarding sense of place.

A courtyard, as we have seen, is a place to come together; in a hot climate it provides a place to breathe, and in a cold climate it can protect against the wind and cold. A **farm at Arisaig** in the west of Scotland epitomises enclosure and protection; it is located deep in a sheltered valley less than half a mile from the fierceness of the Atlantic, its courtyard a further shield for the animals in winter.

Alvar Aalto demonstrated the positive advantages for a building in northern Europe to be closed to the cold north and open to the sunny south. This is most notable in the **Neue Vahr** apartments in Bremen built between 1959 and 1962. The north wall containing the lifts and stairs is almost completely solid, whilst the apartments fan out towards the south. This contrast between a straight line and a fan is a favourite Aalto geometry. Here as elsewhere he exploits its numerous advantages; firstly, the dwellings widen out towards the light giving a greater sense of space, whilst the kitchens, bathrooms and cupboards are in the narrower part; secondly, because of the different angles the dwellings turn their face away from one another and gain more privacy; and thirdly, the shape of the communal entrance hall on each floor makes it a *place,* rather than just a corridor, with each front door recessed within its own porch. The impact of climate is integrated with all the other needs of the residents.

In 1965-67 **Colin St John Wilson** and **M.J. Long** designed a house for the painter **Christopher Cornford**. The client brief asked for more than just use and convenience and sowed the seeds of an architectural idea. He asked for an introspective space that should be central but in contact with other rooms; it should feel protective, in bad weather and at night. At the same time he wanted '*a kind of extroverted aspect*' in relation to the sun and the garden.

The site is on the edge of Cambridge at the end of a cul-de-sac with a view at the back towards open countryside. From the approach road the house has a simplicity that belies the complexity within. This is in response to the client's wishes, and contains a series of overlapping relationships between enclosure and openness, inside and outside, high and low.

3.19 - Cornford house view from south

3.20 - Cornford house living room

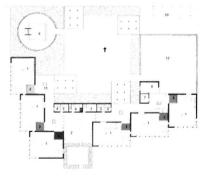
3.21 - Nagele School plan

Essentially the house is square on plan, organised diagonally towards the south, with the artist's studio in a wing next to the front door. On the ground floor the living room is to the north with the fireplace in the corner. Like Neue Vahr it is enclosed on the northern sides by solid walls and it is open towards the south. This openness is ambiguous as there is also a sense of enclosure. This is created by a reduced level (the living room is two steps down) and by three tall Columbian pine posts that define an internal atrium of immense height, magically lit by a clerestory over the fireplace. This is surrounded by an L-shaped ambulatory that connects the entrance with the staircase, and leads into a low kitchen on one side and a dining recess on the other. These embrace the atrium and form an outward facing L-shape in contrast to the inward facing L-shape of the ambulatory. On the diagonal, the living room connects to an open loggia that is an outside atrium defined by three further tall pine posts, and with the kitchen and dining room opening onto it. On the first floor, a gallery from the staircase serves the library and leads towards the main bedroom. The form of the roof gives these rooms extra height and permits high-level windows. They also have windows on to the outside atrium, whilst the bedroom, intriguingly, has an opening panel that gives contact with the living room below.

The difference between the outside and the inside of this house is further marked by the use of materials; the outside walls are fair-faced brick, returned at the ends to exaggerate their thickness, whereas inside they are plastered. These solid walls contrast with the sensitive and carefully detailed use of timber.

In this house, the complexity of geometry exists not for its own sake but to satisfy a series of reciprocal and intentionally ambiguous relationships. It is executed with total consistency, accepting the discipline of pitched roofs and exploiting and enjoying the space below.

Between 1954 and 1960 **Aldo van Eyck** designed a number of buildings whose elegant plans display an important consideration for climate and at the same time demonstrate a subtle system of social grouping. The **Nagele** school is designed as a pin-wheel around a central courtyard. There are four entrances, two from the street outside and two to the halves of the school; each is marked by a free-standing porch over what van Eyck describes as "*a large doorstep*". This leads into a group of three classrooms connected to a central hall. Adjacent classrooms share a small communal space in order to stimulate a varied mix of grouping; it is a non-hierarchical school resembling a village. Within this primary organisation each classroom is protected from the north by a solid enclosing wall with a recessed entrance that serves to emphasise a sense of place. All the classrooms have large windows towards the south and west.

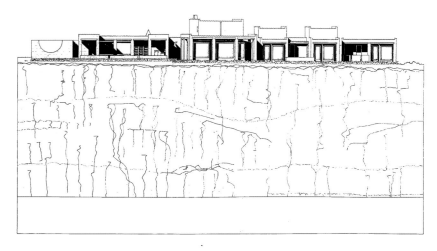

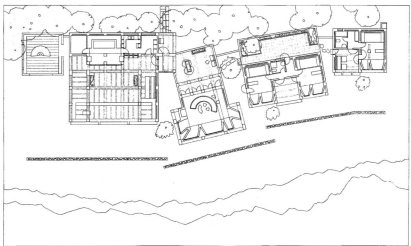

3.22 - Can Lis elevation and plan

3.23 - Can Lis view from sea

THE MAGIC OF LIGHT

The quality of light enriches daily life. Light from the sun is constantly changing in relation to the seasons, the time of day, location, and the weather. The architect, like the painter and the photographer, manipulates light, exploiting its rich palette. Louis Kahn describes light as *"the giver of all presences"*.[3.3] In his many sketches and lectures Le Corbusier has drawn the path of the sun in summer and winter, and so important is this message that it is engraved on a block of concrete outside the Unité d'Habitation in Marseilles.

Two houses by Jørn Utzon in Majorca for his family are particularly notable because they exploit light, and frame views in a very special way. The house called **Can Lis** was built in 1972 after Utzon had resigned from the commission for the Sydney Opera House. It is near the edge of a stone cliff that falls almost vertically into the sea. It consists of five separate pavilions that are very different but united by their architectural expression. It is essentially a place in the sun enjoying magnificent views and many contrasts - inside against outside, dark against light, cool against hot. It is a refuge of peace and calm. To the north it presents a series of nearly blank walls relieved only by an entrance porch, kitchen windows, and carefully planted courtyards.

From the entrance, the kitchen and dining room are to the west at the back of a square U-shaped courtyard facing the sea. This is surrounded by a colonnade that is like a cloister, an apt analogy to a place that has the cool simplicity of a Cistercian monastery. Everything is made of honey-coloured local stone, the walls and columns with the saw marks left as from the quarry, and the floor of slightly darker stone, bare and unadorned. The same system of construction is used throughout; a pair of precast I-beams for lintels, similar single ones for rafters, with arched tiles between, giving a simple richness to the ceilings. The courtyard steps down towards the sea so that the paved floor is at the level of the balustrade, providing a clear view to the horizon. There is thus a choice of where to dine - indoors, under the shade of the cloister, or outside in the open.

The living room is in the pavilion to the east of the entrance porch. To get there you go outside into a small shaded courtyard and through a low colonnade that acts like a narthex into the high living space. It is this room that exemplifies the essence of the house, dramatically emphasising the contrast between inside and outside. The windows, apparently without frames, are set in deep tapered recesses at different angles that channel the view into five separate pictures, giving a measure of suspense and surprise rather than revealing everything at once. These recesses make the bare stone wall appear about two metres thick,

3.24 - Can Lis dining kitchen courtyard

3.25 - Can Lis living room faces the sea

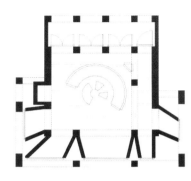

3.26 - Can Lis living room plan

3.27 - Can Lis courtyard faces the sea

exaggerating its cave-like quality and creating a cool interior protected from the glare of the sun. These recesses, together with the columns at the entry, are less than half the height of the room, giving a domestic scale that is reinforced by the large semi-circular seat positioned at the centre. In contrast, a small window high in the west wall emphasises the loftiness of the room and lets in a magical evening light.

The bedroom pavilion next to the living room is similarly entered through its small courtyard. It has two bedrooms embracing a small terrace towards the sea, and each room has windows set in deep recesses as in the living room. The furthermost pavilion is entered through a covered terrace and has one large bedroom with similar windows.

To the south, these pavilions present a classical columnar façade that unifies their internal differences and gives a temple-like quality to each. The most westerly pavilion is a small open square enclosed by walls with large semi-circular openings reminiscent of Louis Kahn. It appears to have no specific function but seems simply to be a place to sit and contemplate, a reflection of the peaceful ambience of the whole house.

After more than twenty years Utzon found the invasion of tourists nearby overpowering, and in his later years he found it onerous to go outside from room to room, especially in winter. He decided to build a second house on a site higher up in the mountains.

Can Felis was built in 1994 and shares many of the characteristics of Can Lis. It presents a nearly blank wall to the north, and consists of three discrete elements, dining/ kitchen, living room and bedrooms, although here they are joined together. The house creates a similar tension between inside and outside, it uses stone throughout though more finely wrought, but above all it embodies the same classical discipline of columns and beams. Entry is under a colonnade through a walled courtyard that leads to a columned porch. The entrance hall does not yet give views of the sea as these are reserved for the main rooms. The living room and bedrooms project forward creating a series of stepped terraces in front of the dining and kitchen area. The upper terrace is covered and supported on a colonnade along its edge like a stoa, so that, as at Can Lis, there is a variety of places to eat and drink. The lower terrace has a long narrow swimming pool, formally arranged.

The living room has a special relationship between inside and outside. It is divided into two with the rear half a metre above the front and the ceiling pitched towards the centre. As in the earlier house the view of the sea is broken up into sections,

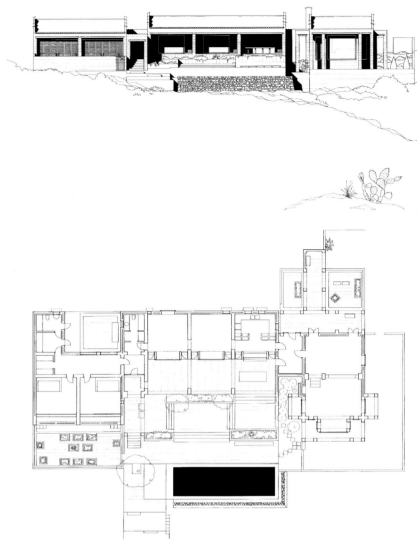

3.28 - Can Felis plan and elevation

3.29 - Can Felis living room

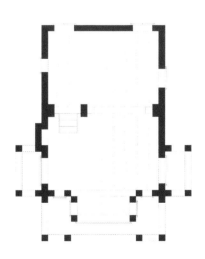

3.30 - Can Felis living room plan

achieved here by three bay windows that are each protected from the sun by external colonnades. This creates a complex pattern of columns with the outer ones extended a further metre below floor level, making it appear like a floating platform above the view.

The bedroom wing has an enclosed courtyard to the north and an open terrace a few steps down towards the view. The walls between the bedrooms extend forward to provide shade and continue the trabeated system of structure. Throughout this house the same repertoire of materials is used as at Can Lis but in a somewhat more refined way. As demonstrated in all his work Utzon took great pleasure in the way buildings are made.

These two houses have a timeless quality and a delight achieved not by reference to fashion or style, but by careful attention to site, to sun and view, to shade and the avoidance of glare, to generous space as well as enclosure, to simplicity of structure and a straightforward way of using materials. All aspects are brought together in mutual support to create a unique and memorable place.

In the **Kimbell Museum** by **Louis Kahn** at Fort Worth Texas designed between 1966 and 1972, it is the quality of light that gives the interior its enduring calm. Its impressive monumentality is achieved by the repetition of a simple form, by the discipline of dimension and human scale, and the careful relationship of materials.

The plan is U-shaped and is made up of long barrel vaults (effectively prestressed beams) arranged in parallel; each is thirty metres long by seven metres wide. The vaults are separated by a low flat ceiling two metres wide that contains sevice pipes. Light enters through a long slot in the centre of each vault and is reflected up on to the polished concrete surface. Some light is diffused through the perforated aluminium reflectors, and in this way glare is avoided. The central entrance bay has four vaults and each of the side bays has six vaults, and in each bay the outer vault is not enclosed but acts as a grand classical portico.

The scale inside is domestic as required by the client to show off medium-size works of art; Kahn referred to it as a *"friendly home"*. To reduce their height the vaults are cycloid rather than semicircular, and their springing is only three metres above the floor. The gallery is spacious, uninterrupted by any permanent walls, and with views across in all directions. Three small courtyards serve to give identity and a sense of place to the whole. Opposite the entrance is a shop with a library behind, and to the side is a snack bar beside the auditorium - Kahn had remarked *"As exhibitions are so tiring, a cup of coffee is a necessity!"*

3.32 - Kimbell Museum entrance porch

3.33 - Kimbell Museum barrel vaults

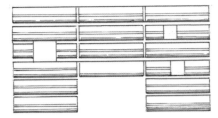

3.34 - Kimbell Museum roof plan

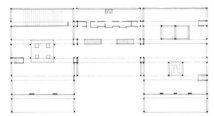

3.35 - Kimbell Museum ground floor plan

3.36 - Kimbell Museum detail

3.37 - Kimbell Museum interior gallery

As with all Kahn's work the monumental presence of the building is achieved by a limited palette of materials. The structure is of concrete, finely crafted and polished from precise shuttering. Walls are of travertine (a material selected to harmonise gently with the concrete) and separated from the vaults by narrow gaps. The gallery floors are made of white oak and the floor under the low ceilings is travertine. Every junction and every detail has been carefully considered by the master. Outside, a formal use of water and groves of Yuapon holly trees serve to settle the building into the landscape.

The Kimbell Museum demonstrates a powerful architecture, elegant in its classical simplicity; this is achieved without any superficial iconic gestures, but is derived from the essential elements of the building.

Sacred buildings evoke a very special mood. The history of the medieval church is not only technical - as demonstrated by the increased height and the enlargement of the windows - but also meaningful, reaching up to heaven, with carvings and stained glass windows telling the story.

The church of **Notre Dame** at **Raincy** by **Auguste Perret** built in 1922-3 continued that tradition; here, the nave and side aisles are separated by tall slender reinforced concrete columns. The nave has a long gently curved barrel vault towards the altar whilst the aisles have a series of barrel vaults running between the columns and the outside. This defines an arched colonnade along the nave and arched heads to the windows. These are made up of an ingenious system of prefabricated concrete blocks ablaze with coloured light. Externally the windows form the whole enclosure without any solid wall; an innovative reinterpretation of late Gothic.

3.38 - Notre-Dame du Raincy interior view

51

3.39 - Notre Dame du Haut Ronchamp exterior from north

3.40 - Notre Dame du Haut Ronchamp exterior from west

3.41 - Notre Dame du Haut Ronchamp view from south west

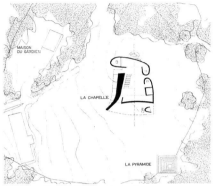

3.42 - Notre Dame du Haut Ronchamp plan

3.43 - Notre Dame du Haut Ronchamp exterior from south

The **Chapel** of **Notre Dame du Haut** at **Ronchamp** by **Le Corbusier** (completed in 1954) is a most dramatic expression of form, space and light. It is sited on a hill in the Belfort gap between the Vosges and the Jura where it stands out against the sky like a bold sculpture. It is orientated traditionally towards the east, and the pedestrian way up to it is from the south. It immediately presents a white concave wall with a random pattern of small openings below an enormous grey roof that projects forward, and to its left stands a convex white tower that has a half-dome at the top. The main entrance doorway, recessed between the concave wall and the convex tower, is faced inside and out with a vivid painting by Le Corbusier enamelled on to steel sheets; the only colour on an otherwise black and white façade.

A building of such sculptural form invites a walk around. From the south-east, the great projecting roof resembles the upturned brim of a hat over the face of the battered walls below. On the south side, it projects about four metres over the entrance, reducing in size to meet the end of the wall at the south-east corner. The east wall is also concave, separated from the south wall by a gap that locates another entrance. The roof here projects around nine metres and shelters the chancel of an outside chapel; it is supported at one end by the south wall and towards the other end by a single column. This dramatic grey curved roof is made of concrete with exposed shutter marks. It appears black on the underside in contrast to the white walls on which it casts long curved shadows. Bright light and deep dark shadows exaggerate the contrasting forms.

From the north-east the section of the roof is revealed in profile, and appears to project behind the wall on the north whose top is cleanly cut off. The face of this wall is flush with one of the towers that is separated from its neighbour by another entrance. The convex plane of the west wall is flush with the towers at the north-west and south-west corners and gives continuity to the form. The top of this wall dips towards a great gargoyle at the centre that discharges into a freestanding pool below.

The footprint of Notre Dame du Haut is a powerful abstraction of the sculptural geometry inside and out. The interior is an inversion of the exterior form and has a mystical quality that is reminiscent of an early Romanesque church but achieved quite differently. The overpowering effect is of subdued light that enters through a random pattern of small windows of different sizes and shapes; these are deeply recessed within chamfered openings in the battered south wall. This wall, together with that at the east end, is separated from the roof by a narrow slot illuminating the dramatic ceiling. This is a convex shape that rises towards the edges and reaches its highest point in the corner to the right of the altar. It is made of dark grey concrete

3.44 - Notre Dame du Haut Ronchamp interior towards east

3.45 - Notre Dame du Haut Ronchamp interior towards west

left untouched from the shutter, and is a continuation within of the great canopy outside. It contrasts with the white walls that have a rough texture similar to the outside. The east wall behind the altar is punctured by small dots of light and by a small square window with a statue of the Madonna visible both from inside and out.

The west wall and part of the north wall flow into three small chapels below the towers that scoop a bright light from above. Intriguingly, this is from three different directions in response to the aspect of the three semi-domes outside, and makes each little chapel a special place.

The floor slopes down towards the curved step into the chancel, and rises again towards the altar. It follows the slope of the ground but is also a reminder of the floor in some of the churches in Burgundy. The plane of the floor emphasises the spaciousness of the chapel, and only a small part on one side is occupied by pews. Its surface is made of polished concrete divided into large random sections, with the central east-west axis clearly defined towards the altar. The platform around the altar is made of a beautiful white stone from Burgundy.

This exceptional late work by Le Corbusier clearly has its genesis in his paintings. Externally the sculptural form is immensely powerful but it is in complete harmony with the space inside. This not only fully satisfies the liturgical needs of the church but also gives it an appropriate presence. The acoustics work well in an architecture that otherwise suggests a respectful silence; a silence and a presence achieved by the subtle manipulation of form and light.

3.46 - Notre Dame du Haut Ronchamp interior north wall

4.1 - Muuratsalo courtyard wall

4 RELATING to CONTEXT

THE LAND

4.2 - Muuratsalo view from below

4.3 - Muuratsalo view from above

The land is a precious resource, together with the sea it is essential for survival. Its productivity depends on the climate, on available technology, on knowledge and skill, as well as on a body of hardworking labour. The city is variously the market place, the centre of trade, manufacture, finance, a place of learning, culture and religion as well as administration or defence. Most of the countryside and all of the city is man-made. In both we have inherited the work of many millions of people who worked for low wages and by hand. In the country they tamed nature into field systems, terraces for vineyards or paddy fields for rice, and they constructed dams, dykes and canals, railway bridges and embankments. In the city they built houses and factories, streets and squares as well as grand buildings; cathedrals, mosques or temples, libraries, theatres, universities, and palaces for the wealthy.

The country and the city are mutually dependent but continually in conflict. In the last two centuries, the tension between the country and the city has been exacerbated by an exponential rate of change; this was due to the increase in population, the rise in industrialisation and greater mobility, most notably in the ownership of the car. All of these impact on the use of land, and, whether in the country or the city, new building makes a dramatic intervention on what exists.

Architects refer to 'reading' a site, which means observing its essential characteristics both within the boundaries and beyond; studying the topography, aspect, views, climate, access, the quality of edges, openness and enclosure, as well as likely changes nearby. Reading a site begins not only with a rational site analysis but also with a sense of wonder, an open receptiveness to the *genius loci*, the positive features to be exploited and the negative aspects to be resolved. This is the beginning of a search for clues as to what might be an appropriate proposal. The ancient arts of feng-shui and geomancy were developed for just this. Every context is different; sometimes it is an idyllic garden or a distant view, sometimes a fine street or square, sometimes a derelict area of a city, and sometimes the extension or repair of an existing historic building.

4.4 - Muuratsalo external view

4.5 - Baron house entrance

4.6 - Muuratsalo plan

4.7 - Baron house plan

4.8 - Baron house exterior detail

In '*The Place of Houses*', Charles Moore, Gerald Allen and Donlyn Lyndon have suggested that there are four ways of fitting a building to the land; *commanding, surrounding, enfronting and merging.*[4.1] A building such as a villa, church or temple in the landscape can be seen to *command,* another might *surround* a courtyard, village green or town square. One building might form an edge or *enfront* a street, whilst another might *merge* into the countryside or urban fabric. These are useful ways of understanding the relation of building to context.

THE RURAL CONTEXT

Houses in the open landscape present a particular challenge. **Alvar Aalto's** summer house at **Muuratsalo,** designed in 1953, is situated on a wooded island in an isolated position enjoying the special relationship between land and water. This raises the question: how best to make a man-made intervention in a natural landscape setting? Aalto's solution was to make a defined domain containing both house and open space, a level platform on an undulating rocky terrain, a formal geometry set in the wild. The plan is a perfect square with the overall form defined by a wall that is high at one side and sloping down towards the other; its enclosure emphasised by its continuity. This form is like a huge monopitched roof that has been cut out to form a great square outside room, an atrium with a large square hearth at its centre - a place to come together around the fire. Surrounding rooms form an L-shaped house where the pitch of the roof provides a high communal living space on one side and lower individual rooms for sleeping on the other - an appropriate and well-established pattern.

Outside and inside are further signified by colour and texture; the plain brickwork outside is painted white whereas the inner walls and the floor of the atrium are made of different sorts of red brick, variously bonded and pointed to make a rich Mondrian-like pattern. Aalto used this not only as an experiment to test different weathering properties but also to provide a homely enclosure. Outside the main house, guest rooms and workshops form a loose chain of small structures along the contours.

The **Baron House** at **Skåne** in **Sweden** by **John Pawson** also stands in open landscape. It is a square house arranged around an external courtyard. It has two predominant axes with the living rooms on the north side, bedrooms to the south, and with the entrance into the courtyard on the east leading across to the front door opposite. Everything about the house is elegantly ordered; the courtyard defines the central part of the living area and is glazed right across, whilst the two ends of the room are partly shielded by the fireplace and the kitchen units, all united within the volume of the pitched roof. The bedrooms are more

4.9 - Bargemon house view from upstairs landing

4.10 - Bargemon house exterior from south-west

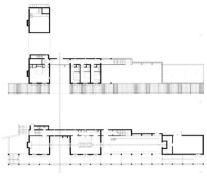

4.11 - Bargemon house plan

4.12 - Bargemon house section

4.13 - Bargemon house swimming pool

4.14 - Bargemon house southern colonnade

private; they are arranged symmetrically about the north-south axis and only their small hallway looks into the courtyard.

The house has a simple corrugated metal roof, white walls and bold black shutters, and from afar it looks like a traditional farm in the landscape. All the windows are the same size from the floor to the eaves, with those on the axes providing views right through the house to the countryside beyond. Large wooden shutters are designed to slide across the windows when the house is unoccupied. This house is meticulously detailed so that the planes of the walls, floors and ceilings meet in exactly the right place and emphasise the beautiful proportions of the three-dimensional geometry. The interior is simple and calm but also discreetly sophisticated; the exterior is low-key and, like Aalto's summer house, settles sedately in the landscape.

Edward and **Margot Jones** designed a family house at **Bargemon** in the Var in the south of France which merges with the landscape and is in complete harmony with its context. The site is in an ancient olive grove with terraces running across it from east to west and with splendid views south over magnificent countryside towards the Mediterranean. The overarching response to the site has the appearance of inevitability; it is a narrow house with the rooms facing the view and arranged in line along one of the terraces. The north wall is almost completely blank with a simple and somewhat understated front door. The plan is organised around two axes: the primary one is along the length of the house and is defined by a fireplace at one end and a formal niche beyond the pool at the other (an intriguing interplay between fire and water) giving a view through the living room, the loggia, the dining room, and the swimming pool; a secondary axis at right angles defines the centre of the loggia and the dramatic view south from the upstairs corridor. Along the whole of the south façade a colonnade of nineteen columns supports a long pergola, broken only at the loggia; this provides shade, frames the view, and unifies the different elements of the plan with a formal presence to the garden. In the climate of Provence a swimming pool is a necessary delight, and its inclusion as a 'room' within the footprint and behind the colonnade is a masterly decision, so different from the bright blue intrusion that often disfigures the landscape. The plan of the first floor reflects the order below, with the main bedroom over the living room, and three smaller bedrooms over the dining room. There are two staircases, an internal stair from the entrance and an external one down towards the pool.

The house is finished with 'crepi', a local method of rendering, and has a monopitch pantile roof. It is an uncompromising house of today that fits in a friendly way with its neighbours. Internally the clarity of the linear plan with its two axes together with the

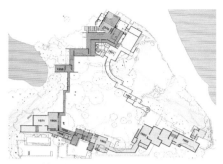

discipline of the grid creates an ordered calm .The effect of the colonnade both inside and out emphasises the overarching intention to exploit the view within a bold classical order, and anchors it in place along the terrace.

Louisiana Museum of Modern Art is in an idyllic garden. It is near the sea at Humlebaek north of Copenhagen, and was designed by **Wohlert and Bo** in stages between 1958 and 1991. The founder Knud Jensen shared with the architects an enthusiasm for the site, as he commented *"The beautiful country helps you to enjoy art in a receptive and pleasant mood, a holiday mood in which everything is fresh and new. This wonderful landscape permits us to pause, repose and contemplate while enjoying the works of art."* At the outset the architects spent weeks living on the site to fully appreciate its essential qualities.

The original house is small and well proportioned. It was built in the 19th century by a nobleman who was married three times, each time to a lady called Louise, hence the name *Louisiana,* which the museum has adopted 'out of respect for such fidelity'. The house became the entrance to the museum, which was designed quite simply as a walk around the garden. From the house a glazed cloister passes between the trees, and at one point it seems to hug the trunk of an enormous beech. It is small in scale, beautifully crafted, with full-height timber mullions and a boarded ceiling, and with views inside and out to carefully-placed sculptures. Not all the secrets of the landscape are given away at once; at each turn surprise views are presented, with glimpses of the lake, a natural dell, a Japanese water garden, leading finally to the openness of the Sound. This contact with the outside in no way detracts from the exhibits; the route alternates between open and closed, low and high, giving both interest and a sense of place to each part.

The cloister leads to galleries that are lit in three different ways; there are those that are side lit, those that are lantern lit, and one that is double-height lit from the end. There is no attempt to achieve even lighting, and the light is ever-changing to give the sort of natural conditions under which many of the works were created. This means that glimpses of sunlight fall on the exhibits, an ideal arrangement for setting off the shape and texture of sculpture. When direct sun is not wanted or when it would do harm, it is simply kept out by blinds or curtains. At the end of the route there is an elegant restaurant built of similar materials overlooking the sea.

New activities and new large acquisitions led to considerable expansion. A square concert hall with seats arranged towards one corner was added near the restaurant, and new exhibition galleries were built towards the south connected to the entrance by another cloister. These galleries are large and high to accommodate works of great size, but to minimise their impact on the park they are cut into the slope of the ground. They are lit by a series of stepped north lights over a flat translucent ceiling.

Later the route was continued further to accommodate the graphics collection and a large meeting hall buried underground. To submerge the graphics gallery and the large hall in this way was a masterly decision; it preserved the view from the park to the sea, whilst at the same time providing an enjoyable walkway under cover around the whole museum.

Louisiana is a fun place to visit, whether primarily to see the paintings and sculpture, attend a lecture or seminar, listen to a concert, or simply to enjoy the park, eat in the restaurant, or picnic by the sea. At every point there is a close link between the works of art and nature, and because of this there is none of that hushed awe or that feeling of exhaustion that we so often experience in an art gallery.

Kerry Hill is an architect practising in Singapore whose work is especially responsive to context. In 1994 he designed **The Datai,** a luxury hotel on a very steep site on the coast of the island of **Langkawi** in Malaysia. Unlike most resort hotels, it is not on the beach but set back on a man-made plateau some three hundred metres away and forty metres above the sea. Elevated in this way it not only catches the breeze but also does not spoil the very thing the guests have come to enjoy.

4.19 - Louisiana skylights

4.20 - Louisiana side-lit gallery

4.21 - Datai Langkawi dining room

4.22 - Datai Langkawi bedrooms

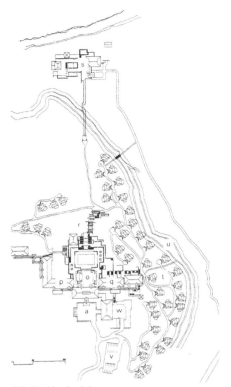

4.23 - Datai Langkawi plan

4.24 - Datai Langkawi entrance

4.25 - Datai Langkawi foyer

4.26 - Datai Langkawi roof detail

Entry is at the top on the axis of the main public concourse, with half the guest rooms in side wings on three floors down, and the other half in villas scattered down the slope. On arrival, the experience is of a powerful spatial horizontality, from lobby to water garden, to lounge, to a view over the swimming pool and the sea beyond, all set below a succession of roofs, alternately high and low, enclosed and open. It is an airy place, with the floor cool and plain in contrast to the beautifully crafted roofs with their exposed purlins, rafters and boarding between. The roofs are supported on timber posts, a straight-forward barn-like construction, traditional but without pastiche. The main dining room is off-centre, without permanent walls, just a great roof with wide overhangs around the edge. It is poised high above the cliff supported on huge tree trunks rescued from the forest. The way down to the beach is by a grand stairway, the way back by electric buggy.

The guest rooms are approached along a separated timber walkway with bridges across to a pair of rooms, giving a free flow of air around. The rooms are furnished symmetrically with a sitting area towards the outside but set back behind its own balcony. The villas are perched above the ground and approached similarly across a little bridge. They are luxuriously planned as a square with bays off at each side for the bed, the bath area, the sitting space and balcony.

In every part of the hotel the opportunity is grasped to provide adequate ventilation. Its quality lies in the careful use of timber exquisitely detailed together with an elegant formality given by the subtle use of axes. There is no pandering to popular images so prevalent in many holiday resorts.

This building demonstrates a useful proposition put forward by the planner Anne MacEwen, namely: "*There are three variables; amenity, accessibility, and cost, and in any situation two of these can only be satisfied at the expense of the third*".[4.2] This means, for example, that if cheapness and accessibility are priorities, then amenity will suffer; if the amenity of a delightful beach must be preserved and economy of resources is a priority, then this will be at the expense of accessibility, and the walk to the beach will be longer; if cheapness and accessibility are priorities, then amenity will suffer. People will not willingly give up their mobility, and without strategies such as this, neither the countryside nor the city will be able to cope.

These buildings, Louisiana and the Datai, together with the houses, are each related to their context in a sensitive and unobtrusive way.

THE URBAN CONTEXT

In the urban context the relation of built form to land is critical. In Britain from the middle of the 19th century the **small town house** has gradually evolved to suit different needs, and it has proved to be highly flexible. The original high densities resulted in a narrow-fronted terrace house. This was a simple box containing two rooms on the ground floor and two rooms above, with the kitchen in a single-storey extension at the back, and the lavatory at the bottom of the garden. Over time a bathroom was added above the kitchen and later an extra bedroom; these extensions left the frontage to the street intact. A slightly more affluent house became semi-detached, with access to the garden at the side, which was sometimes wide enough to accommodate a car space or garage. It is significant that in this way the public face to the street remains unchanged whilst all manner of personal extensions take place at the back.

4.27 - Chimney Pot Park street view

The house where I am writing was built in 1895 and finally converted to its present form in 2008. The original developer made all the houses similar to one another but gave each its own identity by detailing the bay windows in different ways. Over a century lifestyles have changed, and successive owners have been able to adapt the house to their particular needs yet within an overall urban unity.

4.28 - Chimney Pot Park aerial view

Urban Splash, working with architects **shedkm,** have made an innovative regeneration of terrace houses at **Chimney Pot Park** in **Salford**. The streets had become derelict with houses boarded up and covered with graffiti. At the outset the Local Authority considered demolition to be the only option, but gradually, having looked at other small houses that were highly valued, they were persuaded otherwise.

4.29 - Chimney Pot Park sketch drawing

The redevelopment embodies a number of imaginative ideas. Firstly, the streets maintain their footprint and the built form of each house remains the same; secondly, the houses have been turned upside down with the bedrooms on the ground floor and living rooms above, enjoying more sunlight, and including a gallery within the roof space; thirdly, the rear gardens have been made into terraces at the level of the living rooms, with car spaces below; and finally, the form of the chimneys has been kept but they have become rooflights to illuminate the living room. Externally the pattern of windows and front doors remains the same, with brick details over the fanlights and under the eaves as before. Brick walls, slate roofs and metal 'chimneys' (in a gradation of colours from white to black) echo the original. The houses have been drastically but sympathetically adapted to the present-day needs and aspirations of the new residents.

4.30 - Chimney Pot Park skylights

4.31 - Donnybrook Quarter street view

Peter Barber has designed a number of housing schemes in the East End of London; **Donnybrook Quarter** is a typical example. They each originate from a concept of the city made up of streets and squares; they are closely knitted into the existing urban fabric, giving people a strong connection with the local neighbourhood. The density is high, and, as in traditional terraces, the buildings form a hard edge to the street. In other ways they demonstrate a new enlightened approach, most notably in the strong connection between inside and outside. Each house has its own open space whether in a garden, roof terrace or balcony. This creates a profile above street level of separate pavilions which serves both to enrich the façade and to give each dwelling an identity. The terraces are arranged to enclose communal areas designed for children to play and for people to meet and chat. The built form allows the overall plan to have a free geometry adjusted to the edges of the site. Corners are enabled to become distinctive, with smaller or larger dwellings, or with other uses such as a common room, shop or surgery.

In these houses, Peter Barber used simple forms and white painted walls, and in the close-knit layout this provides a high level of reflected light to the outside space. It is a testament to the communal spirit of the residents that graffiti has not yet appeared.

At **Grantchester Road** in **Cambridge,** during 1961-1964, **Colin St John Wilson** designed a pair of houses (including one for his own family) that demonstrates a polemic about the relation of house to street; a public face to the street that is different from the private face to the garden. At the front, a colonnaded ground floor gives a certain formality and grandeur, whereas at the back the L-shaped plan encloses a more intimate private terrace. Wilson's own house is set back to accommodate an L-shaped studio in front on the first floor. The entrance to his house therefore is under a bridge into an atrium, to a further colonnade at the front door. This provides a gradual sequence that recalls the Palazzo Massimi in Rome, designed by Peruzzi four hundred years earlier, with its splendid progression from vestibule to colonnade to cortile.

From the front door, the hallway is low in contrast to the splendid double height of the living room beyond. This has a gallery at the back that is used as a library, with the fireplace nestling more intimately below. The rhythm of the street colonnade permeates the whole house; it is echoed at the entrance, by the columns in the living room, and the glazed wall to the garden. The discipline of the grid serves to relate all the parts of the plan in a harmonious way.

4.32 - Granchester Road house view from the garden

4.33 - Granchester Road house street elevation

4.34 - Granchester Road house living room towards gallery

4.35 - Granchester Road house living room towards window

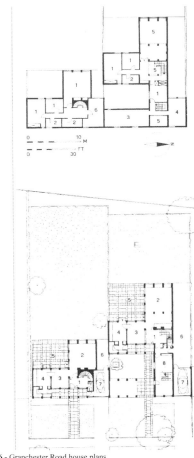

4.36 - Granchester Road house plans

The house was built both inside and out in concrete blocks that were carefully chosen; they were magnificently white when the house was new, but over time they have become a dismal grey due to the dampness of the English climate.

In 'La Ville Radieuse', from the early 1920s onwards, Le Corbusier presented a new vision of the relationship of dwelling to context; this was to live not *on* the land but *above* it. The 'Esprit Nouveau' apartments consisted of two-storey L-shaped houses stacked above one another. Each had its own double-height terrace garden enjoying sun and space above an idyllic parkland. This was followed by a number of significant villas that demonstrated the new polemic, culminating, in 1929, in the Villa Savoye, a house sited in the middle of its own meadow.

This house presents itself as a low, first-floor box elegantly raised above the ground on slender columns set back from the facade. The ground floor contains parking and service rooms together with a spacious entrance hall. From here a gentle ramp and spiral stair lead to the living level above. This forms a U-shaped built form surrounding a square open terrace. The whole is enclosed by a continuous wall and window, giving views in all directions, and making the terrace an outside room. The ramp continues up to the solarium on the roof with its free-shaped walls.

What makes this house so special? Essentially it is the simplicity of form poised above the ground, and emphasised by the expression of the windows. This treatment of the edge gives both enclosure and release, echoed again in the relationship between living room and terrace. Yet within the simplicity, complexity is evident in the arrangement of the elements at the entrance and in the hall above as well as on the roof.

During the three decades after 1920, Le Corbusier studied the implications and possibilities of living high above the ground.

The Unité d'Habitation in Marseilles represents the first example of this new urbanism; a 'vertical garden city'. It is situated to the east of Marseilles in an affluent residential district, and it was designed for middle-income families of different sizes. It is a huge building over 120 metres long and 22 metres wide, rising seventeen storeys above grand and elegantly shaped pilotis.

The essence of the scheme is *la rue intérieure* - the street in the sky. This is at the centre of each three storeys and serves two interlocking maisonettes, one above and one below. These are orientated east-west with deep plans protecting against the Mediterranean sun, and with views towards the mountains on one side and the sea on the other. Similarly-arranged apartments

4.37 - Villa Savoye living room

4.38 - Villa Savoye view from north-west

4.39 - Villa Savoye first floor terrace

4.40 - Villa Savoye entrance hall

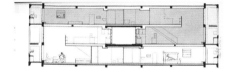

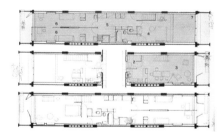

4.41 - Unite d'Habitation section and plans

occupy the southern end of the building. Each of the dwellings has a spacious double-height living room with a gallery at the back and a generous balcony at the front; a system not unlike that in the architect's early houses. The children's bedrooms have a sliding partition between them to make a larger space for study or for play.

The Unité was designed with many communal facilities to enhance everyday living; these included a health centre, crèche, nursery, laundry and youth clubs. Midway up the building, a double-height floor is devoted to shops, a bar, a restaurant and a hotel. Some of these facilities have not been successful as they miss the trade of passers-by. The roof is a place for enjoying the view all around where a gym, a café, a playground and a pool exploit their platonic geometry. They are reminiscent of the Yantra Manta Observatory in Jaipur which Le Corbusier is known to have admired.

The Unité is a monumental building; the form and scale of the pilotis establishes its presence on the ground. Above this, the concrete grid powerfully expresses the scale of the dwelling units rather than, as in so many apartment blocks, expressing the smaller and more repetitive scale of the windows. The vertical rhythm of the single and double-storey balconies, with their concrete balustrades and brise-soleils, creates a deeply modelled façade. This is enriched by the bold articulation of the communal floors and the contrast between frame and wall at the southern end and at the position of the lifts. In this way the Unité stands as a majestic object in the landscape.

The Unité nevertheless stems from a polemic about the city whereby Le Corbusier advocated the death of the street and the city block. His plans for Paris were never realised, and they would have devastated the city. This polemic has been authoritatively challenged.

In '*Genius Loci*'[4.3] Christian Norberg-Schulz emphasises that the city is a place to come together, a place to gather. He points out that traditionally this takes place in streets and squares that are like outside rooms that have a degree of enclosure. In his words "*gathering takes place within a boundary.*"

In '*Collage City*'[4.4] Colin Rowe and Fred Koetter make two intriguing comparisons between the traditional city and Le Corbusier's city of the future. Firstly, they compare the plan of the centre of Parma with Le Corbusier's proposals for the centre of St Die. They demonstrate that the figure/ground relationship is reversed; in Parma the open space is defined by buildings, whereas in St Die the buildings stand in open space. The relation of black and white on the map shows the 'grain' - the relation of built form to the street, the square or open space - and it is this that serves to denote the enclosing nature of the traditional

4.42 - Unité d'Habitation exterior view

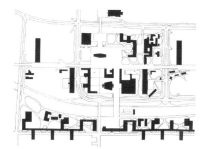

4.43 - Collage City plan of St Die

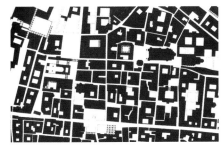

4.44 - Collage City plan of Parma

city in contrast to the wide open expanse of St Die. The authors compare the footprint of the Uffizi in Florence with that of the Unité d'Habitation in Marseilles, (interestingly they are about the same size) and again one is the inverse of the other; the Uffizi surrounds and defines an urban place whilst the Unité stands as an object in space.

Leslie Martin and Lionel March have demonstrated that the city block has significant validity; it is an efficient and economic way of putting built form on land. They point out that a low building around the edge of a site can have the same volume as a high building in the centre. This not only provides useful private space for activities within the site but also presents edges (enclosures) to the public domain outside. It is a pattern that is present in many cities and is still appropriate today. We have already noted that the street and the city block form the basis of Accordia in Cambridge.

In 1973 **Aldo van Eyck** was presented with a difficult context. The **Hubertus House** in **Amsterdam** was required to provide accommodation for about seventy children and twenty mothers in need of care. The original director, Addie van Roijen-Wortmann succinctly defined a complex brief: "*We have a double task…we give them security and protection; we take them out of society and give them an interior which means*

4.45 - Unite d'Habitation roof terrace

73

4.46 - Hubertus House street view

4.47 - Hubertus House entrance

enclosure, but we prepare their return to society, and that means openness…both elements figure prominently in our work". [4.5]

The site is in a 19th-century district in Amsterdam known as the Plantage which contains a mix of residential and institutional accommodation. On its western side is a bland 'functional' building, and on the east a pseudo-classical building that forms part of the new development. The urban design task was to mediate between the two. The new façade has four bays that decrease in width and height towards the east, and thus pay deference to the classical building. The two bays to the west define the majority of the new accommodation whilst the bay to the east is a small extension to what exists. They are all designed with colourful panels between slender columns. The link between the two sides is further enhanced by chamfered bay windows that face one another on either side.

The plan is best appreciated at the entrance floor which is at mezzanine level above the pavement. Mothers are housed in the existing building together with administration, whilst the children are in a terrace of five 'houses' along the western boundary. Two axes at right angles to one another subtly manipulate the relation between them; one is through the gap, and steps sideways to form the route serving the children's accommodation, the other is parallel to the road in line with the lift and stairs. This is a clever move, in effect changing the axis of the existing building ninety degrees in order to connect it to the new.

The five children's houses are each arranged on a west-east axis continuing the theme of chamfered bay windows. They are entered from above with the bedrooms, bathrooms, kitchen and living rooms below in contact with outside play space, and each house is given individuality by curved party walls. There is thus, in plan and elevation, a sense of formality and informality, of openness and enclosure which the director had envisaged.

Between 1991 and 1998, **Benson** and **Forsyth** designed the **Museum of Scotland** in Edinburgh next to the existing National Museum of Scotland. It lies at a critical position within the city, at the junction of Chambers Street with Bristow Place and opposite the entrance to Greyfriars churchyard. It takes its clues from the immediate locality, from the city of Edinburgh and from the history of Scotland which it internally displays. The external wall of warm Moray sandstone relates to the height of its neighbours, and the free-standing drum at the entrance boldly celebrates the corner between the two streets; a reminder also of the Half Moon Battery at the Castle as well as other corners in the city.

The plan demonstrates an essentially simple idea that echoes some aspects of the existing museum; it consists of an inhabited

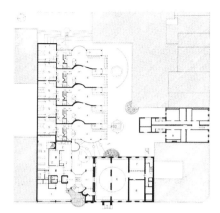

4.48 - Hubertus House ground floor plan

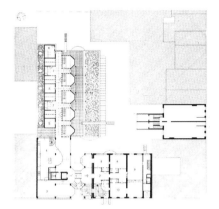

4.49 - Hubertus House mezzanine floor plan

4.50 - Hubertus House rear view

4.51 - Museum of Scotland view from north

4.52 - Museum of Scotland view from west

4.53 - Museum of Scotland view from south-west

4.54 - Museum of Scotland Hawthornden Court

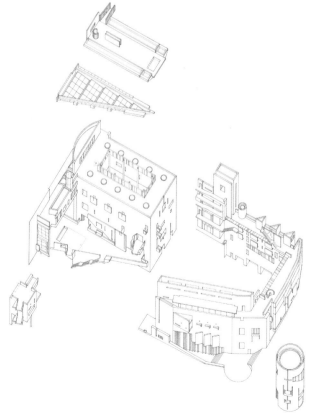

4.55 - Museum of Scotland axonometric of the parts

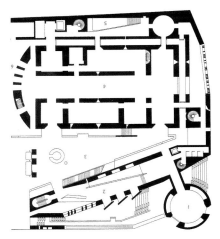

4.56 - Museum of Scotland plan

wall surrounding an inside core. This is revealed externally by stonework surrounding a taller concrete structure with a boat-like form floating above. The core is symmetrical with an apsidal end; it has a nave and aisles with two galleries above, and has clerestory light that is reflected from its inverted curved ceiling. Between the core and the perimeter wall to the north is a high triangular atrium known as the Hawthornden Court. This is the focus of entry from the drum on the outside; it is an impressive top-lit space comparable to the Grand Gallery of the 1861 building by Francis Fowke next door, though with a wall structure rather than a frame.

To describe the building in this way is to outline a strategy, but the experience is much richer. There are recesses and projections, bridges across narrow gaps that let the light penetrate deep down, unexpected glimpses inside and out through narrow slits with splayed reveals that thereby simultaneously enliven the elevations. Visiting this museum is to make a journey through time; the oldest in the basement, the most recent at the top, and from the roof terraces there are views across the City towards the land of Scotland. It is also to make discoveries. There are many ways around the gallery to visit a wide range of exhibits. The great Newcomen Engine holds centre stage with tiny artefacts displayed elsewhere in exquisite cases discreetly lit. This is not a bland shell, a neutral background, nor is it gratuitously self-conscious, a challenge to its contents. It contains a diversity of special places designed to house specific objects in an appropriate way, in subdued or bright light, in high or low space, that is sometimes formally symmetrical and sometimes more casual. This impressive interior is wrapped within the stone facade that presents a frontage related to the two existing streets.

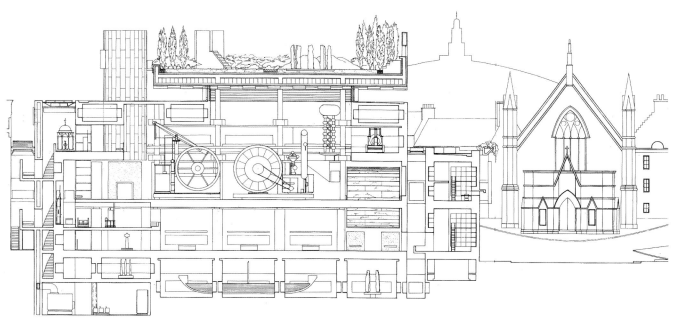

4.57 - Museum of Scotland section

5.1 - Le Thoronet view from west

5.2 - Le Thoronet cloisters

5   RESPECTING MATERIAL and STRUCTURE

We delight in the beautiful colour and texture of materials, we admire the craftsmanship of the well-made object, and we stand in awe at the simplicity, the ingenuity, or the scale of a structure.

Architects refer to the essential nature of a material, and aim to exploit its special quality; Louis Kahn speaks of finding out what a material *"wants to be"*. This means understanding its hardness or softness, whether it is heavy or light, how it behaves in compression or tension, its ability to weather and age, how easy it is to use, and how much maintenance it will require. From experience architects gradually acquire an intuitive understanding of a material, and develop a 'feel' for it - a sensual appreciation of its potential and the way it can be used.

Traditionally, because transport was difficult, local materials tended to be used, and served to give identity to a region. This can be seen in the use of Cotswold stone, London brick or New England weatherboarding. With the rise of industrialisation and greater mobility, the use of local materials has diminished.

Buildings are works of craftsmanship, and whether they are put together by hand or by machine, on site or in a factory, varying ranges of skills are required. Different materials demand different tolerances, and some require specialised tools and equipment. Careful attention is required whenever materials meet or change direction; historically the junction between a wall and a ceiling was often celebrated by an elaborate cornice, and columns were adorned with a moulded base and carved capital; as Louis Kahn commented *"ornament begins with the joint"*.[5.1]

The way a building is constructed is sometimes hidden, as in buildings of the Renaissance. At St Paul's in London, for example, the dome that is seen outside is not that seen within, and the supporting structure is hidden in between. At other times the structure is explicit, as in medieval cathedrals, 19th century railway stations, or the work of architects such as Norman Foster, Richard Rogers, Santiago Calatrava or Renzo Piano. Whether hidden or exposed, a structure has to bring the loads down to the ground, and it is often the expression of this that can generate a powerful architecture.

The properties of a material give rise to different systems of structure. Stone and brick, used in compression require *mass,* and we enjoy the thick walls of a Romanesque church sitting

5.3 - Le Thoronet north aisle

5.4 - Le Thoronet dormitory

5.5 - Le Thoronet cloister steps

heavily on the ground. Timber and steel, used in compression or tension, facilitate a *frame,* and we enjoy the skeletal structures of Glenn Murcutt as exemplified in his book '*Touch this Earth Lightly*'.[5.2] These different systems of structure, whether *mass* or *frame* or a combination of both, serve to set up a discipline that has its own inner consistency, and in this way materials and structure contribute to a particular formal architectural language and to the overarching idea.

STRUCTURES DEPENDENT ON MASS

The Romanesque Abbey of Le Thoronet in Provence was built between 1155 and 1160 by the Cistercians, an order of monks who rejected the luxury and worldliness that the Benedictines had come to enjoy. The new Order prescribed a life of humility, obedience, poverty, hard work and prayer. The Abbey at Le Thoronet was a reflection of this ascetic life and became the simplest of all the simple Cistercian monasteries.

Nowhere else is stone so austerely glorified in walls, columns, vaults and floors. The exterior form of the church expresses the simple geometry of the nave, aisles, transepts, crossing and apse. The western façade is especially severe with no central doorway, no mouldings, no sculpture or decoration, just the precision of a hard limestone wall, carefully aligned and jointed. The unadorned entrances lead into the side aisles. In the upper part of the façade an oculus lights the nave, and another above the choir illuminates the transepts, whilst on the south side two chamfered windows with semi-circular heads light the aisle. The small size of these openings serves to exaggerate the powerful expanse of the wall.

The interior is all stone. This gives a serene dignified presence, a fitting backdrop to the many offices of the day. From the entrance, the grandeur of the side wall sweeps into the half-barrel vault above the aisle. With ultimate simplicity the barrel vault of the nave leads towards the half-dome of the apse. There are no carvings, and only the most discreet mouldings mark a difference between planes or the separation of one element from another. From the south aisle the nave is slightly lower giving emphasis to the texture of the stone floor.

Following the fall of the land, steps lead down from the north transept into the cloister. This gathers together all the facilities of the monastery - the refectory to the north, the cellar to the west, the sacristy to the east, with the dormitory on the floor above. The ambulatory around has an austerity similar to that of the church with a bare stone wall at the back, a plain barrel vault, and a thick colonnade towards the open side. This has bold semi-circular arches divided by a central column and two smaller arches, all beautifully constructed of the same stone. On the north side of the cloister there is a hexagonal pavilion

5.6 - Quincy library exterior in stone

5.7 - Quincy library interior in timber

5.8 - Bourse doorway

that contains a fountain for the monks to use before meals in the refectory. The spacious dormitory has a bold barrel vault and a row of low windows facing towards the early morning light.

The Abbey of Le Thoronet has a formal clarity, a consistency in the use of stone, massive walls and small openings that give a mysterious quality of shade and light. It has been an acknowledged inspiration to many subsequent architects including Le Corbusier and John Pawson.

Henry Hobson Richardson excelled in the use of stone. He travelled extensively in Europe where he studied architecture at the École des Beaux Arts in Paris, and worked in the office of Labrouste. Returning to America, Richardson designed a number of churches including the Brattle Square Church and Trinity Church in Boston, which showed the influence of the Romanesque that was to pervade his life's work. Richardson declared that he was concerned to create an architecture of *'simplicity and quietness'*.

Between 1876 and 1886 Richardson designed suburban libraries in Massachusetts that were all built in rugged stone, and demonstrate his gradual transformation from the Romanesque to a strong and simple architecture of his own. Although there are variations in size and programme, the libraries follow a similar organisation and formal expression, differing mainly because of the context. The **Crane Library** at **Quincy** is typical. The stone exterior has a civic presence with the entry marked by a huge semi-circular arch. The several parts are carefully proportioned and balanced; the long window at the top of the main library contrasts with the plain wall below and with the tall window to the reading room, each giving its distinct pattern of light.

A major delight is the contrast between outside and inside, from the rugged austerity of stone to the warm, precisely detailed and finely crafted timber that provides a homely place to browse and read. Different in expression, the external face and the internal space present an ambience that is both calm and dignified. This follows the tradition established by Christopher Wren at Trinity College Cambridge.

Between 1897 and 1903, almost contemporary with the Glasgow School of Art, **Hendrik Berlage** designed and built the **Bourse** in **Amsterdam.** He had studied architecture at the E.T.H. in Zurich in the 1870s where he was influenced by Viollet-le-Duc, Semper, and also by the work of H. H. Richardson. The Bourse is a bold load-bearing brick building of austere simplicity. It appears to be carved out of the solid; its brick walls define a pure plane where only the window cills project, and the stone lintels and quoins and even the sculptures lie flush with the face of the wall. One of these is at a corner of the building, another lies flat within a brick vault and has its face carved within the

5.9 - Bourse corner

5.10 - Bourse interior

5.11 - Bourse exterior

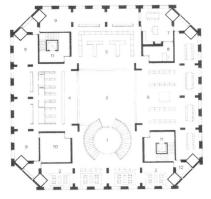

5.12 - Exeter Library plan

5.13 - Exeter Library exterior

keystone of the arch. Positioned in this way these carvings have a dramatically powerful impact. Berlage had written "*before all else the wall must be shown naked in all its sleek beauty, and anything fixed on it must be shunned as an embarrassment*". Influenced by illustrations from Viollet-le-Duc the design of the façades uses a proportional grid based on an isosceles triangle that locates the position and size of each element.

The interior of the Bourse consists of a large central volume surrounded by three floors with arched openings. Every detail is similarly flush, and only the stone corbels project to support the industrial steel trusses. In this building Berlage makes a consistent and simple use of brick that is comparable with H.H. Richardson's use of stone.

The Phillips Exeter Academy Library in New Hampshire by **Louis Kahn** (1965-72) is one of the most significant buildings using loadbearing brick. Here he demonstrates his clear understanding of the nature of the task, the nature of materials, and the nature of light. It has been noted elsewhere that Kahn always searched for "*the essential rather than the circumstantial*",[5.1] and at the Exeter Academy he was concerned to express the essence of '*library*' rather than just '*a library*'; it is both the repository of all human thought and knowledge, and at the same time a place for individual private study.

It is a square building that exploits the tension between the centre and the edges. The centre is a high square atrium bounded on its sides by four huge circles. This space, to quote Louis Kahn, is an "*invitation to the books behind*".[5.2] The circles give a grand scale that is reminiscent of the Reading Room at the British Museum or Asplund's library in Stockholm. They also serve to give identity to each floor positioned at the bottom, middle, or top of the circle. The edges of the building contain individual carrels, private 'dens' close to the light for personal concentration. They are in a double-height space with some carrels on the lower level with communal tables behind, and others on a mezzanine above. Bookstacks occupy the space between the centre and the edge away from the light.

The contrast between the centre and the edge is further emphasised by the contrast between materials; the inside is bold concrete whilst the outside is made more homely by the use of brick. The façades consist of brick columns supporting flat arches where the angle of the bricks at the end of the arches is exploited to reduce the width of the columns on each level above. This gives the columns a subtly tapering effect and at the same time increases the width of the openings. Kahn aptly comments "*a beam needs a column, and a column needs a beam; a beam made of brick is an arch*".[5.3] Each façade is a separate brick plane with a recessed gap at the corner that serves

5.14 - Exeter Library interior

5.15 - Exeter Library carrels

84

to reduce the apparent mass of the building. The human scale is further enhanced by the gentle expression of the timber carrels between the columns. On the inside the use of pine for doors, balcony fronts and furniture gives a warm glow. At ground level the columns create an arcade around the whole building, but strangely, although internally the entry is marked by a grand staircase, on the outside it is hardly celebrated.

As usual in a Kahn building each part enjoys its particular quality of light and shade. After many experiments it was decided to light the central atrium from clerestory windows on each side, giving less glare than rooflights. Each of the carrels has its own little window with large panes of glass above to illuminate the reading tables.

The Phillips Exeter Academy Library is a noble building, where the judicious exploitation of different scales and different materials create appropriate levels of meaning. The Library, as we will see, had a direct influence on the later work of **Michael Hopkins and Partners.**

In his early years Michael Hopkins shared with Richard Rogers and Norman Foster an enthusiasm for framed structures made of steel and glass. This was exemplified in the house that he and his wife Patty Hopkins designed for themselves in Hampstead in 1975, as well as by other buildings over the next ten years.

In 1984 the commission to design the **Mound Stand** at **Lord's Cricket Ground** in London was to herald a more composite architecture combining a structure of mass with that of frame. The origin of this scheme stems from a design by Frank Verity around 1890. This consisted of a tall row of elegantly proportioned brick arches along the line of the adjacent street. Michael Hopkins decided to repair these and extend them along the whole frontage of the new building. They provide a strong base to the light steel structure above and behind. Essentially, this structure consists of a row of six steel columns 400mms in diameter, from which the whole of the upper part of the new building is suspended. The main terrace of seating falls away from the top of the arcaded wall, and extends down to ground level. The open corridor at the top of the wall serves to visually separate the new structure from the old. The next level above is given over to private boxes and dining space for VIPs. This floor is suspended from a storey-height plate girder that spans between the columns for the full length of the building. Secondary lattice girders extend from this beam at right angles to support the upper terrace, which has bars and restaurants behind. This is covered by an elegant tent structure supported and hung from the columns, which Michael Hopkins has described as *"reminiscent of cricket on the village green"*.

5.16 - Lord's Pavillion cross section

5.17 - Lord's Pavillion detail

5.18 - Lord's Pavillion tent structure

5.19 - Lord's Pavillion street elevation

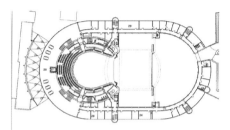

5.20 - Glyndebourne plan

5.21 - Glyndebourne perimiter wall

5.22 - Glyndebourne surrounding colonade

To the street, this building presents a progression upwards from very heavy to extremely light - from the base of load-bearing brickwork, to an open walkway, a wall of glass blocks, and a level of steel louvres, all below the canopy of a tent. The architects spotted the potential of the arcade to establish the order of the whole building, the rhythm of the boxes, the location and proportion of the restaurants and bars, the stairs and service areas, which are all slotted into place with apparent but deceptive ease.

It is the **Glyndebourne opera house,** designed in 1989, that embodies some significant features of Louis Kahn's Exeter Library. It was designed to replace a former building that had become increasingly unsatisfactory over the years. Glyndebourne Festival Opera was founded by John Christie in 1934 to present the highest standard of opera in a magnificent country setting. It established a tradition that still continues, with champagne in the garden beforehand and a lavish picnic in the long interval.

The form of the building has a ruthless simplicity. The simple plan has a semi-circular auditorium at one end and a semi-circular backstage at the other, with the stage and fly-tower near the middle. The whole of the perimeter contains a narrow band of accommodation three storeys high under an impressive low-pitched lead roof. Around the auditorium the façade consists of two levels of brick colonnades below a gallery at the top which has slender steel posts. Each is designed for meeting and chatting, and is used for a picnic when the weather is not good. As the opera house is only used for a short season in the summer, these floors are open to the outside. The foyer likewise is shielded only by a tent structure that spans between the colonnade and the bar, and it has frameless glass doors to the outside. Around the backstage area a band of accommodation contains the dressing rooms and offices. The outside of the auditorium is defined by a circular drum that rises above the main roof; it has a conical roof also clad in lead, with a similar pitch. The fly-tower is a steel and concrete structure covered in lead, and has exposed steel trusses at the top.

It is the quality of detail that gives this large simple building its human scale. The vast expanse of roof has a generous overhang around the eaves, and is given a texture by the gentle steps and standing seams of the lead. The deep open recesses of the façade appear black in contrast to the rich colours of the roof and the walls. The gallery below the eaves is boldly horizontal in contrast to the subtle verticality of the columns. These, together with the projecting drum of the auditorium, are load-bearing and made of hand-made bricks carefully chosen to match the adjacent Elizabethan mansion. The openings all have flat arches whose angled springing is exploited to reduce the width of the

5.23 - Glyndebourne top colonade

5.24 - Glyndebourne exterior view

5.25 - Glyndebourne exterior entrance

5.26 - Mellor workshop

columns above; a similar device to that used by Louis Kahn at the Exeter Library. Hopkins adds a further embellishment by allowing the beams supporting the first floor to slightly project through the face of the columns. The white concrete slab of the top floor is gently arched between the beams and projects to further emphasise the lightness of the gallery.

The inside of the auditorium has the traditional horse-shoe plan. The overarching impression is the golden pitch pine of the balcony fronts which are carefully shaped to reflect the sound. The balcony ceilings, together with the radiating beams around the ceiling, are made of smooth fair-faced concrete. All the different planes and recesses are enriched by pools of light giving a present-day interpretation of the sparkle associated with a traditional auditorium. By contrast the great high backstage is an industrial area with a surrounding brick wall, radiating steel trusses, and a semi-circular rooflight at the apex.

The design of an opera house is complex. The audience have come for a special occasion; they need space to pause and meet their friends, but equally they need to be able to leave with ease at the end of a performance. The performers, the principals and the chorus, as well as the orchestra, all have their particular needs, whilst out of sight are the scene shifters, the lighting and sound engineers, administrators and office staff.

Above all, an opera house requires an environment that facilitates perfection in the quality of sight and sound, and at Glyndebourne both the performers and the audiences are full of praise. To organise this within a simple geometric form is no mean achievement, but nothing has been sacrificed or forced; on the contrary, the ordering of space, structure, and the use of material has given legibility to each part and clarity to the way people move around.

Two other buildings by Michael Hopkins and Partners demonstrate their mastery of simplicity and construction. The **David Mellor Cutlery Workshop,** designed in 1988, has a footprint based on that of a former gas holder. The walls are made of local stone, and its conical roof is clad in lead as in the opera house, with a glazed light in the centre. It appears to float above the wall. Internally, the radiating steel trusses are an appropriate structure for craftsmen making cutlery.

The plan of the **Queen's Building for Emmanuel College Cambridge,** designed in 1993, is semi-circular at each end and equally simple in section. On the first floor, the ends contain an auditorium and a reception room, which both enjoy the inside of the pitched roof with its beautifully crafted timber trusses and pitch pine boarding. The lower floors contain seminar rooms and common rooms, with an arcade all around at ground level.

5.27 - King's Cross west concourse

5.28 - Queen's Building Emmanuel exterior

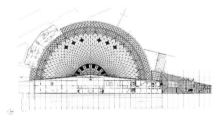

5.29 - Queen's Building Emmanuel interior

5.30 - King's Cross plan at platform level

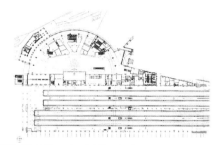

5.31 - King's Cross plan at roof level

At Emmanuel, as at Glyndebourne, the roof is covered in lead. The façade is smooth and flush, made of Ketton limestone, with only the slightest projection in a discreet cornice around the eaves. It is a framed structure, pre-stressed and post-tensioned, where the piers and flat arches are only defined by a minimum groove, and the junction between the piers and the arches is marked by a precast concrete block almost identical in colour with the stone. In the centre of each of these, a steel tube gives access to the tensioning nut of the steel rods, and serves to provide a significant 'decoration' on an otherwise plain façade. These blocks have sloping sides to resist the thrust of the flat arches, and as at Glyndebourne they neatly reduce the width of the piers at each storey.

FRAMED STRUCTURES

We have already noted that the heavy walls of the Bourse in Amsterdam enclosed a large space covered by a steel-framed roof. This was a system that was used in many buildings in the 19th century. Iron and steel had been used to make railway lines and bridges as well as the trains that travelled on them. Stations were built with huge roofs that arched over enormous spans supported on massive structures of brick or stone.

In 1852, at **King's Cross** in London, George Turnbull worked with architect **Lewis Cubitt** to design a train shed covered by two great roofs each, with a span of nearly 30 metres. They were constructed of semi-circular cast-iron arches supported on a brick arcade in the centre, and a long range of brick buildings on the east and west sides. To the south, the shed terminates in two immense brick arches; they are not only a clear expression of the inside structure but also serve as a fitting gateway to the city. A clock tower (useful in a station) forms an impressive centrepiece. When it was built, a glazed canopy supported on cast-iron columns provided a covered waiting place for taxis. In 1970 this whole façade was drastically concealed by an inappropriate extension.

By the end of the 20th century the number of passengers had so increased that a radical reassessment of the station became necessary. This was masterminded by **John McAslan** and **Arup** working with a wide range of different clients - land owners, developers, advisers and statutory authorities. The whole of the existing structure was repaired, the roof of the train shed was made to let in more light, and all the cast iron and brickwork was cleaned and made good. The key intervention was the creation of a new concourse to the west, designed to clarify passengers' routes and sort out the previous congestion. This is a great semi-circular space, partly in response to the curved Great Northern Hotel (also by Cubitt) that had been listed. The concourse is 140 metres across and was the largest single-span structure in Europe at the time; it is low around the perimeter

5.32 - King's Cross platforms

5.33 - King's Cross central structure

5.34 - King's Cross towards existing structure

and rises to a height of 20 metres. In order not to put weight on the west wall of the station or on the hotel, the structure is free-standing; it is a diagrid roof made up of a network of intersecting steel members. Around the perimeter it is supported on seventeen tree-like columns, and in the centre it radiates dramatically down to just four points. Behind these, the central part of the western range presents its façade to the concourse, whereas the side sections are seen through a tall glazed screen. Hidden from view below the concourse is a new ticket hall for the Underground which was completed before the concourse, and which generated a tricky structural constraint. The form and structure of the concourse continues the innovative tradition established by Cubitt in the 19th century.

A curved mezzanine towards the outer edge of the concourse contains shops and restaurants; it is approached by escalators and continues as a bridge through the train shed. This serves as one route to the platforms, with lifts and escalators leading down. A further way to the platforms is through a new wide opening towards the southern end of the new building. The central part contains the booking office where elegant cast-iron brackets have been revealed. Wherever possible the fine 19th century brick and iron details have been retained and highlighted by the contrasting use of glass and stainless steel.

The reinvented King's Cross establishes a wider urban intervention and a new sense of place. The main entrance to the station is into the western concourse and is opposite the entrance to St Pancras station. In 2013, the removal of the 1970 additions in front of the south façade has not only allowed the great arches to be seen but also has provided a new piazza outside the station; a valuable space at a busy road junction. To the north the Central Saint Martin's College of Art and Design occupies further railway buildings; Kings Place contains new concert halls and offices, and to the east 19th-century houses and warehouses provide studios, offices and restaurants.

Next to King's Cross is **St Pancras Station.** This was designed in 1868 by **W.H. Barlow** who had previously worked with Paxton on The Great Exhibition of 1851. He was charged to create '*the most regal entry into London*'. This has both similarities and differences from its neighbour. Like King's Cross it consists of an enormous train shed supported at the sides on brick walls. The roof is different as it has only one span 72 metres wide and 30 metres high at the centre. This is made of wrought iron lattice arches glazed over the centre, and lined with timber at the edges. Exceptionally these arches spring from platform level where passengers stand. Originally the platforms were raised above an undercroft supported on 700 cast-iron columns; a space that accommodated beer barrels brought in from Burton on Trent.

The southern end of the station does not, as at King's Cross, express the internal space. At St Pancras it is fronted by the enormous flamboyant Midland Grand Hotel designed by George Gilbert Scott built in 1873, now renamed the St Pancras Renaissance Hotel.

Towards the end of the 20th century the station was in a dilapidated state covered in years of grime from coal-burning locomotives. The hotel, which had never been a commercial success, was closed and threatened by some for demolition. Early in this century **Foster and Partners** succeeded by **Alistair Lansley** were appointed to prepare a plan for the station, and to provide the terminus for Eurostar trains to and from the continent. New platforms were built allowing the international trains to occupy the original platforms under the Barlow roof. The floor was opened up, allowing light to the undercroft below, which became a sophisticated shopping and restaurant area. A generous concourse was provided at the southern end of the platforms, with further cafés and access to the magnificently restored hotel. Together with the work around King's Cross this became a major contribution to the urban regeneration of the area.

5.35 - King's Cross looking up

5.36 - National Museum of Scotland grand gallery

5.37 - National Museum of Scotland entrance undercroft

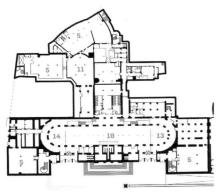

5.38 - National Museum of Scotland plan

5.39 - National Museum of Scotland Chamber Street elevation

The original **National Museum of Scotland** in Edinburgh was designed in 1861 by **Captain Francis Fowke**, who, six years later was to design the Royal Albert Hall in London. Like the stations, this museum presents one face to the city and encloses a different world within. The museum has a classical stone façade with a bold rusticated base and two storeys above; it is a deeply modelled wall displaying appropriate civic grandeur. A monumental flight of steps leads up to the entrance in preparation for the dramatic contrast between the heavy exterior and the lightness inside.

The Grand Gallery consists of a three-storey nave separated from side aisles by tall slim cast-iron columns that support two rows of galleries over the aisles. The whole delicate construction is clear and exploits the nature of cast-iron. This is demonstrated in the capitals and bases of the columns, the junction of beams and balustrades, and the detail of the balusters.

Along the length of the nave, semi-circular arches span between the columns, with bolder arches spanning across. These each support cast-iron rafters, purlins and a glazed roof above. The ends of the nave have semi-circular apses, with the columns and balustrades continuing around to give the gallery a feeling of containment. At each side of the apse, a gently curving staircase connects the different levels. The Grand Gallery brings together elegant simplicity and economy, consistency in the use of materials, as well as a majestic quality of light.

Early in this century **Gareth Hoskins** designed a major regeneration of Fowke's original museum. He renovated the Grand Gallery together with further galleries to the south, and adapted the building to the needs of disabled people. Lifts and escalators were sensitively installed, and a new entrance was made from the level of Chambers Street. The basement then became a dramatically low entrance space with stone vaults. From here, in contrast, the Grand Gallery above now seems even more lofty and ablaze with light. Unfortunately the main entrance doors had to be closed for security, and the monumental stairs from the street have become redundant. When Chambers Street becomes used for pedestrians only, there will be an opportunity to use these steps as an outside auditorium for street shows.

5.40 - Post Office Savings Bank Vienna main hall

5.41 - Pompidou Centre elevation to piazza

5.42 - Post Office Savings Bank Vienna radiator

5.43 - Post Office Savings Bank Vienna light fittings

In 1904 in Vienna, **Otto Wagner** designed the **Post Office Savings Bank**. The building occupies the whole of a city block where the top-lit banking halls are surrounded by offices. Wagner had previously designed major works that were a combination of architecture and engineering, including the Nussdorf Dam and most of the railway stations in Vienna. These projects gave him enthusiasm and experience for the innovative use of new materials.

The Post Office Savings Bank has a symmetrical plan with classical elevations; a heavy base, a projecting cornice and an attic storey above. The base is faced with horizontal panels in strongly modelled granite, and the façade above is clad with sheets of white marble that are fixed with boldly expressed bolts providing a subtle texture to the wall. The entrance is celebrated by a glass canopy on slender posts. These, together with the bolts, the cornice, and the embellishments on the roof are made of aluminium.

The interior of the banking hall is the *tour de force*. It consists of a nave and side aisles each with an elegantly formed glass ceiling. Originally, in the competition design, this was to be suspended by wires from projecting posts, but was later amended to be a glass ceiling of a similar splendid section attached to the truss of a pitched roof. Every element is reduced to the barest essentials and is fastidiously detailed; the shape of the roof is emphasised by slender glazing bars, the columns are clad in aluminium, the floor is divided into a grid marked by marble paving with glass block panels that light the room below; the light fittings and the clock are carefully designed and positioned; the tall aluminium heaters stand like sentries between the openings around the edge.

At the time it was built the impact of the banking hall must have been astounding; it was light, efficient and welcoming compared with the dark imposing interiors of the past. It is now over a hundred years old, yet even if it were built today it would not be out of place. Contemporary with the Glasgow School of Art and the Bourse in Amsterdam it has a timeless quality.

Since the 1960s Norman Foster, Richard Rogers, Michael Hopkins and Renzo Piano were among a group of architects who had a special interest in using new materials and technology in innovative ways. They worked closely with engineers such as Ove Arup, Peter Rice, Edward Happold, and Anthony Hunt.

Richard Rogers and Renzo Piano won the competition for the **Centre Pompidou in Paris** in 1971; it demonstrated a number of attitudes to architecture that were to pervade much of their later work.

The Centre Pompidou is key to the regeneration of a major part of the city. It creates a large piazza sloping down towards the

5.44 - Lloyd's of London interior

5.45 - Lloyd's of London exterior

5.46 - Pompidou Centre service elevation

5.47 - Pompidou Centre gerberette

entrance, reminiscent of the Campo in Siena, a place for buskers and street artists to perform, and for crowds to gather throughout the day and late into the night. From the piazza an escalator rises boldly up the face of the building giving access to each floor and providing varying views over the city. The building is a lively centre for entertainment and information, for exhibitions, music and dance, for many different sorts of culture; it is non-elitist, designed for everyone; Rogers described it as '*a university of the street*'. The front elevation forms a powerful backdrop to the life of the piazza; this is partly due to the drama of the great elevator but also to the legibility of each part of the structure so clearly and elegantly expressed. Events are constantly changing and there is a need for great flexibility, for uninterrupted floor space with the services kept out of the way. These are therefore grouped together at the back of the building; they are exposed, colour coded and celebrated, though their contribution to the urban landscape is questionable.

Richard Rogers has a passion for the way buildings are made. He has a preference for steel, glass and concrete with an overarching concern to express the system of structure and its constituent parts. At the Centre Pompidou, the structure consists of a braced steel frame and concrete floors with a clear internal span of nearly forty-five metres, and a circulation zone of around six metres outside this at the front and back. After many experiments, the brilliant engineer Peter Rice and his team reinvented and modified a system first used in 1866 by Heinrich Gerber in the design of bridges, where short beams are cantilevered from the columns to support the wider span; these became known as *gerberettes*. At Centre Pompidou the *gerberettes* are held down on the outside by vertical steel ties; they have a carefully formed shape designed to embrace the column, support the floor beam, and reflect the loading to which it is subjected. They are made of cast steel, a material that Peter Rice had seen in the work of Kenzo Tange in Japan that mirrored the elegant cast-iron sections used in the great structures of the 19th century. For Peter Rice the *gerberettes* had a special significance; in his book 'An Engineer Imagines' he questions "*what it was that gave the large engineering structures of the nineteenth century their special appeal. It was not just their daring and confidence... one element I had latched on to was the evidence of the attachment and care their designers and makers had lavished on them... the cast-iron decorations and the cast joints give each of these structures a quality unique to their designer and maker, a reminder that they were made and conceived by people who had laboured and left their mark.*"[5.4] He was later to observe "*The scale of the Centre Pompidou would be the scale of the pieces rather than the scale of the whole*".[5.4] Louis Kahn could not have said it better, even though he was to declare how he hated pipes!

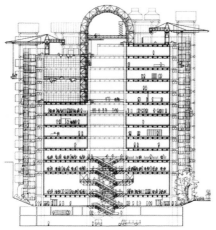

5.48 - Lloyd's of London cross section

Seven years later **Richard Rogers** began work on **Lloyd's of London,** the largest insurance market in the world, and it is interesting to compare it with the Centre Pompidou. The site is in the heart of the City and is tightly constrained. Richard Rogers had hoped that the ground floor would be part of the public domain but the need for security prevented this.

The Room, as it is called, is arranged around an atrium that rises through the full sixteen storeys of the building to a glazed semi-circular vault at the top; it has elevators crossing from side to side to serve the first five storeys. The continuous columns magnify its height. The Room is thus a grand space inhabited by groups of underwriters who work closely together around a desk but are still in contact with others in the market.

Centre Pompidou is made of steel - Lloyd's is made of concrete. Great care has been taken with the design of the junctions using concrete brackets around the columns to support the floors. The building is clad with special refracting glass in aluminium frames.

At Centre Pompidou the main façade presents itself towards the piazza with the services at the back; at Lloyd's the service towers are at the front dominating and concealing the simple form of the Room. The glazed vault of the atrium, which signifies the essence of the building, is visible from only a few viewpoints. The tall towers are complex structures where every element - the exposed service pipes, the toilet blocks, and the spiralling stairs is expressed, all are clad in stainless steel, with the lifts fully glazed.

The Centre Pompidou has a public welcoming appeal; Lloyd's of London is a shiny sophisticated icon with a certain sculptural quality. However, with such a strong celebration of the services, it is difficult to understand quite what the icon represents.

Norman Foster has designed structures of extreme simplicity; we have already noted the elegance of the station at Canary Wharf. This is demonstrated clearly at **Stansted Airport** designed between 1981 and 1991. The plan of the main concourse is organised on a square grid with the supporting structure at every alternate bay in both directions. These have been described as 'trees' with branches arising from a trunk all made of steel. The trunk consists of four robust circular posts connected by circular beams at the top outlining a space slightly taller than a cube. From these corners are attached two systems of structure in compression; one outlines a pyramid over the trunk, the other has branches spreading outwards to a perimeter beam that connects their ends and defines the square bay. From these corners rods in tension connect to the apex of the pyramid. This structure then supports the roof on the square bays on each of the four sides. The roof over each bay

5.49 - Stansted airport

5.50 - Great Court British Museum

5.51 - Great Court British Museum Ionic capital

is a shallow dome constructed as a diagrid with a rooflight in the centre. The elegance of the structure is derived not only from its simplicity but also from the size and detail of the parts. The diameter of each component reflects the load it has to take, and the main branches are subtly tapered towards their ends. The connections between each component resolve the three-dimensional geometry in a straightforward way, carefully related to the process of construction.

The concourse at Stansted is a bright lofty space appropriate for the crowds milling below. Unfortunately other aspects of the airport detract from the delight of this experience. Firstly, there is a long way to walk, and secondly, shops and food stalls have been added, individually designed by others, that compete with the elegance of the space and structure.

In 1994 **Norman Foster** designed a major intervention in the **Great Court** at the **British Museum.** This is a space surrounded by the galleries with the former circular Reading Room of the library towards its centre. With the help of Ove Arup and Partners, Foster designed a fully glazed roof that spans between the galleries and the central building. Its form is a shallow vault all the way round with a diagrid construction. Looking up, the impression is one of great simplicity, but it is in fact the result of skilful geometrical ingenuity; this is because the courtyard is not square but longer on one axis, and the library is towards one end. The library has been clad in white stone, and around its sides rise two gentle stairs that are monumentally wide at the bottom, gradually becoming narrower at the top. These stairs give access to galleries at an upper level as well as to a terrace restaurant. A particular delight is to stand very close to the Ionic capitals on the original building. The diagrid roof casts an intricate pattern of shadows both on the simple circular drum and on the more complex classical façade around.

This has become an impressive and well used civic space - the largest covered piazza in Europe. The original Reading Room was reserved as a privileged domain; now the fabric and the furniture have been restored, and it is open to the public as a library with particular reference to the exhibits in the museum.

5.52 - Tugendhat house view from garden

5.53 - Tugendhat house ebony and onyx partitions

5.54 - Tugendhat house lower floor plan

SMALLER STRUCTURES

For many architects, small buildings have been a vehicle for demonstrating their love of materials which they used in imaginative ways.

As early as 1930 **Mies van der Rohe** exploited the potential of new materials in the **Tugendhat House** at **Brno.** It has an open plan that reads as a beautiful abstraction yet it responded perfectly to the needs and aspirations of its wealthy owners. The site slopes to the south, and the house is entered from the north where it appears to be a simple single-storey building, with bedrooms and playrooms on this floor. A generous spiral stair leads down to the magnificent living space; it is huge, fifteen metres by twenty four, with the south wall entirely of glass giving breathtaking views over the city. There is a conservatory along the whole of the glazed wall to the east.

The structure consists of a widely spaced grid of slender steel columns cruciform on plan and faced in chrome. Within this space there are just two free-standing elements, a pristine plane of a partition made of polished onyx, and a semi-circular enclosure made of dark ebony; these are materials that respond to the changing light. There is thus a suggestion of how the room might be used, a place to eat, to study, to sit around or make music. The furniture shown on the plan demonstrates the generosity of space in each part. In fine weather the great windows to the south can be retracted below the floor. The Tugendhat House abounds in space and light as well as in exquisite materials; for future generations it became an exemplar towards a freer and more flexible way of living.

In 2009, the Tugendhat House became the setting for Simon Mawer's novel 'The Glass Room'.[5.5] Although it is a work of fiction, it gives a fairly accurate account of its history since it was first built. Above all, it contains an evocative description of the quality and atmosphere of the house.

5.55 - Maison aux Marthes first floor

5.56 - Maison aux Marthes ground floor

In 1935, **Le Corbusier** designed a small house that demonstrates a delight in the massiveness of a stone wall in contrast to the slenderness of timber posts. The **Maison aux Marthes** is a basic cheap structure built successively by a mason, a carpenter and finished by a joiner and plumber. It is a long house with seven bays that are each two and a half metres wide and five metres deep. The footprint consists of a bold continuous S-shaped wall half a metre thick built of random stone blocks. Its massiveness is emphasised by small splayed openings below and a narrow clerestory window above. This wall embraces a two-storey timber structure of posts supporting a wooden floor and roof. On each floor two bays at one end are open terraces, whilst the five bays at the other end contain the enclosed living areas and bedrooms with an open access way.

5.57 - Maison aux Marthes south facade

5.58 - Camden Mews south side

5.59 - Camden Mews detail

5.60 - St Mary's Church Barnes exterior view

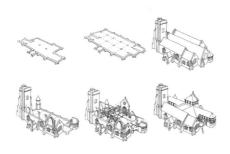

5.61 - St Mary's Church Barnes transition from old to new

For Le Corbusier this is an unusually primitive building yet it has an elegant clarity in its use of materials to express the contrast between heavy and light, solid and void, closed and open.

The work of **Edward Cullinan Architects** is characterised by a studied response to programme, a sensitivity to context and landscape, a careful use of materials, as well as an innovative but appropriate arrangement of form. This is shown in such buildings as the Minster Lovell Conference Centre, Fountains Abbey, and other subsequent work.

Between 1962 and 1964 Edward Cullinan designed and, together with friends, built his own house at **Camden Mews** in London. The site is small and narrow; there is only just enough room for the house and a garage at the side. As the street is to the west, the house is built along the north boundary with the rooms facing south. The living rooms are on the first floor overlooking a terrace above the garage.

As the house could only be built at weekends, the sequence of building became critical. The first task was to complete the roof as quickly as possible so that work could proceed in the dry. The roof spans between the two-storey brick party wall and a row of concrete columns along the south side of the house. The upstairs windows were then hung from the roof that projects beyond the columns. This was followed by the floor and the construction of the rooms below so that the house could then be equipped internally. In his lectures Cullinan enjoys graphically illustrating this sequence of events.

A particular characteristic of this house is in the detailing of the timber construction. Wherever the members are joined, they overlap and are bolted together rather than cut and jointed together in the usual complex way. This was due not only to the amateur builder's lack of skill but also to the precedent of Gerrit Rietveld's 'Red and Blue Chair', an influence shared by many architects at the time. This was a constructional system that would permeate much of Cullinan's later work.

Between 1978 and 1984 Edward Cullinan was involved with the regeneration of **St Mary's Church** at **Barnes** in London which had been destroyed by fire. The Victorian nave and north aisle were completely demolished leaving only parts of the medieval church and tower intact.

The new church became a masterpiece in its plan, section and construction. The most dramatic intervention was that the orientation of the church was changed from east-west to north-south. This enabled the south aisle of the original stone church to become a narthex together with a Lady Chapel. The ends of the former north aisle were rebuilt to make meeting rooms on two floors. The roof of the new nave slopes dramatically down on the eastern side and rises up with a square cupola over the altar. It is the construction of the roof that gives the new church such a powerful and, at the same time, homely presence. Two composite trusses of timber and steel span the length of the church between columns at the south and a new wall at the north. These support rafters that define a complex roof form; the whole is lined with timber boarding. As at Camden Mews the joints between the timber members are lapped and bolted together. The upper meeting rooms at the sides have continuous windows under the eaves, where the mullions consist of a cluster of four members similarly lapped and bolted over the cill and over the plate at the eaves. The timber members of the chancel furniture are similarly jointed demonstrating that this is both a formal and a constructional device.

5.63 - St Mary's Church Barnes courtyard

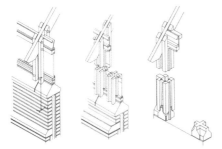
5.62 - St Mary's Barnes detail

5.64 - St Mary's Barnes interior view

5.65 - St Benedict Chapel, Sumvitg view within village

5.66 - St Benedict Chapel, Sumvitg interior

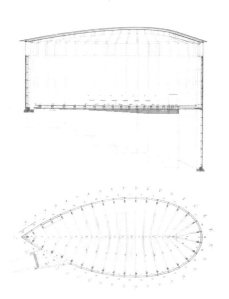

5.67 - St Benedict Chapel, Sumvitg section and plan

5.68 - St Benedict Chapel, Sumvitg entrance

5.69 - St Benedict Chapel, Sumvitg roof interior

St Mary's Church at Barnes is new, quite unlike its predecessor, but its sensitive use of geometry and space, quality of light, and use of material has given it a life and a meaning that is both valued and understood.

The Swiss architect **Peter Zumthor,** before becoming an architect, followed in his father's footsteps as a cabinet maker. The evidence of this can be seen in his design in 1989 for a church in the village of **Sumvitg** on the edge of the Alps in the Ticino.

The church replaces a former Baroque building that was destroyed in an avalanche. The shape of the plan has been variously described as a tear-drop, a leaf or a fish, but the most apt metaphor would seem to be a boat. Looking up at the inside of the roof is like looking into a clinker-built dinghy with its prow towards the entrance, its curved stern behind the altar, and with its rafters radiating from the keel down the centre. Between the rafters, timber boarding follows the line of the perimeter. This provides a rich baldachino over a simple and serene place. The roof is supported around the edge on thirty-seven rectangular columns made of finely wrought timber, and around the top is a continuous clerestory window. The inside wall is painted silver and stands outside the columns, separated from them by thin steel rods. The floor similarly has a gap around the edge separating the horizontal and vertical planes. The entrance is a small lean-to towards the rear of the church near the prow, and from here it is necessary to pass between the columns into the body of the church. There are only six rows of simple pews, and so the spaciousness of the floor and the pattern of the boards can be enjoyed.

Externally, the church is clad with shingles; it stands above the village on such a steep slope that the height of the apsidal end is twice that of the inside. Its approach poses a series of enigmas; the steep path and steps must be perilous in winter, and most surprisingly there is no place outside to linger. It is a masterpiece of understatement, and only a small cross and a simple sculptural bell tower mark its purpose. It rests casually in the landscape like a simple yet highly refined farm building.

Renzo Piano had worked with Richard Rogers on the Centre Pompidou in 1971, and in the decades that followed he was to collaborate with many others designing major buildings around the world including, for example, the gallery for the Menil Collection in Houston, the S. Nicola Stadium in Bari, and the Kansai International Airport; all buildings that are significant because of their technological innovation. In 1981 he founded the **Renzo Piano Building Workshop** with offices in Genoa and Paris, and in 1989 in collaboration with UNESCO, he opened a satellite **Laboratory Workshop** at Vesima outside Genoa. It is a centre for research in horticulture and construction involving

5.70 - Renzo Piano UNESCO Laboratory Workshop workstation

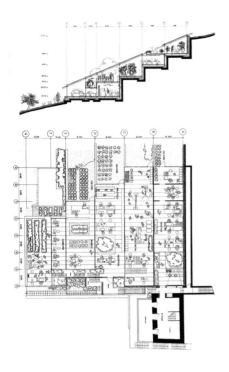

5.71 - Renzo Piano UNESCO Laboratory Workshop

many disciplines. In comparison with most of his other work, it is small, reticent and understated.

The site is typical of the terrain overlooking the gulf of Genoa; it is steep and terraced. Essentially the building consists of a glass roof stretching down the hill, not unlike the many agricultural greenhouses along that part of the coast. The terraced floors below are open to one another for easy contact but they also have a measure of separation.

Apart from the magnificent views, the magic of the building lies in its simple and direct construction. Slender steel posts support laminated timber purlins above the retaining walls, and beams of the same size run down the slope. They are joined to one another and to the square posts by discreet steel plates. Rafters span across to support the glass roof. Technological innovation occurs only in the solar-cells that control the external louvres and blinds that moderate the heat and light. The fully-glazed side walls are without frames; they have slender glass fins to provide stability.

The west side of the plan steps back and provides oblique views of the sea; the east side is straight with an internal stair connecting the different levels. Outside, a funicular connects down to the road below; its cabin is an elegant glass cube giving, on departure, a breath-taking dive towards the sea.

These small buildings are modest without ostentation, yet they display a subtle sophistication in their use of material and the way they are put together, creating an architecture that is both direct and delightful.

5.72 - Renzo Piano UNESCO Laboratory Workshop

5.73 - Renzo Piano UNESCO Laboratory Workshop night view towards the sea

107

6.1 - Säynätsalo informal stairs to courtyard

6 CONVEYING MEANING and DELIGHT

Daily life is full of small signs and rituals that convey meaning. There is the issue of identity; we recognise people from their faces, and we can tell, often quite reliably, what they are like, whether they are cheerful or gloomy, friendly or distant. This is an awareness learnt in early childhood that is gradually confirmed by repeated experience over the years. In the same way, we convey clues to others about our own individuality and personality. The messages we receive and convey are as subtle as they are full of information.

People arrange themselves in groups in various ways. In many societies eating and drinking together is a special joy as well as an important ritual, a sort of communion whether around a table or, as in Nepal, around a sacred stone in the pavement. On a larger scale people delight in congregating together in the market square or on the village green to chat and pass the time of day.

In everyday life the actions and the metaphors we use acknowledge the significance of up and down. We show respect by standing up for a lady, we give a standing ovation, a victor is carried shoulder high or, as at the Olympics, on podiums of different heights. We speak of walking tall, the moral high ground, and Heaven is portrayed as up there, *'a new Jerusalem high and lifted up'*, and Mount Olympus is the home of the gods. Conversely we may bow low, kneel, or lie prostrate; we speak of being in the dumps, downtrodden, and Hell is in the underworld.

The working week may be enriched by a party, a concert or just an evening out with friends. Special occasions call for appropriate celebrations. Some are symbolic related to a particular time such as marriage, birth or death, and are times when we may be overcome by emotion, moved to tears at a wedding, or consoled by laughter at a funeral, for as T.S. Eliot put it *"human kind cannot bear very much reality"*.[6.1] Other events relate to nature - the change of seasons, springtime, harvest or Thanksgiving - to the universe or to the gods; celebrations that are devised to help man be more at home in the world. Dress can contribute to the sense of occasion; we may dress up for a party but not for an evening at home, more formally for a funeral and comfortably casual for a walk in the country.

6.2 - Doorway in northern Nigeria

6.3 - Doorway in India

6.4 - Doorway in Dublin

These aspects of meaning all have a parallel in architecture. The need for identity, the way people relate to one another and to place, the contrast between the everyday and the special, and the expression of character and mood are all significant and all stem from the essential nature of the task.

IDENTITY

In our earlier consideration of the dwelling we noted the need for enclosure, an inside domain separate from yet connected to the world outside, and sometimes, as in the Cornford House, having different degrees of enclosure.

The **entrance** therefore has a particular significance; it is the place of greeting where a visitor is welcomed and invited to come in; it is in-between, the interface between the outside and the inside, the public and the private. All around the world it is celebrated; even in the poorest of squatter settlements some decoration, perhaps just a plant or a painting, often adorns the doorway. In parts of India paintings on the wall welcome the bride home, whilst the number of steps up to the door denotes status. Houses in northern Nigeria are adorned with elaborate carvings that demonstrate the wealth and position of the owner. In a Georgian terrace in London or Dublin a particular house is identified by its individual fanlight above the front door. Sometimes a particular part such as the living room is celebrated on the outside as, for example, in a Regency house where the first floor, the *piano nobile* is elegantly expressed. These discreet embellishments not only express the owner's dreams and aspirations but also establish an individual identity.

Within the urban scene buildings provide enclosure, and streets and squares define places that have their own identity. A hierarchy of roads helps you know where you are and find your way about. In the West End of London, for example, there is an overall grid of main roads; these are so busy with traffic that they act as barriers, whereas in the minor grid of quieter streets there is contact between one side and the other. Often the junction between streets is marked by a clever corner building; it is where you might arrange to meet. These are images that you can carry unconsciously in your mind's eye, and you may get a little bit lost - but not very lost! In a similar way you can relate to the urban squares that break up the grid.

THE EVERYDAY AND THE SPECIAL

Colin St John Wilson has quoted a relevant comment by the Viennese satirist Karl Kraus on the architect Adolf Loos: "*all that Adolf Loos and I have ever meant to say is that there is a difference between an urn and a chamberpot. But the people of today can be divided into those who use the chamberpot as an urn and those who use the urn as a chamberpot*".[6.2] This is an apt metaphor to describe the different role that a particular part of a building or place can be seen to play. We have already seen examples of this; in the Glasgow School of Art where the Library has a presence quite different from that of the workaday studios, and similarly, in the British Library the King's Collection is placed in a jewel-like tower in the centre of the building.

6.5 - Nolli's plan of Rome

Nolli's plan of **Rome** made in 1748 is, like all plans, full of information. It demonstrates the 'grain' of the city, the relation of black and white on the map. It portrays the relationship between enclosed streets and open squares that is part of the city's memorable and magical quality; places where people move about and places where they meet. The Nolli plan is drawn in a way that emphasises the difference between the everyday and the special; the everyday buildings that are private are shown as shaded blocks within the urban fabric, whilst the special buildings that are communal reveal their internal footprints. At that time in Rome there was a proliferation of churches and other public buildings; some, such as the Pantheon, are free-standing whilst others, such as St Agnese in the Piazza Navona, are joined to the buildings on either side and manifest their presence by their height and complexity of form.

Great cities have an identity of their own. In 1934 Steen Eiler Rasmussen wrote a book entitled 'London: The Unique City'.[6.3] It is a title that could be similarly applied to every great city in the world. Some are memorable because of their topography; London and Paris developed along rivers, Edinburgh's Royal Mile strides down the spine of rock from the castle to the palace, Rome and Sheffield enjoy their seven hills, and Sydney exploits its great harbour allowing commuters to come to work by boat; all of these are unique because of their response to the land or the water. Other cities are identified by their role, as centres of trade, education, religion or defence. Some cities contain places that are so significant that they act as icons; the Eiffel Tower or the Centre Pompidou stand for Paris, the Opera House or the Harbour Bridge represent Sydney, and St Mark's Square signifies Venice.

Traditionally, the hierarchy between the everyday and the special is clear; the house and workplace are individual and part of everyday life, whilst the church, library, and theatre are communal and special; in between is a repertoire of buildings that are modestly special, the public house or restaurant, and the shop on the corner. From experience we have come to recognise what these are but it may be necessary to get used to what is new. The distinctions between the everyday and the special remain valid; they not only establish an appropriate symbolic meaning and identity to each particular building but also give legibility to the city as a whole.

6.6 - Säynätsalo entrance

6.7 - Säynätsalo courtyard

6.8 - Säynätsalo roof plan

6.9 - Säynätsalo entrance to council chamber

6.10 - Säynätsalo roof trusses in council chamber

Height signifies a special role. Martin Heidegger famously wrote "*man dwells on the earth but also under the sky*"; it is a simple comment but it has a profound bearing on architecture.

The **Acropolis** in **Athens** dominates the city; it is approached by the magnificent flight of steps between the Propylaea leading up to the Parthenon and the Erectheion which are carefully placed on the gently sloping terrain, together with the beautiful little temple of Nike Apteros magically poised above a high retaining wall.

In the Middle Ages the high towers and spires of great **cathedrals** such as Salisbury, Santiago de Compostela or Siena reached towards heaven. They were lavishly decorated with marbles, bronze and gold expressing the power and authority of the Christian church.

Built in Florence during the Renaissance, the awe-inspiring height of **Brunelleschi's** great dome dominates the whole city; its luminous white marble contrasting with the red roofs all around. In Venice the more modest little church of Santa Maria dei Miracoli glories in its luxurious materials.

In Finland in 1950 **Alvar Aalto** designed a very small and understated Town Hall at **Säynätsalo** that rises gently to its apex**.** It is built of warm and friendly red bricks and finely crafted timber, and it established Aalto as the most humane architect of his generation.

The plan is centred on a raised grass courtyard, a symbolic gathering place for the citizens. Around this are the municipal offices and the Council Chamber with the Public Library as a separate enclosing element. Two generous flights of steps lead up to it; one is at the side of the Council Chamber and is gently formal, whilst the other is more casual with grass between the bricks exaggerating the impression of a mound. At the base is a small group of shops.

To the outside, the Town Hall presents continuous planes of brickwork rising up dramatically to the top of the Council Chamber, its height emphasised by a monopitch roof. In contrast, a single-storey cloister surrounds the courtyard. It is supported on slender steel posts and glazed continuously between dark stained mullions. It is wider at the entrance to form a foyer to the gentle staircase leading to the Chamber above. The floor and the walls of the stairs are made of the same mellow brick as outside, and the ceiling is timber; all illuminated by a narrow clerestory window above. Entry to the Chamber is an awesome experience; it is a room of intense simplicity, a cube with the ceiling rising steeply to one side with one great window opposite, and made with such a small palette of material, brick and timber. Only the roof structure is complex; from the two

6.11 - Seinajoki Council Chamber and Church

6.12 - Säynätsalo stairs to Council Chamber

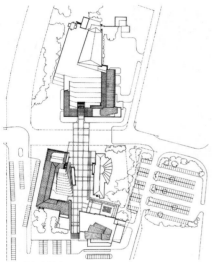

6.13 - Seinäjoki plan

6.14 - Seinäjoki Council Chamber mound

main beams timber struts fan out like the wings of a bird to support the secondary members, with every joint meticulously detailed, giving the Council Chamber a powerful presence.

As usual in Aalto's work, daylight has a special quality giving a sense of place to each part; sun shining between the mullions of the cloister casts a rhythm of shadows along the floor, the narrow band of light above the stairs adds to its welcoming ascent, and the window in the Chamber creates a serene subdued atmosphere. This is a building where the overall disposition of the parts, the sensitive use of brick and timber inside and out, and the control of light, are brought together in concert. Säynätsalo Town hall is very small but also powerfully monumental.

At the **Town Centre in Seinajoki**, designed in 1960, **Alvar Aalto** gave an appropriate meaning and identity to each part of the plan. Essentially it consists of two squares, one secular and one sacred. An elongated civic square serves as a meeting place for the town; it is loosely enclosed by the Town Hall, the Theatre and the Library. From this square a flight of easy steps leads up through a narrow gap to the square in front of the church which is surrounded by parish buildings; a space that can accommodate great crowds for religious festivals.

The two principal buildings, the church and the Town Hall, are signified by their height; the church by its tower and the Town Hall by its Council Chamber. The church is easy to comprehend and, though treated differently, each element is recognisable; the tower is both belfry and look-out and acts as a landmark to the town centre. The church, simpler than most by Aalto, is planned on an axis; it is wedge-shaped, and on both plan and section tapers towards the altar. A row of columns separates the nave from the side aisles; the ceiling has a series of shallow cross-vaults; and tall narrow windows open out at the top into wide arches that give a diffused light onto the curved surfaces. In detail, the columns that are square at the base change section and taper outwards to mark flat arches along the sides of the church, and (as often in Aalto's churches) the lower two metres of the columns are clad in timber to give a human scale. Following tradition, elaborate light fittings provide a richness that contrasts with the plain interior.

The Town Hall on the north side of the square is specially celebrated by its form, material and colour. The form is a development of ideas from the Town Hall at Säynätsalo designed ten years earlier, most notably in the landscaped mound and the steep high roof of the Council Chamber; here, viewed from the south, landscape and building have become one. From the east, the Council Chamber is seen to be on the first floor with the main entrance between the columns at ground

6.15 - Vietnam Memorial Washington the earth gashed open

6.16 - Vietnam Memorial Washington the reflecting wall of names

6.17 - Martyr's Memorial Paris steps down

6.18 - Martyr's Memorial Paris grill towards Seine

6.19 - Vietnam Memorial Washington aerial view

level. As at Säynätsalo, the Council Chamber is gently lit from above. The standard layout of the administrative offices serves as an everyday foil to the more significant event they serve. Unlike all the other buildings that are white, the Town Hall is made distinctive by being clad with shiny bright blue porcelain tiles.

The Theatre and the Library, by contrast, are more reticent buildings and present simple straight façades to the square in deference to the Town Hall. The Theatre has a nearly orthogonal footprint enclosing the fan-shaped auditorium that hardly appears on the outside. Inside, typical of an Aalto theatre, the curve of the fan provides a relaxed foyer space with doors arranged in echelon making it clear which way to go. In a similar way, the Library has rectangular offices towards the square with a long horizontal band of windows covered with closely spaced vertical louvres, and with an understated entrance. The reading room is fan-shaped to give easy supervision from the control desk, but significantly it has been discreetly placed at the back. By underplaying the expression of these buildings towards the square Aalto acknowledged their appropriate symbolic role in relation to the Town Centre as a whole.

In contrast to buildings that rise high into the sky, the **Memorial des Martyrs de la Déportation,** designed by **G. H. Pingusson**, at the tip of L'Isle de France in Paris, is made more poignant by the steep and narrow steps leading down to a crypt-like space which has a barred window at the level of the Seine below. It was created in 1962 in memory of the 200,000 Communists, Jews, and members of the Resistance who died in concentration camps. The chambers below are lined with thousands of tiny lights symbolising those who died.

The **Vietnam Memorial** in Washington, designed by **Maya Lin** in 1981, is similarly dug down; it is as if the earth has been gashed open, and in its simplicity it is a powerful evocation of the horrors of war. It consists of two retaining walls nearly at right angles to one another, one facing the Washington Memorial, the other facing the Lincoln Memorial. Each wall is seventy-five metres long descending from ground level at the ends to three metres at the centre where they join. Nearly 60,000 names of the victims are engraved on the stone which is shiny so that a visitor, reading the names, sees their reflection in the stone - a reminder of the past within the present.

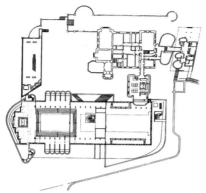

6.20 - St Peter's College Cardross plan

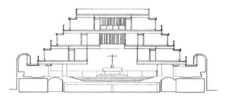

6.21 - St Peter's College Cardross section

6.22 - St Peter's College Cardross refectory

CHARACTER AND MOOD

Architecture conveys meaning and has the ability to set a mood. To quote Le Corbusier *"the purpose of architecture is to move us"*,[6.4] or the philosopher Ludwig Wittgenstein (who once designed a house for his sister) *"architecture glorifies and immortalises something; hence there can be no architecture where there is nothing to glorify"*.[6.5]

A **monastery** has meaning both as a significant place of worship and in the relationship between the individual and community. **St Peter's College Cardross** was designed in 1966 by **Andrew MacMillan** and **Isi Metzstein,** partners in the firm of Gillespie, Kidd and Coia. It is situated in magnificent parkland in a steeply sloping landscape with a lake and specimen trees. It is a seminary for training about a hundred priests, and consists of four connected buildings around an existing 19th-century mansion. These contain accommodation for teaching and recreation, a small convent, kitchens, and, in the main block, student bedrooms above the refectory and chapel. It is this building that most dramatically expresses the meaning of the monastic life.

The entrance to the College is over a shallow pool; this gives a serene approach towards a spiral stair that leads up to the central area between the chapel and the refectory. These are both within an impressive volume that is formed by being below a stepped section on both sides, each containing three floors of study bedrooms. These rooms look outwards towards the landscape and have a wide access gallery on the inside approached by a central staircase. Although the refectory and the chapel are within the same structure, they have significant differences. The access galleries look down into the refectory but they are screened from the view of the chapel. The refectory floor is level, unlike that in the chapel which is stepped down towards the centre, giving prominence to the sanctuary. The refectory has large clerestory windows towards the north, whereas the sanctuary of the chapel extends impressively beyond the main structure. On each side of the chapel five small chapels are lit from above with semi-domes that are reminiscent of the chapel at Ronchamp, designed by Le Corbusier a decade earlier. The sanctuary is the focus of worship; it is lit by a complexity of stepped roof lights giving a special quality of light. Behind the altar but separated from it is a plain curved wall. At the beginning of the Mass, the priests process from a cloister below the chapel up a ramp, and in this way the processional cross appears in front of the cyclorama before they themselves are seen; a moment of spectacular theatre.

The structure of the main envelope is made of concrete with shallow vaults defining the cells; these vaults are continued under the cantilevered floors creating a hint of an arcade in both the chapel and the refectory. The balcony fronts and furniture are made of light-coloured timber in contrast to the concrete. The ceiling of the sanctuary is made of laminated timber beams radiating towards the cycloramic wall; these, together with the light streaming from above, add to its specialness.

St Peter's College contains many meanings created by a series of reciprocal relationships; between the sacred and secular, inside and outside, above and below, as well as essentially between the priest and the collective order. Sadly! After only a short period of use, the College was closed and has since fallen into decay and has been vandalised in a most horrific way. At the time of writing, plans are being developed by Avanti Architects to partially restore and adapt the building to create an education and arts centre.

6.23 - St Peter's College Cardross chapel

6.24 - St Peter's College Cardross cyclorama behind the altar

6.25 - City Hall Murcia façade to piazza

6.26 - City Hall Murcia piano nobile

In 1991 **Rafael Moneo** designed the **City Hall in Murcia.** It is a building that symbolises the role of the State in relation to that of the Church. It is at the narrow end of the wedge-shaped Cardenal Belluga Plaza opposite the monumental baroque cathedral with the Cardenal's palace at the side.

Compared with the vast cathedral it has a very small footprint, yet it has great presence and simple dignity. It is made of a delightful local honey-coloured stone. The façade towards the plaza is completely flush without any mouldings or projections, and stands in contrast to the elaborate and highly modelled cathedral. Essentially, this façade consists of a solid two-storey stone base with a screen of precisely made square columns above. The base has two small square windows and a pair of tall openings, judicially placed. The first two rows of columns above are in front of a two-storey high volume which is expressed by a great double-height opening in the screen; its height exaggerated by a glass balustrade that cuts into the top of the base; a 'grand order' indicative of a *piano nobile.* Above this is a single-storey row of columns with a row of taller columns at the top. There is thus a progression from the heaviness of the base to lightness against the sky. The columns do not form a regular grid but appear to be randomly spaced, giving an intriguingly 'musical' rhythm of solid and void on each level. This serves to create a subtle tension between horizontal and vertical, and most significantly emphasises the planar rather than the columnar quality of the screen. The façade is in no way symmetrical but it achieves a careful balance powerfully expressed by the holes cut into the base and the great void in the screen above. Although it is sensitively composed, this is not the result of arbitrary pattern-making; it is quite properly a reconciliation of the internal programmatic requirements and the external demands of the plaza.

The main body of the building follows the grain of the surrounding streets but the front portion is slightly skewed towards the cathedral. The entry is just around the corner to the north, as Moneo comments *"out of respect for the seniority of its neighbours".* This leads into the foyer with the Legislative Assembly occupying the rear and floor below. All the important civic rooms and their balconies face the plaza so that the dignitaries not only see the life of the city but also can themselves be seen. A terrace on the roof is an appropriate response to the Spanish sun. In front of the building and behind a curved balustrade, steps lead down to a sunken courtyard and café. The administrative offices are at the back presenting more everyday windows to the streets around.

6.27 - City Hall Murcia aerial view

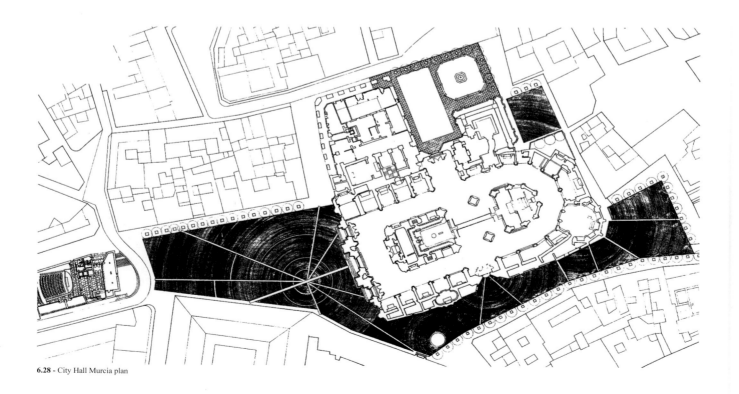

6.28 - City Hall Murcia plan

Moneo has designed a building that both respects its historic setting and signifies its new civic role in a modern democracy. With great skill and sensitivity he has devised an architectural language that is discreet and of the present day without any parody of the past.

CHANGE

Over time society changes and cultural values are modified. This has happened at many different times in the past. During the Reformation, for example, both Catholic and Protestant churches were designed as theatres but each in a different way. The Catholic church became a stage set for the Mass and a splendid visual display designed to inspire the believer, whilst the Protestant church was a sober setting for the preacher to overawe the congregation with the words of the Gospel.

In the 19th century, with the rise in education, impressive libraries and schools began to celebrate a new social order. The growth of major industries gave rise to an unprecedented expression of wealth. The magnificent centre of Glasgow, for instance, is a collective monument to the riches that ship-building gave to the city.

During the late 20th century different values began to emerge: changes in attitude towards religion have pointed towards a more secular society; different attitudes to authority have led to more openness and transparency; different attitudes to equality have challenged established hierarchies, and increased mobility has changed the nature of community. These changes impact on architecture as old icons become redundant and are replaced. It is necessary then to re-establish the role of the icon, but essentially in a way that is imbued with meaning not just image.

Part Two

7.1 - Viipuri Library interior

7.2 - Viipuri Library reading room

7 The NATURE of DESIGNING

ALVAR AALTO'S REFLECTIONS ON THE LIBRARY AT VIIPURI

It is fitting to begin this inquiry into the nature of designing with a short essay by Alvar Aalto. He wrote very little; he did not consider himself as academic but preferred to express his polemic through building. That is what makes his reflections on designing the Library at Viipuri especially revealing and useful.

First, let us look at the building. It was won in competition in 1930 but was almost totally destroyed in the war and stood for a long time in ruins, but it has now been beautifully restored. It is sited in a splendid park next to the cathedral, and the brief was for a lending library and reading rooms, a children's library, a lecture room and administrative offices. On the outside the building is white with stucco walls, and has a clarity of form expressive of the emerging architecture of the time.

The footprint consists of two overlapping rectangles, one containing the library and reading room, the other, the lecture room with the stock room below. From the entrance, the reading room is to the left, and to the right up a half level is the main library. This is on two levels with a wide gallery at head height around the edge, creating a sort of valley in the centre below. At each level the walls are lined with shelves of books. Although the plan is simple, the section is subtly complex, creating different spatial volumes, and the way people move around follows a series of different levels.

The check-out desk is on the gallery level in a central position, and supervises both the library and the reading room. The magic of each room is in the quality of the light from a grid of circular conical openings in the ceiling, which give a diffused shadowless light for both readers and books. The atmosphere is spacious and calm.

The library is high and lit from above whilst the lecture room is low and lit from the side. It is designed for the quality of its acoustic, which is achieved by an undulating timber ceiling designed to reflect the sound.

Aalto was thirty-two years old when he designed this building. He had already designed an exhibition building, a theatre, the printing offices and press for Turun Sanomat in Turku as well as the pioneering sanatorium at Paimio. These buildings, together

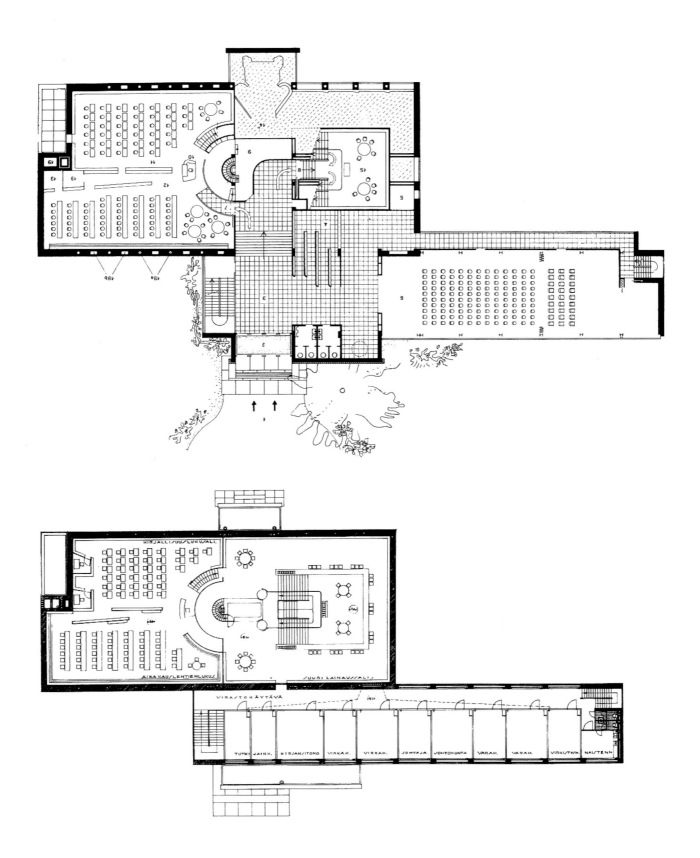

7.3 - Viipuri Library ground floor & first floor plans

with the Viipuri Library, were all essentially orthogonal; he had not yet moved to the freer plan forms that distinguished much of his post-war work.

Aalto's reflections on designing the Viipuri Library are contained in an essay written in 1947 entitled 'The Trout and the Mountain Stream'.[7.1]

"*First and foremost, abstract art has given impulses to architecture in our era – indirectly, of course, but the fact cannot be denied. On the other hand, architecture has provided material for abstract art. Each in turn, these two artistic branches have influenced each another.*

When I personally have to solve an architectural problem I am confronted, almost always, with an obstacle that is difficult to surmount, a kind of 'courage de trois heures du matin'. The cause, I believe, is the complicated and intense pressure of the fact that architectural design operates with innumerable elements that internally stand in opposition to each other. They are social, human, economic, and technical demands that unite to become psychological problems with an effect on both the individual and the group, on group and individual movement and internal frictions. All this becomes a maze that cannot be sorted out in a rational or mechanical manner. The large number of different demands and sub-problems form an obstacle that is difficult for the architectural concept to break through. In such cases I work - sometimes totally on instinct - in the following manner. For a moment I forget all the maze of problems. After I have developed a feel for the programme and its innumerable demands have been engraved on my subconscious, I begin to draw in a manner rather like that of abstract art. Led only by my instincts I draw, not architectural syntheses, but sometimes even childish compositions, and via this route I eventually arrive at an abstract basis to the main concept, a kind of universal substance with whose help the numerous quarrelling sub-problems can be brought into harmony.

When I designed the city library at Viipuri (I had plenty of time at my disposal, five whole years) for long periods of time I pursued the solution with the help of primitive sketches. From some kind of fantastic mountain landscapes with cliffs lit up by suns in different positions I gradually arrived at the concept for the library building. The library's architectural core consists of reading and lending areas at different levels and plateaus, while the centre and control area forms the high point above the different levels. The childish sketches have only an indirect link with the architectural conception, but they tied together the section and the plan with each other, and created a kind of unity of horizontal and vertical structures. I recount these personal

129

7.4 - Viipuri Library view to garden

7.5 - Viipuri Library acoustic ceiling

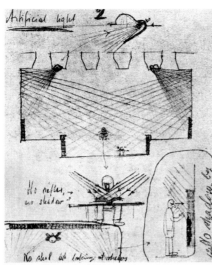

7.6 - Viipuri Library sketch lighting section

experiences without wanting to make a method out of them. But I actually think that many of my colleagues have experienced something similar in their own struggle with architectural problems. The example also has nothing to do with good or bad qualities in the final results. It is just an example of how my own instinctive belief has led me to the fact that architecture and art have a common source, which in a certain sense is abstract, but which despite this is based on the knowledge and the data that we have stored in our subconscious".

In this highly condensed paragraph Aalto refers to a whole range of ways of thinking about design. There is first of all the reference to *"innumerable elements that internally stand in opposition to each other"* and *"the many quarrelling sub-problems to be brought into harmony"*. This is very like our earlier definition of design as reconciliation. Aalto refers to rational thought but he acknowledges that *"the maze of problems cannot be sorted out in a rational or mechanical manner"*; he refers to intuition *"after I have developed a feel for the programme, and its innumerable demands have been engraved on my subconscious… led only by my instincts"*; he refers to the notion of play *"childish compositions"*, the value of drawing and the use of words; he reflects on experience and precedent, and elicits metaphor; *"fantastic mountain landscapes with cliffs lit up"* and he points to the value of abstraction. In this short piece Aalto refers four times to the search for an overall concept. It is this that embodies and clarifies the architect's intentions. It may of course not be one big idea but a collection of ideas working together. This is the most difficult part, to develop a 'story' that is strong enough to be sustained, and to believe in it with sufficient commitment to carry on, and yet be prepared to let it go if necessary later on. Arriving at a concept is the breakthrough in reconciling all the *"quarrelling sub-problems"*. It is this that gives an appropriate role to every part, and once established it provides its own internal consistency.

Aalto uses the analogy of trout spawning far from the sea to describe the distance between the birth of an idea and its realisation. The link between generative ideas and the finished library is not obvious to an outsider; it belongs solely to the designer. In this essay Aalto plays down the use of rational thought in order to emphasise other important aspects of designing, yet the finished library displays a clarity of circulation and an orderliness to every part that is totally reasonable. His sketches of the section show an intense rational study of both acoustics and lighting, yet their genesis was in a moment of play.

In the following sections we will explore different aspects of designing; the value of experience and precedent, the use of metaphor, as well as the search for harmony, all brought together within an overarching concept.

8.1 - Sainsbury Laboratory looking into the laboratories

8   The ROLE of REASON and INTUITION

In his perceptive book 'The Reflective Practitioner',[8.1] Donald Schon seeks to understand the various ways of thinking that practitioners, including architects, use. This is difficult because, as he comments, in this and in many other areas of life *"We know more than we can say"*.

At the outset the architect has to become immersed in all aspects of the task - what is required in response to the programme, the relation to climate, to context, as well as the possibilities and limitations of available resources. This requires the ability to know what to look for, to search for essentials, and in the process to evoke questions that may stimulate ideas. Even within this rational approach a totally objective analysis is not possible since the designer interacts with it and to an extent changes it. As the writer A.S. Byatt put it *"We all remake the world as we see it, as we look at it"*. Different designers therefore interpret the task in different ways. It is often useful to stand back from the detailed requirements and see the task from a wider perspective, which Donald Schon refers to as *"reframing the task"*.

Design is more than problem-solving. It is not like a jigsaw puzzle where a known number of pieces fit together in a certain way in order to achieve a given end result. The designer is more like a novelist who has to devise a story and arrange the sub-plots, seldom knowing at the beginning how it will end. But an architectural design is different from a novel; when it becomes a building it not only serves a useful purpose but also is ever-present in its particular place, and impinges on everyone who comes in contact with it - it cannot just be left on the shelf.

Donald Schon seeks to discover what makes up the '*artistry*' that practitioners bring to their work, and this leads him to discuss those areas that are often dismissed as mere intuition and regarded as beyond description. He proposes that in design, knowing and doing are not separate, and that *"our knowing is in the action"*, the sort of tacit knowing like that used by sportsmen in the field or by musicians working together with a 'feel' for what they are playing. This, as he points out, requires *"reflection and experimentation"*. In designing this is often achieved by the act of drawing.

But where to begin? Many creative artists have recorded the difficulty of getting started. The writer Iris Murdoch has talked

8.2 - Seed Bank exterior view of entrance

8.3 - Seed Bank exterior view of winter garden

8.4 - Seed Bank winter garden

of "*the courage to start, the courage to stick with an idea, and the courage to let it go when it no longer works for you*". The painter Van Gogh has written of his fear of the virgin canvas and the need to splash some colour on to it to make a start.

Architects use many different sorts of drawing. Some are analytical and are often a diagrammatic shorthand towards understanding the programme. Some, like Aalto's early sketches are playful, and they should be looked at carefully as they may contain clues; others are like caricatures that contain the essence of an idea and eliminate what is unimportant. Donald Schon has charted the interesting dialogue that takes place between words and drawings, the thought and the visual interpretation of the thought. He introduces the notion of '*talk back*', pondering a drawing and allowing it to suggest an improvement, a correction, the next step forward; in this way drawings become experiments or explorations where one drawing leads to another. In the development sketches of many architects we can see how the act of drawing has generated the next idea. We can also see, when a sequence of drawings seem to lead nowhere, that it is necessary to try a different tack and reframe the task in a different way. This may require zooming in or out at a different scale, or working from the parts to the whole rather than the whole to the parts, or turning the problem on its head and working backwards from an imagined end result.

Rational thought and intuition go hand in hand, but where does intuition come from? We must admit that often we do not know; just as in everyday life when we might say "*I have suddenly had an idea*" without having any knowledge of where it comes from. It is similar to the way a scientist might think when, after years of painstaking research, he makes a leap in the dark - a leap that must then be rigorously tested. Sometimes intuition lies deep in the subconscious and may relate to early experiences in childhood; it may relate to places hardly remembered but enjoyed like the "*fantastic mountain landscapes*" of Aalto's recollection. Over time the architect can help to stimulate his intuition by constantly observing, recording and reflecting on places visited and enjoyed; memories of awe-inspiring landscapes, cities with magnificent buildings, streets and squares that were sometimes built anonymously and at other times designed by great architects past and present. This is rather like a novelist who makes note of a particular scene that may at some future time be re-lived and re-used. Such observations are valuable, as Hertzberger puts it "*to fill the library of the mind*", to be stacked deeply away so that one day they may be remembered and recalled, not copied, but later transformed in as yet unknown ways. Some of these memories are of actual places and may become useful precedents, others are of a particular mood or atmosphere and may evoke a metaphor.

8.5 - Seed Bank exterior barrel vaults

8.6 - Seed Bank exterior detail

8.7 - Seed Bank exterior conservatory

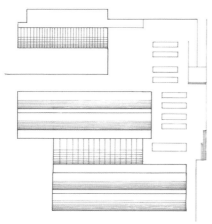

8.8 - Seed Bank plan

The architects **Stanton Williams** have designed two science buildings that had precise briefs. In other hands, with different clients and designers and on a different site, this might have resulted in a utilitarian shed, albeit well insulated and serviced. In the designs that have been built, the technical requirements of the brief have been fully satisfied, but in addition the well-being of researchers and visitors has been carefully considered as well as their relation to a magnificent landscape. The realisation that these particular areas of research have a potentially major impact on the health of the planet influenced the design of the buildings to attain a significant cultural presence.

The **Seed Bank** at **Wakehurst Place** in **Sussex** is owned by the Royal Botanic Gardens at Kew. It contains seeds of all Britain's plants and already houses more than ten per cent of all the world's dry-land plants, those most vulnerable to extinction. As these are from the poorest areas, the potential benefits will be enormous. The plants are stored in a vast underground vault estimated to last 500 years. In addition to the conservation of seeds, the building contains research laboratories and has a permanent team of scientists.

The building is set within an Area of Outstanding Natural Beauty adjacent to a Site of Special Scientific Interest. This gave the necessity of harmonising with the landscape, and the possibility of making the research accessible to the public. As the site slopes five metres from east to west, it was not too difficult to locate the seed storage in a basement and design a discreet low building at ground level.

The main part of the building consists of five barrel vaults; the central vault, the winter garden, is wider and higher with a predominantly glazed roof and contains a public exhibition; on either side two vaults cover the laboratories and offices. A glass lift and a spiral stair at the western end of the winter garden give access from the laboratories to the seed bank below. To the north is a sunken court surrounded by study bedrooms for visiting researchers, together with a library and seminar rooms. Above, on its northern side, is an off-the-peg vaulted greenhouse.

The exhibition in the winter garden explains the research that is going on and the complex arrangements for bringing seeds from around the world. It has glazed sides so that the public can look into the laboratories and see the researchers at work, and some of what they see in their microscopes is displayed on monitors in the exhibition.

The concrete construction is clear and logical. The basement has thick walls to assist the critical temperature control, and similarly the concrete barrel vaults over the laboratories provide thermal mass. There is a limited palette of materials and colour; the columns and beams are concrete, and the external floors

8.9 - Sainsbury Laboratory north façade

8.10 - Sainsbury Laboratory ramp to first floor

8.11 - Sainsbury Laboratory south façade

8.12 - Sainsbury Laboratory ground floor plan

8.13 - Sainsbury Laboratory first floor plan

8.14 - Sainsbury Laboratory second floor plan

and walls are sandstone. The form of the building gives it a calm presence reminiscent of Kahn's Kimbell Gallery. Stanton Williams have succinctly commented: *"Our intention was to create a building in harmony with the landscape, a restrained building that does not 'shout' but sits quietly in the landscape where it is grounded and held by the horizontal line"*.[8.2]

The Sainsbury Laboratory in the **Cambridge Botanic Garden** is a research centre for plant science aimed at understanding how plants are constructed and develop. In recent years the study has been transformed by new scientific and technical advances available to different areas of biology; new possibilities have been opened up and many disciplines have become involved. The building therefore had to contain precise and complex scientific facilities, and at the same time encourage personal interaction between the various teams of researchers. Appropriately, all of this would be in the most beautiful landscape setting of the Botanic Garden. Both the clients and the sponsors envisaged a building of such quality that it would attract the best scientists from around the world.

The architects themselves had to begin with months of rigorous research. As Roger Freedman, Gatsby Charitable Foundation Chief Scientific Advisor to the Sainsbury Laboratory was later to comment *"One of the ways that Stanton Williams really distinguished themselves was that they dedicated quite a long time to understanding what their remit was, what the building had to be. And they also took time to look at the site. When they had digested these issues, that was when they started sketching out general ideas. They shot up in my estimation because of that. They really listened"*.[8.3]

The brief required laboratories, support areas, writing-up areas, meeting rooms, the University Herbarium, a staff restaurant, as well as a café for visitors to the Botanic Garden.

From the outset, both the clients and the architects were conscious of their inheritance from Charles Darwin as well as from John Henslow, the creator of the Botanic Garden. Indeed Darwin's 'thinking path' (his regular walk through the trees) provided the inspiration for the continuous route that brings everyone together in the building. It is a place for relaxation and stimulation away from the intensity of the laboratory.

The overall footprint is L-shaped, designed to embrace the view of the fine trees within the garden. The architects' early sketches reveal the gradual simplification of the plan and the development of the long low section with the Herbarium below ground. The building is approached very discreetly from the north, down a narrow lane off a residential street. From the gateway a drive runs alongside the building to the entry square that is planted with a formal grove of ginkgo trees.

139

The entrance leads into a spacious hall past a lecture room that unusually is glazed on both sides, an indication that nothing is shut away. This is where the 'thinking path' begins; it surrounds the inner courtyard, and has been likened to a monastic or college cloister. On the ground floor there are meeting and seminar rooms as this is an area that can be used for conferences. From here a stepped ramp leads to the floor above; it is wide enough for two people to walk side by side, and its gentle slope serves to encourage conversation. It is reminiscent of that in Asplund's Gothenburg Law Courts. The first floor is the *piano nobile,* a double height volume where the route continues around the courtyard. There are carrel-like spaces along its edge where small groups of scientists can gather to talk and enjoy the view; they recall those in the Glasgow School of Art or the Phillips Exeter Academy Library. The coffee machine is located strategically at the centre. There is a void between the route and the laboratories which are approached by bridges, giving a great sense of openness and spaciousness. The laboratories are raised 400 mms so that they also face the view; the support rooms are behind and the write-up rooms are at each end.

Great care has been taken in the design of the laboratory lighting to admit a shadowless light to the workbenches. At the present time the benches are arranged on a regular grid but this may change because of the requirements of different research teams; the services have been located to allow this flexibility. Similarly, the support rooms have partitions that can be removed or repositioned to suit future requirements.

The building has distinct edges between the outside and inside of the L-shaped plan; the outside façades have tall closely spaced fins to allow flexibility to the rooms, whereas the inner façades have large windows towards the courtyard and the Botanic Garden beyond; they are protected from the sun by huge cantilevered roofs. On all sides of the building the *piano nobile* is powerfully expressed. The public café towards the south has a separate entrance from the garden.

External materials are used in a strata-like manner, with alternating layers of concrete and stone expressing solidity and a permanence that seems appropriate to long-term research. Internally there is a limited repertoire of materials and a restrained use of colour; this serves to exaggerate the splendid colours of the garden that change with the seasons.

The Sainsbury Laboratory is a design where every decision has been given careful thought. Every aspect demonstrates a consistent and rational approach – the design of the laboratories and their ancilliary facilities, the way they relate together and are flexible, as well as the construction and use of materials.

8.15 - Sainsbury Laboratory south-west courtyard

8.16 - Sainsbury Laboratory elevation to Botanic garden

This is matched by an intuitive sensitivity to the needs of people, to space and light, and to the wonderful garden context which gives the research its meaning.

8.17 - Sainsbury Laboratory Darwin walk

8.18 - Sainsbury Laboratory bridge to laboratories

9.1 - Dome of Duomo Florence

9 The VALUE of EXPERIENCE and PRECEDENT

Architects spend a great deal of time considering context, the relation of a building to its surroundings, to the city or the countryside. This is the context of place, but there is also the context of time, the relation of a piece of work to history and tradition.

The essay 'Tradition and the Individual Talent', written in 1917 by T. S. Eliot, provides a good place to start.

To clarify his use of the word 'tradition', he writes; "*It involves… the historical sense… and the historical sense involves a perception, not only of the pastness of the past, but of its presence… This historical sense which is a sense of the timeless as well as of the temporal and of the timeless and the temporal together, is what makes a writer traditional. And it is at the same time what makes a writer most acutely conscious of his place in time, of his own contemporaneity*".[9.1]

To put that in a different way, this historical sense helps us to know where we stand now; it helps us to find our place in time, to give us confidence in what otherwise might seem a confused situation. It also enriches our view of the world because, as the critic William Curtis has pointed out, our perceptions of the past and the present are constantly subject to revision. Once we have seen the paintings of the Impressionists, for example, we can never see nature in the same way again, and so with architecture.

I propose to look at the lives and ideas of a number of architects from different times and place, to see where they came from, to consider the impact of the tradition they inherited, and how they transformed this into something innovative and new, and in that way sowed the seeds of a new tradition for the next generation to inherit. There is considerable diversity in their ideas, with different strands of emphasis as the nature of the task changes and new problems are encountered. What they have in common is that they have each worked in a time of cultural change, and to a degree they have helped to stimulate that change.

Consider first the Renaissance. In the late 14th century and early 15th century in Italy, philosophers, scientists, men of letters, artists and architects became disillusioned with the myths and dogmas of the time, and began to reject the authority of the Church. They came to realise that their values were more in tune with those of classical antiquity.

9.2 - Pazzi Chapel façade

9.3 - Pazzi Chapel interior

9.4 - Pazzi Chapel portico

Brunelleschi was a pioneer among the architects of that time. He was trained as a goldsmith and in 1401 entered the competition for the bronze doors to the Baptistery in Florence, which he won jointly with Ghiberti. These two were supposed to work together but Brunelleschi was a loner and by all accounts a somewhat difficult man, so he decided to have none of it and withdrew. He then travelled to Rome where he measured and made careful drawings of the ancient ruins; he recorded the classical orders and studied their systems of dimension in detail; he came to understand the 'grandeur that was Rome'. Knowing that the dome of the cathedral of Santa Maria Dei Fiori in Florence was going to be completed, he was particularly interested in the Pantheon.

The design of the dome of the Duomo had originally been won in competition in 1367 by Neri di Fioraventi. It had a diameter of 44 metres which was greater than the Pantheon, and it rested on a drum 9 metres high on top of the existing structure which was already 42 metres above the ground. This meant that the base of the dome was the equivalent of about twenty domestic storeys above the ground. The wardens of the cathedral insisted that the new dome should be just like the one by Neri; the trouble was that for the next fifty years no-one knew how to make it! In 1418 a new competition was held, and after a lot of controversy Brunelleschi was declared the winner, with the embarrassing proviso that Ghiberti should work with him. The main difficulty was how to support the dome at such a height while it was being constructed. This was where Brunelleschi demonstrated his innovative understanding of structure, and he devised a way of building a dome without centering. It was consecrated in 1436, eighteen years after its inception, and the architect had survived intrigue, rivalry and ridicule.

While he was involved in this vast enterprise, Brunelleschi was also designing a number of exquisite little buildings influenced by the classical precedents that he had seen on his travels. In about 1430 he designed the **Chapel** for the **Pazzi family** next to the church of Santa Croce in Florence. The simple portico is one of the most memorable facades in the history of architecture. The delicate entablature above six slender columns is broken in the centre by a semi-circular arch that penetrates the plane of the wall. This is so discreetly incised with a classical order that it reads like panelling, and above this the roof is raised as if above a gallery. It is the contrast between the open colonnade at the base, the solid in the centre, and the void at the top which makes the façade so distinctive. Inside, beautifully crafted pilasters barely project from the walls and serve to articulate the plan; above, a play on the geometry of arches and circles creates a space that is both rich and peaceful. Brunelleschi has used the orders and the ordering of classicism in a way that is different from anything done before.

In the centuries after Brunelleschi architects from all over Europe made the Grand Tour to Italy, and thus the architecture of classical antiquity became available as precedents for further explorations. We will note Christopher Wren's innovative use of the classical orders in the **Library** at Trinity College Cambridge.

Forward then to the 20th century. **Charles Edouard Jeanneret** was born in 1887 in the Swiss town of La Chaux-de-Fonds which was the centre of the watch-making industry and also of Art Nouveau. Jeanneret went to the local art school where he was greatly influenced by his teacher Charles L'Eplattenier who taught him to draw as well as to design and engrave the back of pocket watches, and who suggested he might become an architect. Jeanneret designed his first villas in La Chaux-de Fonds in 1905 and 1908. It is fascinating to note that these were contemporary with the Glasgow School of Art, and that this was the architect who, twenty years later, was to design the Villa Savoye, one of the most seminal houses of the century!

Two experiences were about to change his life. Firstly, his own Grand Tours to Italy, Greece and Constantinople where he carefully made the drawings that are gathered together in the first volume of his complete works. These drawings reveal how his critical and incisive eye could pick out the essentials which he was later to use as precedents. The second experience was to work for a time in the offices of Auguste Perret and Peter Behrens where he learnt about the possibilities opened up by reinforced concrete and mechanisation. In 1920 Jeanneret changed his name to **Le Corbusier**.

9.5 - Le Corbusier sketches

'Vers Une Architecture' was written in 1923 and translated into English as 'Towards a New Architecture' in 1927. It is a passionate rallying cry for a modern architecture in a new world of mass production. In places it reads like the refrain of a poem repeated again and again:

> *"A great epoch has begun.*
> *There exists a new spirit.*
> *There exists a mass of work conceived in the new spirit;*
> *it is to be met with particularly in industrial production.*
> *Architecture is stifled by custom.*
> *The 'styles' are a lie".* [9.2]

'Towards a New Architecture' is also a passionate eulogy about the architecture of ancient Greece and Rome as well as Byzantium and the Renaissance. Le Corbusier devotes many pages of text, photographs and drawings to a lyrical appreciation of the Parthenon and the relationship between its parts. He records his careful observation of every form and detail - the dramatic horizontal impact on the landscape of the stepped base, the verticality of the columns emphasised by their fluting, both made optically more satisfying by their almost imperceptible

9.6 - Doric Capital

9.7 - La Tourette chapel

curvature. Referring to a Doric capital, he comments *"the fraction of the inch comes into play. The curve of the echinus is as rational as that of a large shell. The annulets are 50 feet from the ground, but they tell more than all the baskets of acanthus on a Corinthian capital "*.[9.2]

From writing like this we can see how the highest aims of classical architecture became engraved on his memory. He delights in pure Platonic forms, prisms, cubes, cylinders, pyramids and spheres: *"Architecture is the skilful, accurate and magnificent play of masses seen in light "*. He sees this in the great monuments as well as in the little church of Santa Maria in Cosmedin with the subtle geometry of its pulpit and ambo; *"This is the pure and simple beauty that architecture can give"*. Le Corbusier later said *"the past was my only real master "*, and from this strong sense of tradition he developed innovative ideas for the future.

'Towards a New Architecture' has been an inspiration to many architects although his persuasive dogmatism has led others astray. As in a political manifesto there are memorable catch phrases such as *'a house is a machine for living in'*, which, when taken out of context, ignores the fact that Le Corbusier saw in the machine the same qualities of elegance, economy and precision that he admired.

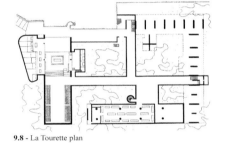

9.8 - La Tourette plan

9.9 - La Tourette view from north-west

In 1953 Le Corbusier was asked to design the **Monastery of La Tourette** on a steep hillside near Lyons. The plan is arranged around a courtyard from which the cloister crosses from three sides to the chapel. The elements that form the monastic life are clearly expressed; the monks' cells are at the top, the communal facilities including the refectory and library are below, and the chapel occupies the whole volume of one end. The Dominican Abbot suggested that Le Corbusier should first visit the monastery at Le Thoronet in Provence to appreciate the austerity of the Cistercian Order, its bare stone simplicity and the mystical quality of light. The chapel in the Monastery at La Tourette is in no way a copy of Le Thoronet but it captures the essence; it is a long high space made of bare concrete; the way it is lit gives a quiet contemplative atmosphere. Le Corbusier has transformed an old precedent into a place that is new, appropriate and imbued with meaning. Externally, the plain bare concrete expresses enclosure with no concession to the world outside.

Gunnar Asplund was born in Stockholm in 1885. He was therefore an almost exact contemporary of Le Corbusier. At the age of twenty he attended the Royal Institute of Technology in Stockholm and in 1910 he transferred to the Royal Academy. After a year there a group of students, including Asplund and Lewerentz, rebelled against the old-fashioned conservative Beaux Arts teaching, and set up their own atelier with four part-time practitioners as their tutors.

9.10 - Woodland Chapel view through trees

9.11 - Woodland Chapel portico

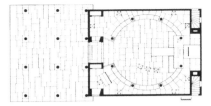

9.12 - Woodland Chapel plan

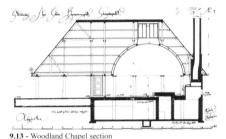

9.13 - Woodland Chapel section

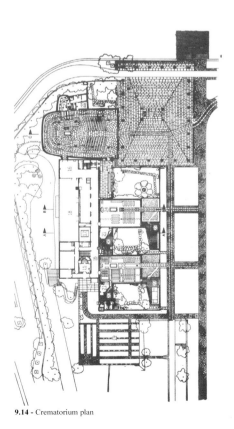

9.14 - Crematorium plan

Asplund designed his first houses and schools around 1912, and in 1913 set off on his Grand Tour of France, Italy and Greece that was to have a profound influence on all his subsequent work. In a lecture afterwards he made the telling remark "*it is more important to follow the style of the place than that of the time*". Like Le Corbusier he made sketches of everything he regarded as significant, drawing plans, sections and elevations as well as details of a classical repertoire. His sketches in Italy were drawn in the same way as those of his later buildings.

On his return to Sweden, he and Lewerentz won the competition for the **Stockholm** Woodland Cemetery, and in 1918 Asplund designed the small **Woodland Chapel**. It is a project that shows the architect's sensitive respect for tradition. It is a finely crafted barn with a steep shingled roof without gutters, a simple geometrical form given a dignity and grandeur by a deep portico two-thirds of the size of the chapel. This has a low flat timber ceiling supported on three rows of four plain circular timber columns painted white. The generous proportions of the portico transform the barn into a classical temple from which it is distantly derived. Inside, a circular space below a semi-circular dome is lit from a central rooflight, and reinforces the solemnity of the occasion. The circle is defined by eight columns, fluted versions of those outside, with capitals reminiscent of the Doric order but without an entablature; a drama enhanced by the contrast between low and high, dark and light. This is a classical idea distilled to its essential simplicity.

Asplund's greatest masterpiece, **The Crematorium** in **Stockholm,** was created between 1935 and 1940. An abstraction of the hill up to Calvary is made by a man-made landscape that leads up to a simple granite cross on the skyline. The noble portico, a monumental entrance that is twice the size of the main chapel, recalls a classical temple. It is a simple trabeated structure with slightly tapering stone-clad columns, flush with the beams and without moulding. This supports a roof with a timber ceiling dished towards an opening in the centre with a Resurrection monument below. This great portico, seven bays by five, is placed asymmetrically to the chapel entrance, and is a free-standing structure, a device used by Lewerentz in his Chapel of the Resurrection that emphasises the portico as a meeting place. It respects the emotional needs of the mourners, presenting an appropriate dignity and formality to them on their arrival, and it powerfully embodies Asplund's aim to create '*a building that does not threaten but invites*'. To quote James Codrington Forsyth: "*If ever the Modern Movement had its Parthenon, it must be Gunnar Asplund's Woodland Crematorium in Stockholm. Aloof from the city, it rises, like its ancient counterpart, to heights of aesthetic purity coupled*

9.15 - Crematorium Calvary Hill and Cross

9.16 - Crematorium portico

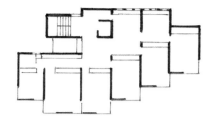

with deep emotion; and though it has little in common with everyday building, it nevertheless serves as a symbol for the civilisation that gave birth to it".[9.3]

Asplund died at the age of fifty-five, the year the Crematorium was completed, and was one of the first to be cremated there. Now, after so many years, the building is as modern and as much part of a tradition as it was then.

Colin St John Wilson was born in 1922. After studying at Cambridge and the Architectural Association, in 1948 he went on his Grand Tour to Italy and, like his predecessors, filled his sketchbooks with careful analytical drawings. As a student of that generation he was enraptured by Le Corbusier. This informed his work at the London County Council from 1950-1955 where the twelve-storey blocks of maisonettes on the Bentham Road Estate pay a clear tribute to the Unité d'Habitation.

In 1956 Wilson moved back to Cambridge to join Leslie Martin in practice and teaching. Around this time Alvar Aalto visited Cambridge, just when Wilson was beginning to question the doctrinaire philosophy of his former guru, and this was to change the direction of his life.

The first building for which the work of Aalto became a precedent was the **William Stone Tower for Peterhouse College** in Cambridge which has a close affinity with the Neue Vahr apartments in Bremen. In both buildings the north side is solid, containing the lifts, stairs and service rooms, with its back to the cold, whilst the south side is open to the sun and the view. In the Aalto building the rooms are arranged in a fan-shape whereas in the Wilson building they are orthogonal and arranged in echelon. This early work is closer in form to its precedent than are those later on.

In 1958 **Leslie Martin, Patrick Hodgkinson** and **Colin St John Wilson** designed student housing at **Harvey Court** for **Caius College** in Cambridge. It clearly has its genesis in two precedents; firstly, the plan of traditional Cambridge colleges which combine privacy with a sense of community, and secondly, the Town Hall at Säynätsalo by Alvar Aalto.

Harvey Court has a square raised courtyard surrounded by three floors of student accommodation, and with a common room, breakfast room, kitchen and storage below. The east, north and west sides face inwards, while the south side faces out towards a garden. Each floor is stepped back giving generous balconies to all the rooms. As at Säynätsalo there are two flights of steps up to the courtyard; the entrance stair is from the east, and a more generous and gentle terrace stair leads into the landscape. From the courtyard, two entrances lead into a circulation gallery

9.20 - Harvey Court view of north elevation

9.21 - Harvey Court entrance steps

9.22 - Harvey Court raised courtyard

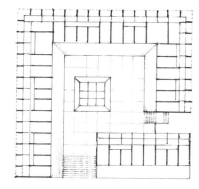

9.23 - Harvey Court plan

that runs around the external sides of the building, and serves the rooms at that level. From this gallery, flights of stairs on the outside wall give access to a group of rooms on the level above, and from there continue upwards to serve another group on the top floor.

Harvey Court is designed on a very pronounced grid. On the inside this is expressed by the floor pattern of the courtyard and by the projecting party walls between the windows. On the outside this presents a highly modelled façade with heavy buttresses that stands proud of the staircases and overshadows the glazing to the access gallery. It is built of a beautiful brick similar to that used traditionally in Cambridgeshire together with carefully crafted joinery. The design follows an unbuilt scheme for student housing in the middle of Cambridge, and in its present location it makes little response to its context and addresses the street in a somewhat austere way. This has subsequently been softened by planting.

From the late 1950s onwards Wilson was influenced by other precedents. He had great respect for the writing of the painter Adrian Stokes which gave a philosophical basis to his work. He became impressed by the work of 19th-century architects such as Butterfield, Waterhouse and Street, as well as the theoretical writing of Pugin and Ruskin that became known as The English Free School. These architects had opposed a rigid classical symmetry in favour of a more flexible approach that could respond more easily to the internal requirements of a building. This had been decried by some historians as merely 'the battle of the styles' but it had an influence in America on H. H. Richardson and Frank Lloyd Wright, as well as on architects in Austria, Holland and Scandinavia. These historical precedents were to inspire Wilson's final design of the British Library which appropriately sits alongside St Pancras Chambers by George Gilbert Scott, one of the major works of The English Free School.

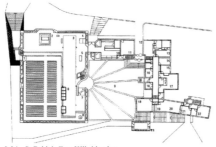
9.24 - St Bride's East Kilbride plan

9.25 - St Bride's East Kilbride elevation

9.26 - St Bride's East Kilbride entrance

9.27 - St Bride's East Kilbride north wall inside

Andrew MacMillan and Isi Metzstein, partners in the office of **Gillespie, Kidd and Coia,** have demonstrated the way a wide range of precedents have conditioned their thinking and their work. The influence of the masters of the Renaissance, Charles Rennie Mackintosh, the City of Glasgow, Italian hill towns, as well as the work of Le Corbusier and Alvar Aalto can all be seen hinted at in their work.

This is shown clearly at **St Bride's Church** in East Kilbride completed in 1963. The church stands on a promontory, and the treatment of the approach with its steps, campanile and piazza is reminiscent of a town in Tuscany. The ground of the piazza is marked by a fanned pattern of brick paving centred on a circular brick threshold. The entry is further celebrated by an undulating wall that serves to change the direction towards the font at the rear corner of the church. A long free-standing gallery, together with the position of the confessionals, emphasise this route that then subtly turns back towards the altar.

Externally, the rectangular mass of the church, the tall campanile, and the low presbytery complement one another. Like many of the churches by MacMillan and Metzstein it is built of brick inside and out. The walls are exaggeratedly thick; at the entrance the brickwork is corbelled on one side, and the east wall has a random pattern of niches that scoop light from above, bringing to mind the chapel at Ronchamp by Le Corbusier. Here as elsewhere there is a complexity of brick bonding, where soldier courses are cleverly used to link the different sizes and shapes of openings.

The church is lit in a variety of ways to give a particular quality to each part. In addition to the niches at the side, diffused light over the whole ceiling enters through a timber grille below steel trusses. Three triangular funnels projecting above the roof are arranged to direct light onto the sanctuary variously in the morning and the evening, whilst a shallow band of top light neatly tucked behind the baldachino illuminates the wall behind the altar.

What makes this simple rectangular box a sacred place? It is the contrast between inside and outside, with the undulating wall of the porch providing a pause between secular and sacred. It is the contrast between simplicity and complexity, the use of brick throughout, subtly detailed to enrich the planes of the walls and floor. It is the contrast between bright and subdued light defining a memorable sense of place, the location of the font, the high altar, the lady altar and the mortuary chapel, all placed as if inevitably. These are the qualities that give the work of MacMillan and Metzstein a timeless quality, untouched by fashion and by the superficialities of style.

Alas! twenty years after it was built, the campanile was in need of repair and it was decided that it should be demolished as this was the cheaper option. Because of this, East Kilbride has lost a significant landmark, and the church has lost the focal point of entry to its piazza.

John Pawson's work has an austere simplicity. His design for the **Monastery of Our Lady of Nový Dvůr in Bohemia** is in the tradition of Cistercian building from the 12th century without ornament or ostentation.

The site is that of a derelict Baroque manor house with its farm buildings surrounding a courtyard. As usual in Pawson's work the context provided some early clues for the design. But first it was necessary to gradually discover and understand the essence of a monk's way of living - a life of mostly silent contemplation regulated by seven religious services a day, interspersed by work on the land or in the workshop. From the outset Pawson was conscious of the awesome responsibility of designing a home for monks who had solemnly vowed to live there for the rest of their lives.

As in the 12th century, the core of the monastery is the cloister that links the several parts of a monk's life; prayer, eating and sleeping, study and meeting together. Pawson had known Fountains Abbey in Yorkshire since he was a child living nearby, and later often visited the Cistercian Abbey at Le Thoronet in Provence, a building that became a stimulating precedent. The medieval cloister required an arched colonnade to support the vaulted roof, but Pawson was concerned to reduce the cloister at Nový Dvůr to its ultimate simplicity. With the advance of technology he was able to cantilever the barrel vault from the surrounding structure, to do away with columns, and have an uninterrupted view into the cloister garden. The cloister has a pristine wall of glass to shield against the cold winters. This spare simplicity makes the cloister a place for quiet contemplation as the monks move around individually or in groups.

The discipline of pure planar geometry, of few materials and the absence of colour follows through into the church. In contrast to the dramatic horizontality of the cloister this is a vertical space, twice as high as it is wide. It is ingeniously lit by indirect light brought down within the double side walls, articulating the different parts of the church and directing the view towards the altar. The plain semi-circular apse, like that at Le Thoronet, is an embellishment to the strict Cistercian rule. Everything is white, including the monks' habits, except for the dark wood of their stalls, the warm glow of light fittings, and the altar furniture.

9.28 - Nový Dvůr Monastery view from cloister

9.29 - Nový Dvůr Monastery chapel

The refectory on the west side of the cloister is a restoration of part of the Baroque structure and has the original columns and cross vaults. Meals are eaten in silence listening to a sacred reading. The scriptorium is essentially a library for private study, it is a high white room with dark wooden furniture. The spines of the books appear as a rare glimpse of colour in this reclusive world.

An existing separate building has been converted to a guest house. The ground floor is a low columnar structure with cross vaults and is used for communal activities. The guest rooms are on the first floor, and enjoy the inside volume of the roof that steps down low over a study area by the windows. On each floor the accommodation for families and visiting priests is kept separate. In due course a simple free-standing chapel will be built with subtle lighting around its altar, a low-key companion to the main church. Workshops are planned on lower ground to the south-east of the cloister, designed as an inhabited terrace in deference to the main building, and linked by a covered walkway.

The monastery at Nový Dvůr is a present-day interpretation of the essence of Cistercian architecture; it is in no way a pastiche nor is it a style. It is a view of architecture that has permeated all the work of John Pawson before and after this particular building. For him this attitude to architecture is not just a preference, it is a conviction and a commitment. It is interesting to note that in 2006 he made an exhibition in Le Thoronet. For this he designed a series of benches and located them in strategic positions inside and outside the Abbey. Each of these focussed on a particular aspect of architecture; such as context, landscape, circulation, order, light and geometry. In the catalogue these were illustrated by photographs of part of the Abbey together with examples of his own work. The link between Cistercian architecture and that of Pawson was made overt, each based on ruthless simplicity.

In summary, each of these architects inherited a tradition, and each in their own way, because of different constraints, and with new ideas and aspirations, worked towards a new tradition. As we extend our view to other architects of today we find great diversity, different emphases and intentions, but we also discover common ground, a concern for real issues, continually renewed and reinterpreted. The purpose of precedent is not to copy the past but to inspire a vision for the future.

10.1 - Municipal Orphanage plan

10.2 - Municipal Orphanage exterior view from south

10 The USE of METAPHOR

Metaphor is used in design in a number of different ways. Sometimes it may appear to be far removed from the task on hand and is not necessarily apparent to the user, but it often serves to open up new ideas and different ways of thinking about the task. Donald Schon refers to this as a "*generative metaphor*".

We have already noted **Alvar Aalto's** allusion to metaphor in his account of the genesis of the Viipuri Library: "*I pursued the solution with the help of primitive sketches, and from some kind of fantastic mountain landscapes with cliffs lit up by suns in different positions I gradually arrived at the concept*".

Aldo van Eyck has recorded how he has often made use of metaphor. He was born in 1918 and lived in England until 1935. His father was a poet and, together with his English teacher at school, imbued in the young Aldo a love of William Blake. In an early project for a school he used as his inspiration two lines from the 'Songs of Innocence and Experience'*: "When the voices of children are heard on the green/ and laughing is heard on the hill",*[10.1] a metaphor that served to raise the level of his thinking high above the immediate requirements in the brief.

Between 1947 and 1955 Aldo van Eyck designed around **sixty children's playgrounds** in the city of Amsterdam. They tended to be variations on a theme using elemental shapes, circles, squares, triangles, and hexagons, often incorporating a sand pit, concrete benches to sit on or transform into a table, a climbing frame, and sometimes a simple roof; a repertoire that he was to employ again and again. It was the quality of these playgrounds that led the Director of the **Municipal Orphanage in Amsterdam** to approach him to design a new building.

As was the case with the Glasgow School of Art, the Director was very clear what he wanted, and from the outset was adamant that he did not want any hint of an institutional building. He was concerned to make a *home* for children who had lost their parents; a view that van Eyck found very sympathetic, and the two men shared ideas as the design developed from 1955 to 1960.

The brief called for two groups of children, juniors and seniors, each with four houses for different ages; it also required areas where children could come together in various groups as well as within the community as a whole. Aldo van Eyck came to

10.3 - Municipal Orphanage aerial view

159

10.4 - Municipal Orphanage view from east

10.5 - Municipal Orphanage view of exterior

10.6 - Municipal Orphanage view of entrance courtyard

see this as a small city, an embodiment of his famous aphorism '*a house is a tiny city, a city is a huge house*'. This became for him a powerful generative metaphor that evoked a new way of interpreting the task; it suggested the possibility of an urban centre, streets, mini-squares, and houses with their own individuality. For Aldo van Eyck this raised issues of inside and outside, closed and open, large and small applicable both to the whole and the parts. As the building has long since ceased to perform its original purpose and at the time of writing is unoccupied (changes unrelated to the quality of its architecture), it is necessary to study the plan in detail, to walk around it and note both its classical ordering and its relaxed freedom.

The entrance to the Orphanage is from the north under a bridge into a square; here the Director's office is in a strategic position easily accessible to the children. Two streets lead off in diagonal directions at right angles to one another each serving the four houses that are arranged in echelon. The streets follow the pattern of the houses, alternately narrow and wide, open and closed with a richness of different views, and providing a variety of different places for stopping to chat or to play. But the discipline of the geometry is not rigid; at three critical points the glazed wall to the street follows a diagonal to ease the flow of people around the corner. As in many cities the plan is laid out on a grid but here the pattern is loose and open; it calls to mind the architect Christopher Alexander's comment that "*a city is not a tree it is a semi-lattice*". The grid generates a repetitive structure of more than three hundred small domes, each about three metres square, punctuated by eight large domes, some ten metres square, that rise majestically above the others and define a special place in each house.

The single-storey houses for the younger children are along the street to the south, whilst the houses for the older children are on the western street, partly on two floors. In response to the climate all the houses have solid walls to the north and large windows towards the south. The houses for juniors have two living areas arranged diagonally comprising a play-room under a large dome and a sitting room under four small domes; the bedrooms are in a wing to the east gathered around a small covered verandah. Each house has a large open patio to the southwest, and although it belongs to the house it makes a strong contribution to the street. This has a glazed wall and doorway that offers a welcome to children from other houses. The houses for senior children are L-shaped, with two living areas on the ground floor enclosing an open terrace partially covered by the floor above. The first floor is square and contains the bedrooms surrounding a sitting area under a large dome. These domes at first-floor level provide a regular rhythm along this street in concert with those along the other street. As in the junior houses, each house is given its own identity by a particular activity such

10.7 - Drie Haven communal areas

10.8 - Drie Haven entrance to dwelling

as a pancake kitchen, workshop or puppet theatre that can be enjoyed by the home group as well as by visitors. The system of the plan is not an order of symmetry but of balance, and this gives a freedom of use as in a city.

Furthermore, there is a strict classical discipline in the way the building is put together, with its simple geometric forms, the uniform use of concrete, brick, glass and glass blocks, as well as the constant eaves level that serves to give a human scale.

When **Herman Hertzberger** began the design of **De Drie Hoven**, a home for elderly people in Amsterdam, he asked himself the question '*what does it mean to be old?*' and his answer was two-fold, the need for privacy and the need for contact; a neat architectural task! This led him to concentrate on two elements, the front door and the kitchen, and the relation of these to the access inside the building which he called 'the street'. He described it like this; "*A resident might feel lonely living by themselves, and might long for someone to drop in, and similarly, a neighbour might be looking forward for someone to talk to. The Dutch (or stable) door provides a suitable invitation. Half open it is both open and shut, open enough for a passer-by to have a few words, yet closed enough to prevent any intrusion. When the door is shut, the resident wants privacy*".[10.2] In the same way the kitchen has a window onto the street whilst the other rooms, the living room and bedroom, enjoy their privacy. Hertzberger made another clever move; at the entrance to each little house, the street widens out to form a small porch - a realm that is both part of the street and part of the dwelling, where residents can put their own furniture and sit and chat to passers-by. Furthermore the streets converge on a big hall called 'the village green' where everyone can meet if they wish. These several metaphors served to generate a non-institutional homely ambience.

The early sketches by **Enric Miralles** for the **Scottish Parliament** demonstrate the way a concept arises from a very powerful metaphor. When he presented his proposals to the competition committee in 1998, he chose to present a series of thirteen evocative sketches describing how he would approach the task, rather than showing a building design. Each sketch contained hand-written notes that summarised his underlying thoughts.

Inevitably he was impressed by the site. It is at the lower end of the Royal Mile that stretches along a ridge from Edinburgh Castle at the top to the Palace of Holyrood at the bottom. It sits below the overwhelming Salisbury Crags to the east and the more modest but monumental Carlton Hill to the north. Miralles sought to emphasise that the new Parliament should not only be woven into the historic centre of the city but also be embedded

10.9 - Scottish Parliament Miralles sketch

10.10 - Scottish Parliament Mirralles sketch

10.11 - Scottish Parliament entrance interior

10.12 - Scottish Parliament garden lobby

10.13 - Scottish Parliament garden lobby skylight

in the land and landscape of Scotland. He illustrated this with the powerful metaphor of branches of a tree springing from the landscape above, with its leaves sprouting on the site of the new Parliament. There are also sketches of upturned boats that had taken his fancy at Lindisfarne; images of leaves and boats that were to inform the geometry of the developed design.

Essentially, Miralles was concerned to distance his design from that of a grand gesture, the pompous monumental building that to him and his clients signified the authoritative Parliament of the past. In contrast, he described his aim to create a university campus, a place for the interplay of ideas, for exploration and discussion. To this end he proposed a collage of different places each responding to its varying needs; the leaves in the drawing were annotated relating to the main chamber, the committee rooms, and the place for public presentation.

Gradually the concept developed; he carefully drew a view of Queensbury House, the one existing building that would be retained. He sketched a garden, a place of repose, and again and again redrew the link down from the Crags, each time with a greater emphasis, culminating in the assembly chamber and showing a hint of its form. He commented "*it is crucial to meditate on the iconography of our Parliament*".[10.3] From here on, the drawings explored a series of abstract forms that showed the seeds of what would later be built. This is a remarkable record of an important and serious journey.

How does the final building fulfil these aims? Inside is to experience a series of quite different spaces, each with its own form, structure and light, designed for the various ways that people with different roles meet one another, and in response to many layers of meaning.

The public foyer is a long hall with three fan-shaped barrel-vaulted ceilings that are engraved at random with crosses of St Andrew. It is a simple crypt-like space anticipating the lightness and intricacy of the garden lobby above.

The garden lobby is the central concourse that everyone must pass through day by day into all the different areas of Parliament. This is the place where politicians, the public and the press come together. Its complexity is appropriate for the exchange of ideas that it encourages, a place for meeting sometimes by arrangement and sometimes by chance. It is an overwhelming place unlike any other. It is here that the metaphor of leaves is most strongly felt. Thirteen rooflights of varying heights and sizes reach upwards admitting light from different angles, all beautifully crafted in timber and steel. Between them, the ceiling plunges dramatically down subtly modulating the space below, and supported on bold concrete columns of different shapes. Walls and windows set up different

10.14 - Scottish Parliament debating chamber

10.15 - Scottish Parliament members rooms from outside

10.16 - Scottish Parliament entrance

10.17 - Scottish Parliament façade to street

10.18 - Scottish Parliament Queensbury House

10.19 - Scottish Parliament entrance façade

rhythms and different patterns of glazing, with every element working in concert to create a bustling ambience.

To the west, the lobby leads to a range of private rooms on several floors at right-angles to Canongate. They are used by Members of Parliament, and are accessed from a wide corridor - another place for casual conversation. Miralles was concerned to make these rooms places for individual thinking, and quite unlike those in a standard office block. They are cave-like with barrel vaults and with a personal 'den' against a projecting window which contains a built-in seat and a desk on three stepped levels. It will be interesting to see if such a prescribed way of working will, over time, withstand the differences between individuals.

The garden lobby gives access to the regenerated 17th-century Queensberry House that contains the offices of the presiding officer as well as the Donald Dewar reading room. It also gives access to the four boat-shaped towers of different heights that contain committee rooms and offices. It is here that the legislative work of Parliament takes place. These rooms, like the lobby, have their own character; they are each different in plan with a variety of dramatic sections.

From the lobby, a ceremonial stair leads up to a glazed walkway that gives access to the Debating Chamber. The plan of this room follows an elliptical arrangement of seating that is designed to foster togetherness and cooperation, rather than the confrontation at Westminster; it also conceals party boundaries that can change at any time. It is a high room with huge rooflights arranged to illuminate the wall behind the rostrum. The walls are lined with timber panelling and have large windows to provide views out. It is the complexity of the roof structure that gives the room its special quality; inverted trusses of laminated oak and tensioned stainless steel with elegantly formed joints, and with light fittings and cameras adding yet more sparkle. The whole is beautifully made.

Each part of the building is unique, but the building as a whole is more controversial. The internal circulation is confusing, and the complex junctions between the different spaces are unresolved. Externally from the height of Salisbury Crags, the form that signifies the different parts of the building has a dynamic quality. It nestles within the urban fabric whilst discreetly addressing the open landscape, and from this viewpoint it relates directly to Miralles' initial sketch. However at street level the significance of the grass roofs of the tapering barrel vaults and the long canopy is not apparent, and from below their meaning is lost. Unfortunately while it was being built, there arose the need for increased security, and this reduced the celebration of the two entrances.

10.20 - Castle Drogo distant view

The Scottish Parliament has been likened to the Berlin Philharmonie by Hans Scharoun; neither is monumental, and both have an internal complexity. But there is a significant difference; in Berlin the outside is underplayed and is a simple expression of the volumes within; in Edinburgh the outside is adorned with a range of applied patterns made of many materials. These are variously interpreted as different symbolic references; to some people they add richness but to others they appear superimposed and arbitrary, and seem to detract from the clarity of the overall idea.

Enric Miralles died just after final approval was given to the scheme. It is only conjecture how the building might have developed and changed had he lived. As with a novel, design work needs to be subject to continual editing, and this is difficult without the original author. Nevertheless the Scottish Parliament is the result of very serious thinking. It is a response to what an architect regarded as the essence inherent in the programme; to make a Parliament building that is representative of a new more open democracy.

Sometimes a **literal metaphor** forms the basis of a design. It may be consciously in the designer's mind or it may become apparent afterwards and may simply be a useful description. **Castle Drogo** in Devon by **Edwin Lutyens** (designed and built between 1911 and 1930) is literally a castle, for that is what the client expressly wanted. Julius Drewe was the founder of the Home and Colonial Stores and by the age of thirty-three he was rich enough to retire. He chose a site at the top of an escarpment looking down into the Teign valley and out over Dartmoor to emphasise its fortified position. Lutyens wrote to his wife "*I do wish he did not want a castle, but a delicious lovely house with plenty of large rooms in it*".

From afar Drogo appears simply as a granite outcrop, but nearby from the Teign valley it reveals itself as a castle of timeless quality. The entrance drive is high up from the north, with the castle at first hidden by trees but then suddenly coming into view with Dartmoor beyond. From the outset the design went through a number of drastic changes with the early schemes centred on a large entrance courtyard with symmetrical buildings on either side. These proved to be too lavish both in space and cost and, even after work had begun on site, the plan was cut in half. Although this caused the organisation of the plan to be compromised, it greatly enhanced the image of a castle.

Castle Drogo was designed as a country house for entertaining. Circulating along elegant galleries and up and down very gentle stairs was part of the enjoyment of the equally elegant guests. The slope of the site and the location on the edge of the

10.21 - Castle Drogo main corridor

10.22 - Castle Drogo stairs to dining room

10.23 - Castle Drogo domed ceiling

10.24 - Castle Drogo kitchen

10.25 - Castle Drogo scullery

escarpment gave opportunities for dramatic changes of level and height that Lutyens was keen to exploit. From the entrance hall a gallery makes a gradual progression up towards the drawing room, and then at right angles down a grand flight of steps to the dining room. The gallery is delineated by arches and barrel vaults related to the window openings, with a saucer dome marking each change of direction. Over the stairs a coffered barrel vault leads the eye upwards to appreciate the awesome change of height, from four metres at the top to eight metres at the bottom, in a space only two and a half metres wide. The stairs are lit by a tall window at the half-landing and by a dramatic high bay window at the bottom, both made up of a system of repeated lights. The bay window defines a small but special place marking the entrance to the dining room. It also gives a subtle borrowed light to the drawing room above. It is somewhat surprising that, within the grandeur of the whole, the carefully crafted living rooms and bedrooms have a homely quality due to their scale, proportion, and light.

It is the severe circulation spaces that are most castle-like. In certain places the whole wall is made of granite, in other areas the skirting and the edges of the openings are of granite, with the varying block sizes forming an abstract rectilinear pattern against the plastered walls. In some of the corridors the window mullions are extended inwards for nearly a metre above a window seat, and in sunshine these thin slabs cast deep shadows and create a lively rhythm.

Castle Drogo, like other great houses of the period, was kept going by a large staff for whom convenience was not a high priority. They had to walk a long way from the kitchen to the dining room, although facilities in the kitchen area were of a high order. Lutyens clearly enjoyed designing the lighting and ventilation of the pantry, kitchen, scullery and larders in different ways; a bay window above the sinks in the pantry, a round lantern over the kitchen, semi-circular clerestory windows over the scullery, and an ingenious octagonal light-well to ventilate the larders.

Externally the granite is more rugged than inside, but less so than Mr Drew would have liked. Indeed when he tried to insist on rough granite Lutyens replied "*The big blocks are right for the lower courses but quite impossible to carry them up… I am very keen about your castle but must fight you when I know I am right*". The looseness of the plan on various levels allows the separate elements of the building to be different in height. The walls are generally slightly battered though the bay windows are vertical; many of the corners are chamfered, and together these add to the castle-like image. The windows are placed apparently at random but they are appropriately positioned for the spaces within; each elevation is carefully composed. The window

10.26 - Castle Drogo elevation overlooking Dartmoor

system is made up from the module of the individual light repeated horizontally and vertically, and this gives a unity to the varied pattern.

In dramatic contrast to the rest of the building, the south elevation is an overwhelming *tour de force*. It cannot be seen from the entrance terrace, and it is necessary to walk around the building and see it from below. Built on the edge of the escarpment, this narrow façade rises nearly twenty metres high and is innovative in every way. In contrast to the chamfered corners elsewhere, the plane of the wall is cut back forty-five degrees at the corners to produce a knife-edge arris against the sky. As the windows increase in size at each storey, they form a discreet bay window at the top formed by the cut-back in the façade. The effect of this play with three-dimensional geometry is to powerfully exaggerate the height of the façade precisely at the point where the ground falls steeply away. This is unlike anything anywhere else; a pure invention of the mind, it confirms Lutyen's motto '*metiendo vivendum*' (by measure we live). It was his particular vision to transform the south front of a castle into the prow of a mighty ship.

Below the terrace and approached by a tunnel under the entrance hall is the chapel. This was built on part of the foundations of the abandoned building. It is low and mysteriously dark; the chancel is at a lower level with two massive columns only a metre high supporting simple vaults. This crypt-like space contrasts dramatically with the lofty spaces in the building above.

In this building Edwin Lutyens carried the metaphor of castle to its limit, and at the same time he seized the opportunity to be uniquely innovative.

Hans Scharoun designed three schools that are like villages. Although the three plans are different, they each embody what he regarded as the essence of the educational programme, namely, that a lot of learning takes place outside the classroom. They each consist of streets that have a measure of complexity delineating different zones, and providing places to pause as well as to pass through. Along the streets are the different 'buildings' that together make up the school.

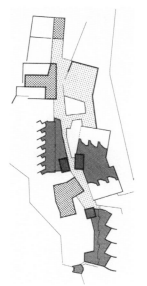

10.27 - Darmstadt school plan

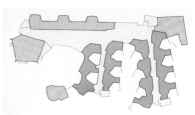

10.28 - Lunan school plan

The primary school at **Darmstadt,** which was never built, has a linear plan with the assembly hall and administration at either side of the entrance, three groups of classrooms (for the primary, middle and upper schools) distributed along its length, and the gymnasium conveniently located towards the middle.

The **Geschwister** school at Lunen is a secondary school for girls. Its footprint consists of a wide main street with two side streets leading off at right angles. The assembly hall is at the entrance, the science rooms are on the north side of the street with the administration at the far end, and the classrooms for the lower and middle schools are on the side streets to the south. The upper school classrooms together with the art and craft rooms are on the first floor.

The school at **Marl** is centralised with five streets radiating from the assembly hall. Four of the streets have classrooms on one side and specialist rooms on the other; the fifth street has offices and administration.

The plan of the classrooms within each group is different according to their perceived educational needs, and each group has its own communal area giving a sense of identity. As in Aldo van Eyck's Orphanage the streets are alternately narrow and wide, closed and open, but unlike the regular grid of the Orphanage, in these schools the streets meander at different angles as if they had been built over time. This is a formal device that Scharoun used again and again. Although no part of the geometry of the plan is orthogonal, there is a sympathetic rhythm in the repetition of the parts.

Scharoun designed from inside out, carefully satisfying the educational requirements of each part and assembling them in different ways with his own humane vision. The overall form of these schools is not a carefully contrived composition, rather it is just what it has been allowed to become, accentuating its likeness to a village.

In all his work **Hans Scharoun** enjoys the complexity of non-orthogonal geometry. In the **Berlin Philharmonie** (1956-63), as in his schools, this is not just a capricious idea; the geometry is an appropriate response to the requirements of the programme.

In a concert hall the clear sound of the music is paramount, and this has generated the essence of this design. In a traditional concert hall most of the audience sits on raked seating behind the conductor, with those at the back a long way away. In the Philharmonie the orchestra is in the centre with seating all around within a complex volume enclosed by multi-faceted walls. This complexity nevertheless has a symmetry that reflects the symmetrical relationship between the conductor and the orchestra. The audience is divided on a series of terraces at

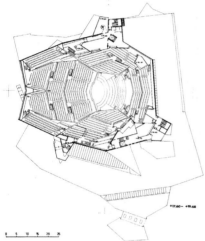

10.29 - Scharoun Philharmonie ground floor plan

10.30 - Scharoun Philharmonie top floor plan

different levels and at different angles. This has a number of advantages; firstly, the division of an audience of two thousand people into groups of about three hundred gives a sense of intimacy; secondly, the balcony fronts, like the enclosing walls, are nowhere parallel to one another so that direct reflections of sound are avoided; and thirdly, the bold sloping balustrades between the terraces create a lively view, a landscape of people enjoying themselves; and lastly, each terrace has its own access making arriving and leaving easy without congestion or hassle.

The ceiling is in two halves meeting at a point high above the orchestra, and each half is convex to reflect sound where it is needed. In contrast, its edges are low above the seats at the top of the auditorium; it is therefore both grand and intimate. Peter Blundell Jones has described the design metaphorically: "*The construction follows the pattern of a landscape, with the auditorium seen as a valley, and there at its bottom is the orchestra surrounded by a sprawling vineyard climbing the sides of its neighbouring hills. The ceiling, resembling a tent, encounters the 'landscape' like a 'skyscape'. Convex in character, the tent-like ceiling is very much linked with the acoustics, with the desire to obtain the maximum diffusion of music via the convex surfaces*".[10.4] Musicians and audiences alike are rapturous in their praise of the acoustic quality as well as the overall ambience.

From nearly symmetrical positions in the auditorium, stairs lead down towards the entrance on the right side of the hall. To achieve this they turn through a complexity of different angles cleverly placed so that they indicate a clear way to go, changing

10.31 - Scharoun Philharmonie interior

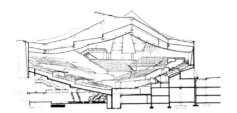

10.32 - Scharoun Philharmonie section

10.33 - Scharoun Philharmonie foyer

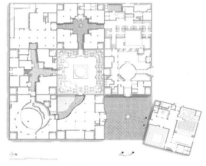

10.34 - Cultural Centre Jaipur plan

direction at generous landings that are different in shape and size, getting wider as they converge '*like tributaries to a river*'. These are places to stand and chat, to see and be seen, as well as to enjoy the dramatic three-dimensional space with all its rich complexity. As at the Royal Opera House in London an orchestral evening is a special occasion, a social and festive event before and after a performance.

The Berlin Philharmonie and the State Library, also by Scharoun, are located close to the pristine steel and glass form of the National Gallery by Mies van der Rohe, and together they form part of an important cultural centre. The exterior of the concert hall is a direct expression of what goes on within rather than a self-conscious civic gesture, nevertheless the scale of the tent-like form over its high undulating walls gives it an appropriate grandeur.

Charles Correa designed two buildings between 1980 and 1990 with overtly literal metaphors; the Jawahar Kala Kendra (the Cultural Centre of Jaipur) and the Vidhan Bhavan (the State Assembly in Bhopal). These are based on a mandala, the mystical diagram of nine squares that was the core of temple planning where each square represented a planet.

The Cultural Centre in Jaipur is based on the plan of that ancient city where, because of the topography, one square was displaced. In Correa's design one square is cut adrift and set at a forty-five degree angle and serves to mark the entrance. The whole is a model of the cosmos and each square has its planet's appropriate symbol, colour and particular opening to the sky. Each square has an entrance to its neighbouring squares, and is enclosed by a high wall that drops down at each corner to express its autonomy. This pattern of courtyards is appropriate to a museum: internally each square is very different and provides a particular place for exhibits from different places, and it allows for a variety of ways around the galleries. Most significantly the metaphor of the mandala evokes memories of the great Indian tradition. There are many references to precedent - the central

10.35 - State Assembly Bhopal view over valley

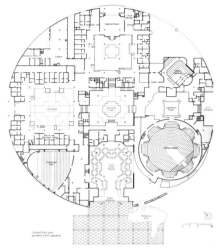

10.36 - State Assembly Bhopal plan

10.37 - Jeweller Shop Vienna

10.38 - Travel Agent's Shop Vienna

square, for example, which is used for performances has stepped terraces for seating reminiscent of bathing ghats. Each square is carefully designed for its use, and the architectural language hints at tradition but transforms it to the present day.

The State Assembly in Bhopal is based on a mandala of nine squares superimposed on a circle. This serves as an ordering device that defines the two major axes and locates the different points of entry. Each square has its own meaning and character, its own degree of formality and grandeur, and a special quality of light from its particular opening to the sky. Again there are many references to metaphorical precedent: the central courtyard has a spiral pattern in the floor under a circular opening evoking a nebula, the Lower House resembles a great stupa, and, as in the Cultural Centre, the seating in the entrance court recalls a ghat. Whilst the circular form emphasises the powerful presence of the building sited on top of a hill overlooking Bhopal, internally the arrangement of parts of the plan are somewhat compromised.

In these two buildings the metaphor provides the starting point and leads to a memorable and meaningful organisation. The mandala is a literal description of the design rather than an analogy, and in this respect the way the metaphor is used is very different from that which generated the Orphanage in Amsterdam or the Philharmonie in Berlin.

Two shops in Vienna by **Hans Hollein** clearly demonstrate the difference between the generative and the literal metaphor. The **Jeweller Shop** is an abstraction, it is what you choose to make of it; to some people its beautifully crafted shiny materials suggest the precious goods for sale, to others it is an Aladdin's cave, and to the designer it may be something quite different. The **Travel Agent** on the other hand is a literal representation of places you might like to visit, with sand and palm trees, pyramids and a classical temple. The Jeweller Shop is more subtle and powerful, whereas the Travel Agent is more obvious and accessible.

11.1 - Church at Seriate west elevation

11 The SEARCH for HARMONY

11.2 - Church at Seriate entrance porch

11.3 - Church at Seriate double apse inside

11.4 - Church at Seriate double apse outside

11.5 - Church at Seriate centre of ceiling

GEOMETRY

Over the door of Plato's Academy were written the words '*Let no man ignorant of geometry enter*'; words that could well adorn every architect's studio. Indeed all the buildings described in these pages are graphic examples of three-dimensional geometry. Some architects enjoy the elegance of simplicity, and endeavour to reduce each design to its bare essentials, whilst others embrace complexity, and express the intricacy of every part.

Simple geometric form marks the work of **Mario Botta.** This is evident in his early houses but it is most powerfully expressed in his sacred work.

The Church in the **Pope XXIII Pastoral Centre** at Seriate was designed and built between 2001 and 2004. It is a large high church in contrast to the adjacent low pastoral centre that has a long colonnade along the side. Unusually for an Italian church it is surrounded by a lawn defined by precise hedges.

The form of the church is generated by a disciplined play with light and geometry. The organisation of the plan is a square divided into sixteen small squares, with the four central squares forming a flat ceiling. From the sides of this ceiling four huge skylights rise up at forty-five degrees to the high external walls, whilst from its corners four roofs slope down at the same angle and continue down to the corners of the building. This results in a form that is both simple and complex, where the junctions between the planes meet with exact precision. The whole building is made of a warm red Verona stone that has a rough texture and catches the light with a sparkling glow. Th e entrance picks up the same geometry, and has the traditional arrangement of a large central door leading into a glazed porch, and with small doors at the sides for daily use. The edges of the porch define the diameter of a semi-circular paved threshold, and from the apex of the doorway a long line is cut vertically in the stone wall ending in a discreet cross. There are no mouldings, and the only protrusion on the façades is a shallow double apse at the east end that houses the reredos.

The interior is powerfully illuminated by reflected light from above. The structure of the roof is expressed and delineates a bold cross on the flat part of the ceiling. The form of the

11.6 - Church at Mogno view of altar and reredos

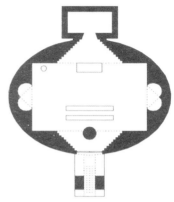

11.7 - Church at Mogno plan

11.8 - Church at Mogno distant view

11.9 - Church at Mogno external form

11.10 - Church at Mogno entrance from outside

sanctuary is a reminder of the threshold outside; its plan is a segment of a circle and the size and shape of the opening containing the double apse echoes that of the porch. This contains a delicate depiction of the Crucifixion in low relief by Giuliano Vangi, and is illuminated from above. This carving, together with the sanctuary and a two-metre high dado around the whole church, is in finely polished Verona stone. The rest of the surfaces are clad with panels made of narrow timber slats covered in gold leaf; these few materials add to the simplicity of the overall form. The height of the dado and the corner ceilings give human scale to a very high space. The altar, pulpit, and holy water stoup all enjoy the same simple geometry and are beautifully made. As the elegant wooden pews occupy only about a quarter of the floor area there is a great sense of spaciousness.

In this large building Mario Botta has inherited the spiritual simplicity of Romanesque architecture and has reinterpreted it with grace.

The Church of San Giovanni Battista in Mogno was designed in 1987 following an avalanche that had demolished the previous church in the beautiful Valle Maggia in Ticino. From across the valley the circular glazed roof stands out above the few houses in the village. The building is clearly special, but from this distance it is not immediately apparent what it is. A closer view reveals an elegant striped cylinder made of alternate rows of grey Riveo stone and white Peccia marble. The top of this is sliced off at a steep angle rising high towards the east, in a way reminiscent of a church tower. The glass roof is raised slightly above the walls and projects to form a delicate cornice.

The entrance is on the low side of the church from a small paved courtyard. It is celebrated by a clever combination of elements: a pair of arched buttresses that support a series of stone steps forming a canopy over the door; and over the buttresses a simple steel structure containing the bells. Rainwater from the roof cascades dramatically down the steps into a trough at the base.

Externally the church is a pure ellipse with the main axis across the shorter dimension. Inside it is more complex; the floor plan is rectangular with bays cut into the thickness of the wall. The entrance bay is chamfered under a heavy low lintel that has a stubby column in the centre; the bay behind the altar is similarly chamfered but under a semi-circular arch that has the quality of a grand Romanesque doorway. The chamfers are made by stepping back successive rows of the grey and white stonework. At each side of the church a simple arch reveals a semi-dome over a small apse with seating around. The effect of light streaming at an angle across the striped walls is overwhelming. Externally the walls are vertical, but internally they taper and

11.11 - Church at Mogno entrance from inside

11.12 - Vuoksenniska Church distant view

gradually define an ellipse which, because of the particular angle, makes the roof a perfect circle. A massive pair of stone arches span from the low entrance to high above the altar; they give lateral support and serve to emphasise the loftiness of the church. It is small but spacious with just two pews and a simple marble altar; the expanse of the striped floor is shown to advantage. The only embellishments are a crucifix, a Madonna, a holy water stoup, and some candlesticks.

Botta has discreetly exploited a simple geometry, he has used a limited range of materials, and has manipulated light in such a way as to create a calm and quiet place.

Complex geometry can result in dramatic and flamboyant architecture, such as the ancient Roman temple at Baalbek, the exuberance of Bernini and Borromini in Italy, the fantasies of Fischer von Erlach and Balthazar Neumann in Germany, and the fine craftsmanship of Art Nouveau in Brussels, Paris and Nancy.

In many of his plans **Alvar Aalto** demonstrates a preference for a free form, often fan-like, stemming from an orthogonal geometry. We have already noted this in the plan of the apartments at Neue Vahr in Bremen and in the library at Seinajoki. It is never just a preconceived idea, it is a response to the needs of the programme.

The **Church** at **Vuoksenniska (1957-59)** is one of Aalto's most complex small buildings. Located in the industrial city of Imatra, it was required to be used for a variety of social gatherings in addition to its liturgical function. To this end the church is capable of being divided into three; when it is used for small services that part can seat around 300 people, but when used as a whole it accommodates around 800.

The church is asymmetrical, and the plan has the hint of a fan. The side towards the street is parallel to the building opposite, but the straight west wall of the church is splayed at an angle, and from this springs the dynamic form of the church. The east side of the church facing the forest, unlike the west, is dramatically curved. From the sanctuary on the north there are three interlocking volumes; on plan they become wider towards the back of the church whereas in section they become lower. The ceiling curves down to the ground behind the altar creating an illusion that the three crosses are suspended in space. The complex curves were determined by careful acoustic research; they recall the lecture-room ceiling in the library at Viipuri. The three parts of the church can be separated when required by massive concrete walls 400mm thick that slide on an oiled track.

There are further spatial and functional refinements; firstly, on the axis of the altar there is a processional route towards the south door; secondly, within the sanctuary the straight west wall

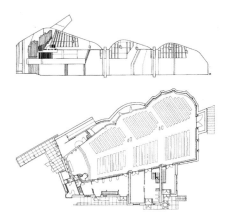

11.13 - Vuoksenniska Church section and plan

11.14 - Vuoksenniska Church interior looking east

11.15 - Vuoksenniska Church exterior from north

curls round to subtly embrace the pulpit; and thirdly, on the opposite side of the sanctuary there is a magnificent great organ and a gallery for the choir.

As usual in an Aalto building there is a dramatic use of light that changes with the weather and the time of day. The altar is illuminated by two vertical slit windows concealed from the congregation by concrete louvres, and each of the three volumes has high-level windows on the east that follow the curve of the wall and are sloped inwards to aid the acoustics. The floor of the sanctuary is white marble, and the nave has red quarry tiles. The walls and ceiling internally are white; externally the walls are finished with white rendering, and the roof is covered with copper. In an industrial city with many very high chimneys, the tower required a distinctive form; it is hexagonal on plan with buttressed corners that become fins towards the top, and is surmounted by a tall delicate cross.

The church at Vuoksenniska invites comparison with Ronchamp, built a few years earlier. Both are complex and innovative, breaking away from established tradition. Le Corbusier's church is a completely free sculptural form whereas Aalto's follows a more consistent geometry. Internally, both buildings create a calm ambience by their form and the sparse use of materials; externally, at Vuoksenniska the expression of the roof, made of a conventional material, anchors the building more strongly to the local tradition.

DIMENSION

Architecture depends on dimension; things made must first be measured; but in what ways does dimension contribute to harmony?

Plato and **Pythagoras** believed in the mathematical and harmonic structure of the universe and sought the implications of this on everything man-made. In his 'Ten Books on Architecture' **Vitruvius** claimed that architecture imitates nature, and in particular that it relates to the dimensions of man and hence to the order of the cosmos. This idea was taken up by architects of the Renaissance, and was summarised by Leonardo da Vinci in his famous drawing of '*Vitruvian Man*', an ideal man with arms and legs outstretched inscribed within a circle and a square.

Around 1450 **Alberti** wrote 'Ten Books on Architecture' where he is explicit that the ideal plan for a church is a circle, and the ratio of the parts should be such that '*nothing could be added or taken away without detriment to the whole*'. The ratios he described were applicable to the section and elevation as well as the plan; they were expressions of an overarching harmony, and his inspiration was in classical antiquity.

11.16 - Santa Maria Novella west elevation

The architectural historian Rudolph Wittkower has analysed the façade of **Santa Maria Novella,** built in 1456 in Florence, and found it to be an assembly of squares, double squares, and one and a half squares. The whole composition fits within a square that is divided in two to give the height of the two storeys. The lower storey consists of two squares, and that above fits into one square, whereas the scrolls follow the diagonal of a further square. It must be acknowledged, however, that to the viewer it is the magnificence of materials and the precision of workmanship that inspires the greater sense of awe.

In his scholarly 'Four Books', **Palladio** acknowledges his debt to Alberti. In particular he reiterates the way that proportions in architecture correspond to intervals in music; the harmony produced by the one is the same as in the other. For Palladio, this provided a system of dimensions that he was to use both in his splendid villas and in his churches. For him, as for many Renaissance architects, this was regarded not only as an aid to design but also as the only basis for an architecture that is in harmony with the universe.

11.17 - San Giorgio Maggiore west elevation

The Venetian church of **San Giorgio Maggiore,** begun in 1565, enjoys a splendid magnificence. On the island directly opposite the Piazzetta San Marco, it has one of the most distinctive locations in the world. Seen across the broad expanse of water, it stands out dazzlingly white against the warm brick of the other monastery buildings next to it. The nave is expressed as a classical temple with a grand order of half-columns on high bases; interpenetrating behind this, as it were, is a lower temple that expresses the aisles and has a smaller order with its entablature carried right across.

Inside there is a simple clarity; the plan is a Greek cross with a central dome illuminated by windows in the drum. The nave, the chancel and the transepts are celebrated with a grand order and have barrel vaults with semi-circular windows cut into them. The aisles are lower with a smaller order and with cross vaults. As on the façade, the grand order consists of half-round columns on high bases whereas the smaller order has flat pilasters rising from the ground.

The architectural historian Deborah Howard was interested to explore whether buildings designed in accordance with musical proportions produced an exceptional musical acoustic. She arranged for the choir of St John's College Cambridge to sing in several positions in the church, but nowhere was the sound as good as in a simple rectangular space! Nevertheless, the splendid architecture of San Giorgio Maggiore has a consistency inside and out that is enhanced by the discipline of dimension.

Three hundred and fifty years later **Le Corbusier** was to become consumed with issues of dimension. In 'Towards a New Architecture', he emphasised the importance of the *regulating line*. By superimposing a right-angled triangle on the façades of such buildings as the Capitol in Rome and the Petit Trianon at Versailles, he affirmed that this served to regulate the proportions of the parts. Later he applied this to the elevations of his own buildings, notably, the Ozenfant house and the Maison La Roche; the thesis being that this fixes things and avoids what is arbitrary.

For the next two decades he worked towards a '*rule of proportion*' that could be used universally, and the result was the '***Modulor***'. As with Vitruvius this was based on the dimensions of an ideal man, but rather than with arms and legs outstretched, Corbusier's man held one arm above his head. The Modulor was based on the *fibonacci* series of numbers where the third number in the series is the sum of the previous two. There is evidence that this is a system that applies to much of the natural world. Le Corbusier devised two scales denoted as red and blue; the red scale was based on the height of a man (1830 mm), while the blue scale was related to the top of his raised hand (2260mm). Combining these two scales gave a series of measurements related not only to different human postures, but also to the length, breadth and height of rooms as well as the size of every element.

The first use of the Modulor was at the **Unité d'Habitation** in **Marseilles,** built between 1947 and 1952, where all the dimensions, the size of the dwellings, the timber window frames, and the kitchen fitments relate to the Modulor. To demonstate the importance of this proportional system, Le Corbusier's ideal man is engraved on the concrete wall at the base of the lift tower, standing proudly with his arm upraised. Le Corbusier's aim, like that of Alberti and Palladio, was to make a building where all the parts are in harmony with one another and with the whole.

11.18 - The Modulor depicted at L'Unité d'Habitation

11.19 - Katsura Palace interior

11.20 - Katsura Palace exterior

11.21 - Katsura Palace plan

11.22 - Katsura Palace view out

The **repetitive grid** is a simpler system for ordering the plan. This is exemplified in the traditional Japanese house and especially in the magnificent **Katsura Imperial Palace.** Here, as in humbler dwellings, the plan is based on multiples of the *tatami,* a mat that measures approximately 1800mm x 900mm. Rooms are described by the number of mats, for example, 4.5 mats (2700mm x 2700mm) or 8 mats (3600mm x 3600mm). Because of this, rooms and pavilions can be joined together to create a free, even meandering, plan. The principal room has a slightly raised recess, the *tokonoma,* a sacred place where a special picture, a candle or pot of flowers is displayed. The *tokonoma* is usually the size of one mat but in a grand palace it might be two mats long.

The Japanese way of living in a traditional house is unique as there is no furniture, and families and guests sit on the floor; a small table is brought in for dining, and a mattress for sleeping; equipment that is stored in cupboards measuring about one mat. Because of this, the rooms are spacious and uncluttered with sliding doors between, and are used for many different purposes; a very flexible arrangement. The height of rooms and the size of all the timber members are similarly prescribed. The discipline of the plan is continued in the elevations, and results in a simple repetition of the panels, and a rhythm that gives a timeless quality.

The Royal Palace stands in a beautiful garden with an idyllic lake; close contact between house and garden is essential to this way of life, as much of daily living takes place on the verandah. In addition to the main house there are tea houses, waiting rooms and a temple casually placed around the garden, with the paths meandering freely and creating a lively contrast to the order of the house. The texture of the paths, the detail of the bridges, and the placing of individual rocks and lanterns all add to the total ambience of peacefulness and repose.

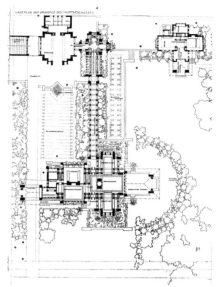

11.23 - Martin House plan

11.24 - Martin House front elevation

11.25 - Martin House porte-cochère

Frank Lloyd Wright used geometry and dimension to create an architecture that has a rigorous order and yet has great freedom and flexibility. From an early age he became fascinated by geometry, and he has recorded the deep impact that attending a Froebel kindergarten had on him. They used to play games making patterns with squares, circles, and triangles, or with blocks of wood that they arranged on a table marked out with a four-inch grid. Later he was captivated by Owen Jones' book *'The Grammar of Ornament'*, written in 1865, from which he devised other patterns using intersecting tartan grids; his interest in order had begun. Thereafter he was to use a grid (which he preferred to call a *'unit system'*) as a basis for most of his work whether in buildings, furniture or glass; it served to provide a consistency of scale as well as a rhythm to each part.

Frank Lloyd Wright designed a great number of suburban houses. The **Martin House,** built in 1904, demonstrates most clearly how he exploited the discipline of the grid. It is complex but made up of simple elements, it is asymmetrical yet abounds in symmetry, with continual changes of axis from one room to the next. This intricate plan is covered by simple hipped roofs with a low pitch that, because of their wide overhang, appear to float over the structure below. Within the whole asymmetrical composition, the house addresses the street with a stately symmetrical façade. The library is at the front and the dining room beyond the living room at the back, all in an open plan; this defines a north-south axis. The living room and its huge covered porch are centred on the fireplace on an east-west axis. The entrance to the house is somewhat hidden away; it is approached by steps along the face of the building that turn in towards the hall and set up a new north-south axis. From the hall the living room is on the right entered on either side of the fire place; the reception room is on the left arranged with its axis on the fireplace. The entrance hall is continued in a splendid covered pergola down to the conservatory at the bottom of the garden; this is a grand symmetrical building that has a cross axis leading towards the garage, again organised north to south. On the other side of the garden is a small cottage that is similarly orientated.

The grid is emphasised by bold brick piers made of narrow bricks with deeply recessed joints, and expressed both on the inside and outside of the house. Internally the brickwork is only visible up to door-head height - a level that is carried systematically throughout the house, and serves to define a human scale.

The **Robie House,** built between 1906 and 1908, further exploits the 'unit system'. It is on a corner site in a Chicago suburb facing a park. The client was aged twenty-seven, the director of a bicycle firm, and was very clear that he wanted to be able

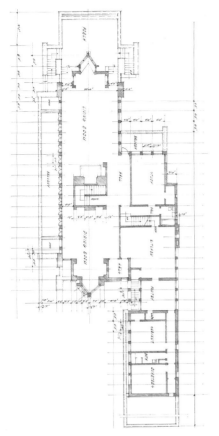

11.26 - Robie house plan

11.27 - Robie house exterior view

11.28 - Robie house living room

to see passers-by but not be seen himself. To this end Wright placed the living areas on the first floor with the bedrooms above, and with the playroom, billiard room and entrance on ground level below. The plan consists of two long volumes sliding past one another, with that at the front containing the living and dining room, and the kitchen and servants' rooms at the back.

As in previous houses, Wright opened up the plan and eliminated doorways wherever possible. Living and dining are therefore part of one big room divided by the fireplace and stairs. This is designed on a square grid five units wide and fifteen units long with bay windows on axis at each end. The centre of the ceiling of the room, three units wide, is higher than the edges that each occupy one unit in width; these are at door-head height giving this large room a sense of intimacy. At the southern end is an enclosed terrace covered with a huge cantilevered roof; a feature that also occurs outside the main bedroom on the floor above. Over the living room this roof extends at the sides with wide overhanging eaves to shade the continuous row of windows. The roof thus gives expression to the powerful horizontality of the whole composition - a horizontality that is echoed by the windows, the balustrades, and the concrete copings.

Internally, beams cross the room follow the line of the ceiling and, together with the light fittings, accentuate the rhythm of the windows. These have geometric stained glass patterns that serve to add to the privacy of the interior. The chimney breast has a wide opening above the fireplace enabling the ceiling to be seen continuously. The whole house has great clarity in its form, its materials, and in its manipulation of light and shade. The use of a repeated dimension (Wright's 'unit') serves to generate a satisfying rhythm that pervades throughout the whole building.

THE ELEGANCE OF THE PLAN

In 'The Trout and the Mountain Stream' Aalto stresses the close relationship between abstract art and architecture. This is embodied in the plan that is full of information; it is an abstraction that distills the essence. The plan of every good building has this quality, whether it is the Parthenon, the Colosseum, Sainte-Chapelle, the city of Fatehpur Sikri, or any of the buildings described in these pages. In a medieval cathedral such as Wells in Somerset, it is fascinating to contemplate the necessary accuracy involved in setting out the plan in readiness for everything that will be built above. This accurate geometry will determine the pattern of the vaulting, the rhythm of the columns, the weight upon the buttresses as well as the magic of light from the windows. The plan is decided in advance but built decades later, and in this way it anticipates the building.

11.29 - Matisse Chapel of the Rosary in Vence interior

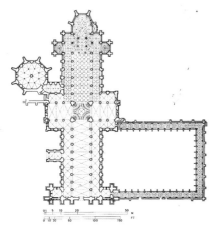

11.30 - Wells Cathedral plan

Wells Cathedral was built in stages between the late twelfth and fourteenth centuries. Each generation made its own modifications whilst respecting the geometry of what had gone before. The plan represents the order of all the parts - the overarching symmetry of the church itself, the rhythmic procession of columns and vaults in the cloister, the high majestic vault in the chapter house springing from its central pier, and its approach by monumental winding stairs. The plan can be described as elegant in just the same way that a mathematician refers to an elegant proof.

The **Chapel of the Rosary** at **Vence** in Provence was designed between 1943 and 1949 by **Henri Matisse**. He had been very ill and was cared for by a nurse who later became a Dominican nun called Sister Jacque-Marie. In gratitude to her he decided to design a chapel that would be a complete work of art, in its plan, its lighting, its use of materials and colour, as well as its murals. He meticulously designed every detail including the altar furniture, the confessionals and the vestments.

The geometry of the plan consists simply of two rectangles intersecting at right angles. The longer one, the nave, accommodates a lay congregation, the shorter one, that I refer to as the choir, contains three rows of pews for the Dominican nuns. As these two spaces are equal in width, their crossing defines a square in which the sanctuary is raised up one step. The altar is placed diagonally so that the priest standing behind it addresses both the lay congregation and the nuns. He stands on a semi-circular platform raised a further two steps - a neat play of pure geometry. The altar and platform are made of granite in contrast to the marble floor. The whole room is executed with minimal simplicity; there is no expression of structure, just an emphasis on the pure planes of the floor, the walls and the ceiling. This is the reticent space that Matisse illuminates with his magnificent colours of stained glass, and decorates with his huge images drawn in black lines on white ceramic tiles.

On the axis of the choir facing the nuns' pews there is a large stylised drawing on tiles of St Dominic, and on the axis of the nave behind the altar is a two-light stained glass window depicting the Tree of Life. On the right hand side of the nave is a huge drawing of the Virgin and Child, and on the end wall behind the congregation is a great representation of the Way of the Cross, bringing together in one composition what are usually the separate Stations of the Cross. Matisse painted these full-size on paper while sitting in his wheelchair, and they were then transferred on to the tiles. Cartoons that he made for these are in a gallery behind the chapel. There is a sequence from an early portrait of a monk through many simplifications, to an abstraction which portrays not a particular monk but the essence

11.31 - Barcelona Pavilion exterior view

11.32 - Barcelona Pavilion interior pond and statue

11.33 - Barcelona Pavilion exterior pond

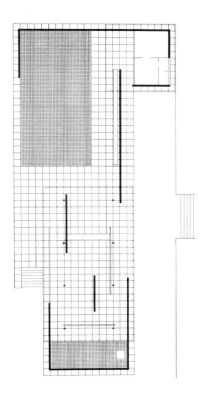

11.34 - Barcelona Pavilion plan

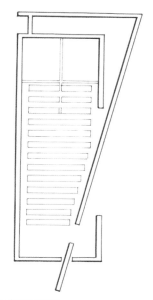

11.35 - Church of the Light plan

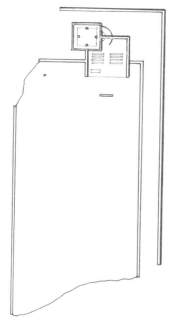

11.36 - Hokkaido Church plan

of the Saint who founded the Order. There is a similar sequence from the portrait of a beautiful lady (perhaps Sister Jacque-Marie) to an abstract depiction that is Mary the mother of Jesus. These images are reduced to their most elementary forms, and because of this they have a most powerful presence. For many architects something similar takes place, as can be seen from their early sketches. These may be the playful childish doodles to which Aalto refers, but they often show how an idea seems to be coaxed from one drawing to the next.

Apart from the Tree of Life window behind the altar, the chapel is lit by a series of windows behind the nuns' pews and on the left side of the nave opposite the image of the Virgin and Child. These form a row of narrow windows from the floor with semi-circular heads nearly up to the ceiling; they are cut deeply into the thickness of the wall without any mouldings. Matisse devised the forms of the stained glass from paper cut-outs. Their vibrant colours form a rhythmic pattern across the windows and cast coloured light across the room onto the black and white panels, and these in turn reflect their images onto the shiny marble floor. It is this above all that gives the chapel its unique magic. In contrast to the boldness of the windows and ceramic panels, Matisse designed a very delicate crucifix and candlesticks on the altar in order not to impede the view of the priest during Mass.

Externally the form of the chapel is equally simple and reticent. A low double-pitched roof is centred over the nave and extends downwards over the choir. The tiles are mainly glazed white with a bold echelon pattern of blue tiles along its length, and with the eaves consisting of three rows of tiles in the traditional Provençale manner. From the ridge, a tall decorated cross and bell tower signifies that this is a chapel.

The German Pavilion in **Barcelona** by **Mies van der Rohe** has no use other than itself; it has no need to respond to programme or climate, it simply enjoys the formal relationship between the parts and between materials. The plan distills the essence of the building - space expands and contracts, long horizontals are

11.37 - Hokkaido Church exterior view

11.38 - Church of the Light interior looking west

11.40 - Church of the Light interior looking east

11.41 - Church of the Light exterior

11.39 - Hokkaido Chapel looking out

11.42 - Chapel by Siren looking out

expressed in the roof, pavement and water, and pure planes of walls contrast with the slender steel columns. The interplay of gorgeous materials and one solitary sculpture all contribute to an atmosphere of quietness and calm.

As Aalto points out, architecture has a direct relationship to abstract art. In the 20th century the paintings of artists such as Piet Mondrian and Ben Nicholson might be regarded as building plans, and the work of architects like Mies Van der Rohe and Tadao Ando could be displayed as paintings.

The Japanese architect Tadao Ando, whose work is reduced to ultimate simplicity, reveals his delight in the elegance of the plan. **The Church of Light** in **Osaka** is based on a simple rectangle intersected by a long wall at an angle. This is a splendid abstract pattern but it is not just a wilful device as it appropriately defines the use; the outside of the wall leads towards the entrance and provides a porch, whilst the inside of the wall gives access to the vestry. At the points of intersection, a full-height window cuts into the rectangular volume with a slit of light along the top subtly illuminating the dim interior. The theme of light is taken up behind the altar where narrow slits of light are cut vertically and horizontally across the whole wall forming a cross. The simplicity of plan is echoed in the simplicity of elevations both inside and out.

Tadao Ando similarly exploits simple geometry in the plan of a **church** in **Hokkaido.** This abstract composition consists of two overlapping squares that relate to a rectangular lake, and two enclosing walls that stand at right angles to one another. The landscape has been mounded so that the entrance is on the first floor in a square glass box that is enclosed by four huge concrete crosses nearly touching at the corners. From here a semi-circular ramp leads down to the square church below. The whole wall opposite is glazed, giving a view into the lake with a simple cross rising out of it. The great window can slide to one side so that on occasion the church can open out to the landscape. It is reminiscent of the chapel at Otaniemi by Kaija and Heikki Siren. In all Ando's work the precise use of bare concrete without mouldings or projections adds the simple abstraction of the plan to the third dimension.

THE SIGNIFICANCE OF THE ELEVATION

Elevations play an important role; often we see the outside of a building that we never enter; we see the form and the façade and we make a critical judgement. It may have a regular rhythm or a balanced asymmetry, it may be flat or deeply modelled, it may consist of a wall with windows cut into it or a system of columns and beams or arches, it may have a gradation from a heavy base to a lighter top, or it may present a front or a back that represent a different domain between public and private.

11.43 - Trinity Library Cambridge view towards court

11.44 - Trinity Library Cambridge view towards the backs

11.45 - Trinity Library Cambridge interior

Sometimes, though not always, the elevation may tell you what a building is, or at other times it may just signify its importance.

How does the elevation come about? It requires deep thought; nothing arbitrary or wilful will do. In the middle of the 20th century it was proposed that the elevation should automatically express on the outside what goes on within, and should honestly express its structure. This is a simplistic rationalisation which, as we have seen, history contradicts. Essentially the elevation is an interface between inside and out, it comes about by the *reconciliation* of the internal demands of the building and the external demands of the street, the square or the landscape. This requires a sensitive understanding not only of the needs of the building but also of the immediate surroundings.

The Library at **Trinity College Cambridge** by **Christopher Wren** is a magnificent room with two faces, one towards the College, the other towards the beautiful park known as 'The Backs', with each face cleverly acknowledging its different context.

The Library is sited in Nevile's Court that lies to the west of Great Court and is entered through the screens between the Hall and the Buttery. The north and south sides of the Court were originally built between 1605 and 1612 and extended westwards some sixty five years later. They are three storeys high with a wide cloister at ground level that has semi-circular arches to the court and a plain back wall relieved only by doors to the staircases. The Library started on site in 1676 and completes the west side of the court. It consists of one great room raised above the ground and entered by a separate pavilion at the north end.

The interior is exquisite. Everything is placed symmetrically; bookcases some 3.6 metres high line the walls and project about 2.7 metres into the space forming thirteen study bays on each side with tall semi-circular-headed windows above. The bookcases have fine cornices and magnificent carving in the panelling, coats of arms, swags and cherubs. White busts on pedestals stand on the floor at the end of each bookcase with a further row above; their whiteness contrasting with the dark wood. Large black and white marble tiles form a diagonal pattern to the central aisle, whilst a raised timber floor between the bookcases adds to the sense of enclosure of the bays. Above the bookcases Corinthian pilasters support a rich entablature below a large-scale coffered ceiling. All the elements - the bookcases, sculpture and carving, the floor, walls and ceiling - form an overarching order and contribute to the richness and grandeur of this long room.

Externally, Wren demonstrates his skill in manipulating the classical orders, and at the same time he resolves an ambiguity between the elevations and the section. This is intriguing in two

11.46 - Trinity Library Cambridge doorway to Backs

11.47 - Trinity Library Cambridge view into Nevile's Court

11.48 - Trinity Library Cambridge bookstacks

11.49 - Gothenburg Law Courts exterior view

ways: firstly, the bold horizontal line below the library windows would appear to mark the level of the first floor, but it is in fact the top of the bookcases that occupy the wall space below; and secondly, the two façades each respond to their different contexts rather than to the interior; they act as an interface between the symmetrical room inside and the two different worlds outside.

The east elevation towards the Court is essentially open with a low colonnade related to what exists. Its face is rich and deeply modelled, consisting of two superimposed orders of bold pilasters, Ionic above and Tuscan below. Between the lower pilasters is a sub-order supporting an architrave and a row of semi-circular arches that are filled in with carved panels. Between the upper pilasters the Library windows have semi-circular arched heads.

By contrast the outside west façade is essentially a wall. The large windows of the Library are similar to those on the inside but they fit into a plain rectangular frame as if the wall has been carried up into a cut-out grid, an 'order' but without classical references. At the lower level the wall appears as a strong base where three entrances are marked by Doric columns supporting an entablature, with their low door openings fitted just below the floor. A series of unglazed openings light the undercroft, similarly set low within the expanse of the beautiful Ketton stone wall.

What does the difference between these façades achieve? The openness of the east side continues the cloister and emphasises the inside; its overt classicism celebrates the grandeur of the library and its historic contents. The solidity of the west side emphasises the edge, the boundary between the College and The Backs, penetrated only through doorways; its face is simplified, more reticent, in some ways more austere and yet still monumental.

When **Gunnar Asplund** won the competition for the extension to the **Law Courts** in **Gothenburg** in 1913, he was faced with the daunting task of relating the new to the old. It was to take twenty-four years to come to fruition, and a wide range of drawings reveal a difficult journey.

The existing Law Courts were in a neo-classical building around a courtyard with its main entrance facing Gustave Adolphe Square to the east, with the river to the south, and Kristine Church to the west; the site for the extension was to the north. The plan was organised on the east-west axis from the portico.

In Asplund's first design, a new monumental entrance was formed facing the river, creating a strong south-north axis. The extension was around a second courtyard with the Courts on the

11.50 - Gothenburg Law Courts progress sketches

11.51 - Gothenburg Law Courts across square

first floor approached by a bridge from the existing building. The façade to the square was simply an extension of what existed.

In 1915 the plan was modified and the entrance reverted to its original position facing the square. This set up two axes; one related to the entrance, the other to the position of the Courts. This is an arrangement that was sustained through the many changes that were to follow. At this time different designs for the façade towards the square showed variations on a continuous classical theme.

Over the years many alternative plans were explored. In a 1919 scheme the west side of the existing square was removed, opening it up to the church; in 1920 the new courtyard was made circular. A whole range of studies was made of the elevations, some with one entrance others with two, some with one continuous built form others with two pavilions. By 1925 the organisation of the plan was established in principle. It had a staircase within the new courtyard leading to a gallery that served the four Courts. Alternative elevation studies continued to be explored, and even in 1934 pilasters with classical capitals

198

11.52 - Gothenburg Law Courts interior looking north

11.53 - Gothenburg Law Courts interior towards stair

11.54 - Gothenburg Law Courts new staircase

still appeared. This is somewhat surprising because in 1930 Asplund had already pioneered the Stockholm Exhibition that heralded a new architecture.

From 1935 onwards the introduction of a framed building gave a new freedom to the plan, the sections and the elevations. The heavy columns between the two courtyards were removed, and the new floor is supported on widely spaced slim columns set back from the edge. A huge glazed screen on both the ground and first floor separates the original open courtyard from the new covered one, though the same stone floor throughout provides continuity. The entrance to the new part is in the corner of the old cloister, and leads to the free-standing glazed lift and the foot of the stairs. This is exceptionally long with low risers and wide treads giving a gentle gradient. This leads to a gallery around the courtyard providing a generous space in which to sit and wait, well lit from above and elegantly furnished. Two rectangular courts are on the sides of the gallery, and two with curved sides are at the end. All the walls on the outside and inside of the Courts are lined with timber. Inside the Courts the jurors sit behind a subtly curved desk that is raised up two steps with witnesses placed to one side; this gives a degree of formality but without the pomposity often associated with a Court. The whole interior is designed to alleviate stress and create an atmosphere of calm. It is an architecture more appropriate to the new times.

The framed structure allowed a new reconciliation between the existing elevations and the new. Both stand on a granite plinth, the horizontal lines approximate to the existing order, the vertical lines create a similar rhythm, and the Court is expressed as a *piano nobile* with discreet carving above the windows. A clever move was to shift the windows from the centre of the structural bays towards the old building, thus giving a dependence of the new to the old. Peter Blundell Jones has commented: "*Asplund tied together old and new in such a subtle way that each profits from the other: the old building is actually better for the experience and the new one could not live without it*".[11.1] Designing the elevation in a way that would reconcile the internal requirements of the Law Courts with the existing façade had been a long struggle, but it was demonstrably worth it.

In these various ways the plan develops in three dimensions in section and elevation, and in turn the section and elevation moderate the plan. Gradually the relationship between them is resolved, '*tied together*' in Aalto's words, and a consistent concept is realised.

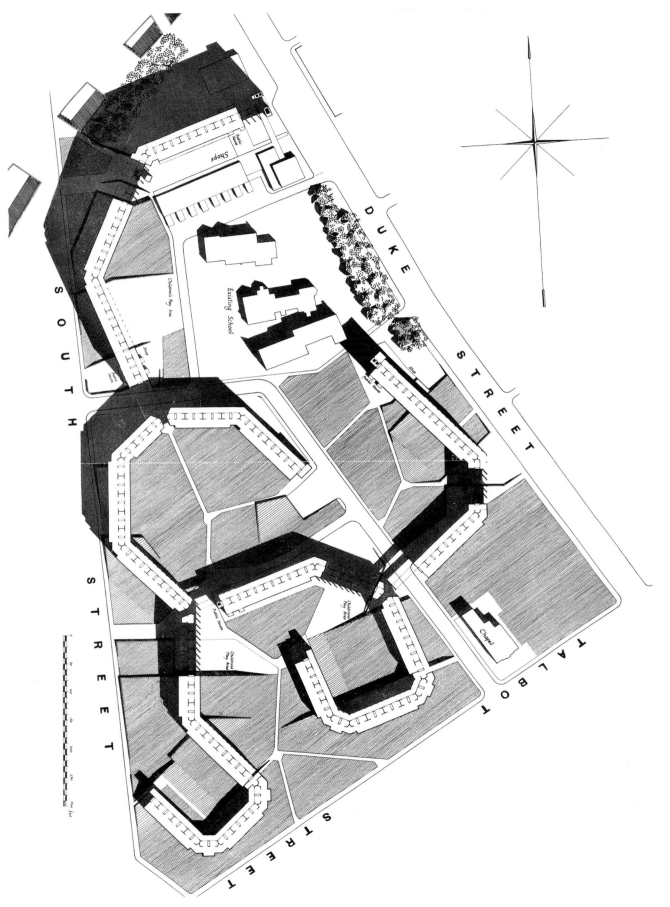

12.1 - Park Hill plan

12 REFLECTIONS

In this book I have addressed aspects of architecture and designing that I regard as significant, and I have illustrated these by a selection of work that has given me inspiration. It is now appropriate to reflect on the way that these issues relate to my own design work. This gives an opportunity to consider how they operate together.

I should first relate where I came from. I consider that architects of my generation qualified at a privileged time. It was just after the war when hopes were high, and among all the professionals, geographers, economists, sociologists, planners as well as architects, there was a sense of optimism and a deep social concern to make a better world albeit within a climate of frugality. Little had been seen or built for many years; even then the Unité d'Habitation by Le Corbusier and the Town Hall at Säynätsalo by Aalto were still only under construction. It is not surprising that these factors had such a powerful influence on our way of thinking and our work.

12.2 - Park Hill before redevelopment

From 1952 onwards **Jack Lynn and I** worked in the Sheffield City Architects Department and designed a major slum clearance development at **Park Hill.**

Sheffield at that time was still a thriving industrial city with major steelworks, coal mines, and cutlery workshops where working hours were long and hard. On the Park Hill site people were living at 400 per acre (1000 per hectare) in two-storey back-to-back houses around a courtyard with a communal water pipe and W.C. The houses were so close together that the sun could hardly penetrate. Yet for all the hardships (and perhaps because of them) there was great neighbourliness; despite the dirt and the closeness, people took a certain pride in their houses, and most of them wished to go on living in the same locality.

12.3 - Park Hill aerial view of site

12.4 - Park Hill past elevation

The Park Hill site is in a commanding position in the centre of the city; it is on a plateau sloping gently from south to north with a steep bank on the west down to the railway station. The long continuous blocks of Le Corbusier's '*Ville Radieuse*' were an influential precedent, and by similarly using a constant horizontal roofline, the new housing was designed to relate at the southern end to the scale of the existing houses, and at the northern end to the scale of the city. This was the strategic move that gives Park Hill the powerful urban impact that it has.

12.5 - Park Hill view of southern end

12.6 - Park Hill view of northern end

12.7 - Spengen Holland deck

12.8 - Byker Newcastle deck

202

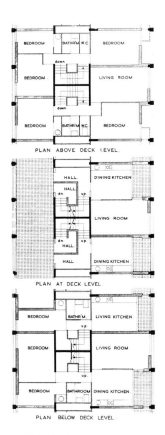

The idea of 'the street in the air' became fundamental, but unlike Le Corbusier's '*rue intérieure*', at Park Hill it is in the open air. It aimed to facilitate the sort of neighbourliness that exists in a street on the ground where there is a choice of neighbours, room to stand and chat, and space for children to play. These wide decks, as they became known, are quite unlike the narrow access balconies in a conventional slab block of the time. The decks connect the whole scheme together and form a meandering route across the site. Because of the slope they run to ground at different places in the direction of a nearby park. Unlike the Unité, at Park Hill the built form creates enclosure, and in response to the light, the space between the buildings gets bigger as the building increases in height down the hill. Furthermore, in order to give the dwellings the best orientation, the deck changes from one side of the building to the other. These moves together serve to give different parts of the scheme their own identity; the experience of living in a four-storey building looking onto a small courtyard is different from living higher up with more distant views. This is not to suggest that all these benefits were spotted in advance; sometimes one move evokes another with surprising results.

The dwellings are grouped in a cluster three stories high and three bays wide containing two flats below the deck and two maisonettes on deck level and above, each with its own generous balcony. This gives a deeply modelled façade where the scale of the repeated cluster and the boldness of the concrete structural grid relate well to the immense size of the building (aspects that were inherited from the Unité). Each three-storey band served by its deck has its own different colour to emphasise its identity, and each is named after a former street on the ground. In order to signify their own home the residents then adorned their threshold in some special way just as they had done previously.

For the first decade or so the residents regarded Park Hill as paradise compared with what they had before. The decks worked as intended, there was great conviviality, children played there, residents stood or sat and talked, and the milkman brought his trolley along to deliver the milk. In hindsight I realise they have one major shortcoming; streets in the air, as on the ground should have windows onto them to enrich both the dwelling and the street. In this way one can see passers-by, keep an eye on the kids and watch out for any vandalism. We did not know then about the deck housing built in Spangen in Holland over forty years before. Much later Ralph Erskine was to incorporate this very successfully at Byker in Newcastle.

Over the years things began to go wrong; the three industries that had made Sheffield great, steel, cutlery and coal, ceased to exist; the management of Park Hill changed, the building fabric was allowed to deteriorate, and it was used as a place to house

12.13 - The Courtyard Ewelme living room

12.14 - The Courtyard Ewelme studio

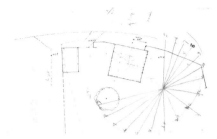

12.15 - The Courtyard Ewelme sun diagram

12.16 - The Courtyard Ewelme early elevations

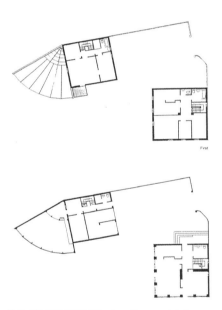

12.17 - The Courtyard Ewelme plans of houses and studio

12.18 - The Courtyard Ewelme tartan grid

difficult tenants. In addition society was developing a growing drug culture with increased violence. Park Hill was threatened with demolition but in 1998 it was listed by English Heritage and its future, if not guaranteed, was likely to be assured.

From 1962 onwards **Cailey Hutton and I** worked together in practice where, because of the reputation of Park Hill, we designed a number of houses and communal housing schemes.

The **Courtyard** at **Ewelme** in Oxfordshire was designed for my own family. The site is an orchard on the south side of the village street where the houses form a continuous edge. The new house follows the pattern of its neighbours and continues the character of the street.

The house has a square plan with its diagonal facing due south towards the view. Following the precedent of Aalto's apartments at Neue Vahr, the walls on the north-east and north-west sides are solid to protect against the cold and noise, whilst in contrast the façades to the south-east and south-west are more open towards the sun and view. An early sketch demonstrates the way the movement of the sun lights the house in different ways at different times in the year. The ground floor is arranged so that the living room enjoys the sun throughout the day, the dining kitchen benefits in the morning and the study in the evening. Although these rooms have openness to the garden, the solidity of the columns gives a sense of enclosure. When required, the kitchen, living room and study can be shut off as separate rooms but at other times double doors from floor to ceiling give a more open plan - a good place for a party! On the first floor the main bedroom is at the south corner with two single rooms on each side; these have removable partitions between them so that the house can be changed from five bedrooms to four or three. In deference to Louis Kahn, the service rooms, the bathroom, utility and cloakroom, occupy the north corner; and the rooms they serve, the living rooms and bedrooms, are towards the south.

The house is organised on a tartan grid where the overall square is divided into spaces that are square, square and a half, or double-square, a discipline that gives a consistent scale to the whole. The narrow bands of the grid accommodate the columns, the fireplace, bookshelves and cupboards. Externally, the pure geometrical form, a pavilion with a pyramidal roof and a colonnade on two sides, gives the house a certain formality towards the garden.

In keeping with the rest of the street, the house is made of a mellow red brick with timber windows and a slate roof. Internally, the walls are fair-faced brick painted white, the

12.19 - Bond Keltz House view from south west

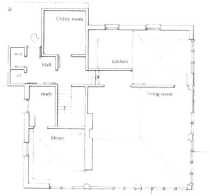

12.20 - Bond Keltz House upper floor plan

12.21 - Bond Keltz House lower floor plan

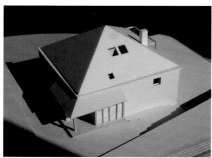

12.22 - Bond Keltz House model from north

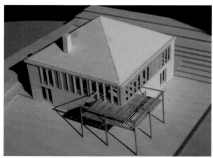

12.23 - Bond Keltz House model from south

ceilings are boarded, the hall is tiled and the rest of the ground floor is made of hardwood. The timber ceiling and floor give a homely warm feeling in contrast to the walls.

The front door is celebrated by a generous flight of brick steps from a gravel courtyard. This is surrounded by a brick wall with a smaller square building along one side. This contains garages and a flat above, similarly organised on the diagonal.

This building leads into a fan-shaped studio that follows the skew of the site. It is a plan that has desks around the perimeter and is well suited to the working arrangement. The walls and floor are brick, and the roof is made of laminated timber beams with boarding between.

The house and studio work well; they fit in with the village and make the most of the sun and the garden, there is a sense of enclosure yet also of openness, of privacy but also of welcome; the simplicity is enhanced by the use of materials and by the quality of light.

The **Bond/Keltz** house designed thirty-five years later is a further development of the square plan. It is in a valley in Devon facing south with views overlooking the sea. Unlike the Courtyard at Ewelme, which is in the context of a village street, this house is a pavilion in the landscape. The diagonal similarly faces south, allowing the same disposition of solid walls to give protection from the cold north and openness to the sunny south. The entrance is within a covered porch at the north corner of the house, and because of the slope of the land it is at a half-level between the two floors.

In order to capture the best view, the living areas are on the first floor with the bedrooms below. The large square living room is at the southern corner and enjoys the inside of the main pyramidal roof. As this is very high at the apex it allows a cantilevered gallery to sit above a quarter of the living room with the fireplace in the cosy space below. The dining room and the study are at each side with mini pyramids under the roof giving them their own autonomy. All the sloping ceilings are lined with timber boarding to create a homely atmosphere.

The house is organised around a consistent geometry. The square porch leads into a double-square hall that indicates a change of direction up towards the living room. The staircase down to the bedrooms below is less prominent; it is to one side and is illuminated by a dramatically tall light-well leading to a square hall below.

Externally, the windows of the living room, dining room and library appear as a continuous timber frame, a *piano nobile*, in contrast to the rendered masonry elsewhere. It is further enhanced by the timber terrace that wraps around the south

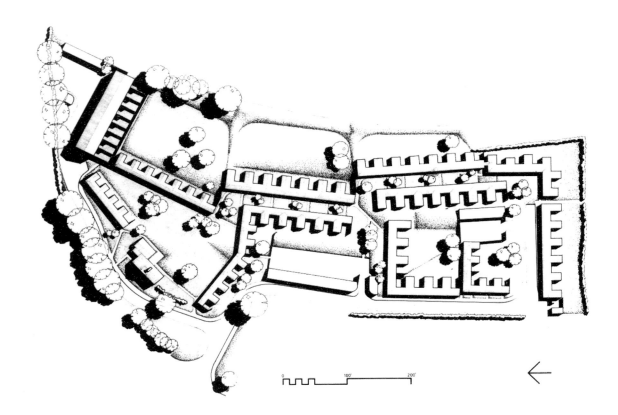

12.24 - Dibleys Blewbury plan

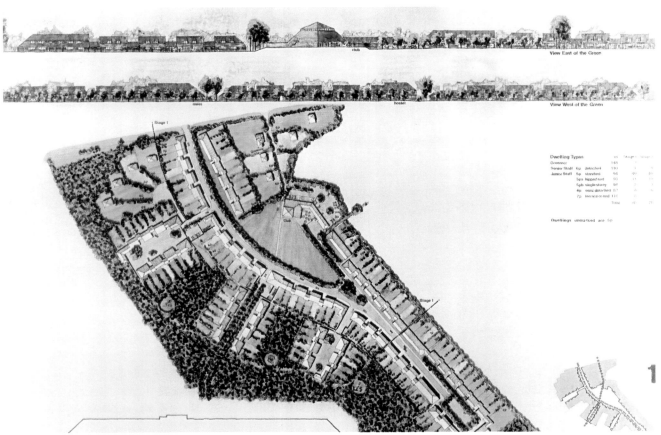

View East of the Green

View West of the Green

Dwelling Types			Stage 1	Stage 2
Governor		148		
Senior Staff	6p detached	110		
Junior Staff	5p standard	94		
	5pa hipped end	90		
	5pb single storey	96		
	4p semi detached			
	7p terrace or end	110		
	Total			

Dwellings unmarked are 5p

12.25 - Prison Officers Housing plans

12.26 - Dibleys Blewbury view of pedestrian street

12.27 - Dibleys Blewbury private courtyard

corner of the living room. This not only serves to express the upside-down organisation of the house but also to celebrate the southerly aspect and the view.

At **Dibleys** in the rural setting of **Blewbury** in **Berkshire** we designed a 'village' for elderly people where relation to the sun was a prime consideration. The central focus is a large old house that was intended to become a communal centre; it has a village green in front and a pattern of pedestrian streets leading from it; these are laid out with grass and trees and with mini squares as they change direction.

Each single-storey cottage is L-shaped on plan, designed around a small sunny courtyard that the residents have made their own with a riot of colourful plants. The living room and bedrooms look out onto this whilst the kitchen, next to the front door, looks out onto the street giving a measure of contact with passers-by. The cottages have a homely scale like that of traditional almshouses achieved by the low eaves at door-head height.

A competition can be used to investigate a particular issue, and that for **Prison Officers' Housing** provided a vehicle for exploring *identity* and *place*.

The brief was hierarchical; it called for about sixty houses for officers and eight houses for senior ranks together with community rooms and open space for play. So often housing consists of identical rows of identical dwellings in nowhere land. Here two factors contributed to the plan; the irregularity of the site, and the concept of a village green. Some houses enfront the street leading to the green, others surround it, and others are in short culs-de-sac that lead off fan-wise, with detached houses for senior ranks at the northern end of the site. Communal facilities are at the head of the green. A forest separates the housing from the view of the prison wall.

The housing at **King Street in Cambridge** relates to its urban context and forms two new edges to a city block. It is designed around a garden courtyard which all the residents pass through on their way home. It therefore serves as a gathering place with seats in the shade or in the sun. We had in mind the Begijnhof in Amsterdam, a former convent dating from the 14th century, a quiet and peaceful place behind a busy shopping street.

The courtyard is bounded by three-storey buildings on the north and the south which are stepped down towards the centre to allow in maximum light. The north block is raised above a car park, and above this the dwellings have private terraces looking down into the garden. The south block along the street has bay windows raised slightly above the pavement to give the residents privacy whilst still allowing a view of passers-by. The corner is

12.28 - King Street Cambridge street view

12.29 - King Street Cambridge courtyard towards east

12.30 - King Street Cambridge courtyard towards south

12.31 - King Street Cambridge courtyard at west end

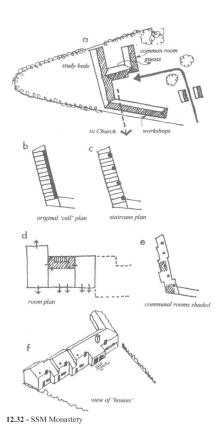

12.32 - SSM Monastery

celebrated by its height, stepping down at the side to enclose the courtyard from the street. It is built of a brick similar to that used in the surrounding buildings, and is a low-key intervention in the urban scene.

The design of the **Monastery** for **The Society of the Sacred Mission at Milton Keynes** evoked an unexpected use of metaphor. It is for an Anglican Order that previously had run a theological college. The Church of England decided that study for the priesthood should be in a university, and the monks had to rethink their vocation. They advertised their availability, and the Bishop of Oxford suggested that they might discover a role in the new town of Milton Keynes that was starting to be built. They found a redundant vicarage opposite a splendid church by Robert Hooke (a contemporary of Christopher Wren) and proposed to develop it, but they were unable to formulate a brief. They had previously been busy teaching, and found it difficult to envisage how they would now spend their time and what their new home should provide. After much deliberation we asked our clients the question: "*if instead of talking to us you had approached an estate agent, what sort of redundant building might you consider; a stately home, a railway station, a warehouse, a school or perhaps a farm?*". The idea of a farm captured their imagination; the farmhouse could be used for guests, the cowsheds for living, the barns for a workshop, and so on. The final building is nothing like a farm but the metaphor released a whole range of exciting new possibilities.

The design of the study bedrooms raised a further surprising response to precedent. Initially these were arranged on two floors along a corridor reminiscent of a cloister, but this was considered institutional "*it would make us feel we are in cells!*" These 20th-century monks saw no reason why the rooms should be identical, and looked forward to the choices that variety would give. The corridors were replaced by a staircase system rather like that in an Oxford or Cambridge College with three rooms above and three below with each room different. This gave a configuration unlike that envisaged at the outset; it had evolved into five 'houses' that in turn were given their own identity with a separate communal facility in each.

In 1988 I joined **Barry Gasson** in a limited competition for the **British Ambassador's Residence** in **Moscow.**

The brief described two distinct parts; a series of grand rooms for receptions and state banquets, together with separate private accommodation for the ambassador. It was required that the building should have a presence appropriate for the Queen's representative in a foreign land, but it should also provide maximum security especially at the entrance.

12.33 - King Street Cambridge courtyard at west end looking north

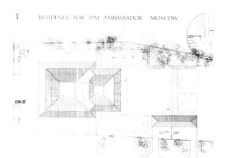

12.34 - Ambassador's Residence Moscow site plan

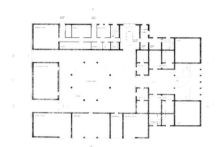

12.35 - Ambassador's Residence Moscow ground floor plan

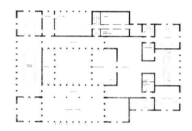

12.36 - Ambassador's Residence Moscow first floor plan

south elevation

section a-a

12.37 - Ambassador's Residence Moscow cross section

east elevation

12.38 - Ambassador's Residence Moscow long section

The driveway enters into a square courtyard towards a well-protected front door. A spacious hall then leads to an easy grand staircase to the floor above, with access from a half-landing to the outside for garden parties. On the first floor a large reception room connects at the sides to a library and to the guest suite. Straight ahead on the axis is the winter garden overlooking the courtyard; this is a special place reminiscent of a splendid balcony on the previous Residence that had views over the river to the Kremlin. All the state rooms are arranged around the courtyard and are defined by the form of the roof.

The ambassador's private apartments are around a smaller private courtyard on the floor above and are also defined by the roof. The two elements of accommodation thus have a similar geometry and, arranged in this way, they overlap to encompass a whole.

It transpired that the Russian Government agreed to extend the lease of the magnificent Residence overlooking the Kremlin, and the competition designs were never built.

After Park Hill was listed, in 2005 the imaginative developers **Urban Splash** working with architects **Hawkins Brown** and **Studio Egret West**, and landscape architects **Grant Associates**, began to prepare proposals for regeneration, and in 2011 the first stage was complete. They had to address the dilemma of reconciling authenticity and change. This was new, different and difficult. It went far beyond the repair of the structure though that in itself is impressive. After years with a bad reputation it needed to demonstrate a fresh start, to attract new residents, two-thirds of these would rent or buy from the open market whilst others would be existing Park Hill tenants.

In the 21st century, living is required to be more spacious, and the dwellings now have lower occupancy and more open plans, with views right through and light from both sides. Double glazing allows larger windows, and the brickwork has been replaced by brightly coloured aluminium panels. This controversial proposal required approval from English Heritage who applied the 'squint test'- *if you half shut your eyes, does it still look like Park Hill?*- an intriguing way of assessing authenticity! At first the colours seemed a bit bright but they demonstrate a pristine new beginning, and they continue to indicate the different deck levels, the 'streets in the air' which are part of Park Hill's essence. The change to the elevations when the panels are open is a witty device.

A new entrance provides a welcome to Park Hill. It is a splendid monumental space four storeys high, and from here the journey up in the glass lifts is a delight with views over the city to the moors beyond. At night the building is brightly illuminated, and the shiny steel stairs spiralling upwards adds sparkle. The way

12.39 - Park Hill regenerated deck

12.40 - Park Hill regenerated dwelling entrances

that the entrance, the lifts and stairs are set within the structural frame shows masterly respect for what existed before.

The arrival at each level is similarly spacious, and the access still has the qualities of the original deck even though the dwellings encroach on it a little. This is very clever; it not only gives useful space inside but provides a significant threshold, a public/private place to each group of four dwellings.

The choice of materials, the detailing and workmanship show great care. This is evident in the entrance doors, the stairs and windows as well as the design of the kitchens and bathrooms. These benefit from more resources than were originally available. It is refreshing at this time that the whole design is free from gimmicks and there is a consistency and inevitability to each part.

Urban Splash and their architects have got the balance right between respect for authenticity and the embrace of change. What they have done gives real meaning to the word 'regeneration'; it represents a new vitality. I sense, in those who have been involved, the same enthusiasm and excitement that Jack Lynn and I enjoyed half a century ago.

12.41 - Park Hill regenerated lifts & stairs

12.42 - Park Hill regenerated elevation

12.43 - Park Hill regenerated spiral stair

215

References

Introduction
0.1 D'Arcy Thompson *On Growth and Form* Cambridge University Press 1971

1 The Nature of Architecture
1.1 William Buchanan, Ed. *The Glasgow School of Art,* Glasgow School of Art Press 2004
1.2 Denys Lasdun in conversation

2 Facilitating Activity
2.1 Aldo Van Eyck discussion with Singapore students
2.2 Herman Hertzberger lecture to Bristol students
2.3 Stefan Collini *What Are Universities For?* Penguin 2012
2.4 Colin St John Wilson in conversation

3 Modifying Climate
3.1 Paul Oliver *Dwellings: the House across the World* Phaidon 1987
3.2 Charles Correa discussion with Caribbean students
3.3 Brownlee and De Long *Louis I Kahn: In the Realm of Architecture* Rizzoli 1992

4 Relating to Context
4.1 Moore, Allen, Lyndon *The Place of Houses* Holt, Rinehart & Winston
4.2 Anne MacEwen in conversation
4.3 Christian Norberg-Schulz *Genius Loci Towards a Phenomenology of Architecture* Rizzoli 1980
4.4 Colin Rowe and Fred Koetter *Collage City* MIT Press 1983
4.5 Francis Strauven *Aldo van Eyck: The Shape of Relativity* Architectura and Natura, Amsterdam 1998*

5 Respecting Material and Structure
5.1 Brownlee and De Long *Louis I Kahn: In the Realm of Architecture* Rizzoli 1992
5.2 Philip Drew *Touch this Earth Lightly* Duffy & Snellgrove 1999
5.3 Richard Saul Wurman *The Words of Louis Kahn* Rizzoli 1986
5.4 Peter Rice *An Engineer Imagines* Artemis 1994*
5.5 Simon Mawer *The Glass Room* Little Brown 2009

6 Conveying Meaning and Delight
6.1 T. S. Eliot *Burnt Norton* Faber Poetry 2001
6.2 Karl Kraus *Die Fackel* Magazine 1913
6.3 Steen Eiler Rasmussen *London The Unique City* Jonathan Cape 1948
6.4 Le Corbusier *Towards a New Architecture* Architectural Press 1946
6.5 Ludwig Wittgenstein ed. G.H. von Wright *Culture and Value* Blackwell 1984

7 The Nature of Designing
7.1 Alvar Aalto *The Trout and the Mountain Stream* ed. Göran Schildt, translated by Stuart Wrede, reprinted courtesy of The MIT Press from Sketches 1985*

8 Reason and Intuition
8.1 Donald Schon *The Reflective Practitioner* Maurice Temple Smith Ltd 1983
8.2 *Stanton Williams in Sussex* Architecture Today 117
8.3 John Parker et al *The Sainsbury Laboratory: Science, Architecture, Art* Black Dog Publishing 2011*

9 The Value of Experience and Precedent
9.1 T. S. Eliot *Tradition and the Individual Talent* from *Points of View* Faber and Faber Ltd 1945*
9.2 Le Corbusier *Towards a New Architecture* Architectural Press 1946
9.3 James Codrington Forsyth *Woodland Crematorium* AJ Masters of Building: Erik Gunnar Asplund 1988*

10 The Use of Metaphor
10.1 Aldo van Eyck in discussion with Singapore students
10.2 Herman Hertzberger lecture to Bristol students
10.3 Ian Balfour *Creating a Scottish Parliament* Finlay Brown 2005
10.4 Peter Blundell Jones *Monograph Hans Scharoun* Gordon Fraser 1978*

11 The Search for Harmony
11.1 Peter Blundell Jones *The Gothenburg Law Courts Part 2* AJ Masters of building Erik Gunnar Asplund 1988

Thanks are due to these publishers for permission to use their quotations.

** Every effort has been made to trace and contact copyright holders of all the quotations; any errors or omissions will be corrected in subsequent editions.*

Glossary

Aedicule - a small room or structure often framed by columns

Ambulatory - a place for walking

Annulet - small ring encircling a column

Apse - a semi-circular or polygonal recess, especially in a church

Arris - sharp edge formed by the angular contact of two plane surfaces

Atrium - inner courtyard

Axis - a line dividing a regular figure symmetrically

Baldachino - canopy over an altar

Barrel vault - usually semi-cylindrical vault

Battered - receding slope of wall or column from ground upwards

Box girder - a truss in the form of a box

Brise soleil - a projecting fin to provide shade

Cantilever - a beam or structure supported at one end

Capital - head of pillar or column

Carrel - small enclosure for study

Chancel - part of church often containing the altar reserved for clergy and choir

Chamfered - bevelled edge or corner

Clerestory - part of church wall with windows above aisle roofs

Coffered - ceiling with sunk panels

Colonnade - row of columns

Console - kind of bracket or corbel

Corbel - projection jutting out from wall to give support

Cortile - courtyard

Cycloid - curve traced by a radius of a circle as it rolls along a straight line

Dado - lower part of wall finished differently from upper part

Diagrid - a grid arranged on the diagonal

Doric, Ionic, Corinthian - the Orders in classical architecture

Echelon - staggered formation

Echinus - the curved part of a Doric capital

Entablature - the part of a classical order above the column

E.T.H. - Swiss Federal Institute of Technology in Zurich

Fair-face concrete - concrete left unadorned as from the shutter

Finial - ornament finishing off the apex of a roof or gable

Funicular - worked by a cable from a stationary engine

Genius loci - the spirit or ambience of a place

Ghat - steps above river where Hindus burn their dead

Grain - pattern or texture of built form on the ground

Keystone - voussoir at summit of arch locking the whole together

Lintel - horizontal beam over door or window

Loggia - open-sided gallery or arcade

Lunette - aperture in arched ceiling to admit light

Monopitch - roof with single pitch

Mullion - vertical bar dividing lights in a window

Narthex - western portico in early Christian churches

Oculos - a circular opening in a dome or wall

Pergola - covered walk often with plants over

Piano nobile - usually the first floor containing the principal rooms

Pilaster - a column engaged with the wall

Platonic geometry - geometry based on pure forms, such as squares, circles

Programme - description of requirements

Rectilinear - bounded by straight lines

Reredos - screen behind the altar

Solarium - place enclosed by glass for enjoying the sun

Soldier courses - bricks or stones laid on their ends

Springing - the beginning of an arch from a wall or column

Stupa - a relic shrine

Trabeated - system of construction with columns and beams

Transom - horizontal bar across a window or top of a door

Truss - supporting structure of roof or bridge

Unwrought timber - timber that has not been planed

Further Reading

Balfour Alan *Creating a Scottish Parliament* Finlay Brown 2005

Blundell Jones Peter *Hans Scharoun Monograph* Gordon Frazer 1978

Boesiger/ Girsberger *Le Corbusier 1910-1960* Tiranti 1960

Botta Mario *Prayers in Stone* Editrice Compositori 2005 RIBA 2006

Brownlee & De Long *Louis I Kahn: In the Realm of Architecture* Rizzoli 1992

Buchanan Peter *Renzo Piano Building Workshop* Phaidon 2007

Buchanan William Ed *The Glasgow School of Art* Glasgow School of Art Press 2004

Butler A.S.G. *The Architecture of Sir Edwin Lutyens* Country Life 1984

Casamonti Marco *Rafael Moneo* Motta 2008

Cruickshank Dan Ed *Erik Gunnar Asplund* AJ Masters of Building 1988

Curtis William *Modern Architecture Since 1900* Phaidon 2001

Dal Co Francesco *Tadao Ando Complete Works* Phaidon 2000

Davies Colin *Hopkins 1 & 2* Phaidon 2001

Eliot T. S. *Point of View* Faber & Faber 1945

Fleig Karl *Alvar Aalto Vol 1* Tiranti 1971

Frampton Kenneth *Tadao Ando* Museum of Modern Art 1993

Hale Jonathan *Ends, Middles, Beginnings* Black Dog 2005

Heathcote, Hall, Merrick, Sorrell *Transforming King's Cross* Merrell 2012

Hertzberger Herman *Buildings and Projects 1959–1986* Arch-Edition, Den Haag

Hertzberger Herman *Lessons for Students in Architecture* 010 Publishers 2001

Hertzberger, van Roijen-Wortmann, Strauven *Aldo van Eyck* Stichting Wonen 1982

Holmdahl, Lind, Ödeen, Eds. *Gunnar Asplund Architect 1885 – 1940* The National Association of Swedish Architects (SAR) 1950

Johnson Philip *Mies van der Rohe* Martin Secker & Warburg 1978

Keys & Laslett Eds. *Dwelling Accordia* Black Dog 2009

Khan Hasan-Uddin *Charles Correa* Concept Media 1987

Latham Ian & Swenarton Mark *Dixon Jones* Rightangle 2002

Le Corbusier *Towards a New Architecture* Architectural Press 1st publ. England 1946

Luchinger Arnulf *Herman Hertzberger 1959-86* Arch-Edition Den Haag 1987

Macleod Robert *Charles Rennie Mackintosh* Hamlyn/ Country Life 1968

Martin Leslie *Buildings and Ideas 1933-1983* Cambridge University Press 1983

Mawer Simon *The Glass Room* Little, Brown 2009

Menin Sarah & Kite Stephen *Colin St John Wilson An Architecture of Invitation* Ashgate 2005

Moore, Allen & Lyndon *The Place of Houses* Holt, Rinehart & Winston 1974

Morris Alison *John Pawson Plain Space* Phaidon 2010

Norberg-Schulz Christian *Genius Loci Towards a Phenomenology of Architecture* Rizzoli 1980

Oliver Paul *Dwellings: The House across the World* Phaidon 1987

Pardey John *Utzon Logbook 111* Edition Blondal

Pfeiffer Bruce Brooks *Frank Lloyd Wright Selected Houses* A.D.A. Edita 1991

Powell Kenneth Ed. *Richard Rogers Architecture of the Future* Birkhauser 2006

Pulvenis de Seligny Marie-Thérèse *Matisse The Chapel at Vence* Royal Academy 2013

Rasmussen Steen Eiler *London The Unique City* Jonathan Cape 1948

Rice Peter *An Engineer Imagines* Artemis 1994

Rodger Johnny *Gillespie Kidd & Coia Architecture 1956-87* RIAS/Lighthouse 2007

Rota Italo *Mario Botta Architecture and Projects in the 70's* Academy Editions 1981

Rowe Colin & Koetter Fred *Collage City* MIT Press 1983

Schildt Göran Ed. *Alvar Aalto* MIT Press 1985

Schon Donald *The Reflective Practitioner* Maurice Temple Smith Ltd 1983

Stierlin Henri *Encyclopaedia of World Architecture* MacMillan 1983

Stonehouse Roger *Colin St John Wilson Buildings and Projects* Black Dog 2007

Strauven Francis *Aldo van Eyck The Shape of Relativity* Architectura & Natura, Amsterdam 1998

Taylor Brian Brace *Geoffrey Bawa* Mimar/Butterworth Architecture 1989

Thompson D'Arcy *On Growth and Form* Cambridge University Press 1971

Urban Splash *Transformation* RIBA Publishing 2011

Weston Richard *Alvar Aalto* Phaidon 2002

Wilson Colin St John *Architectural Reflections* Butterworth Architecture 1992

Wilson Colin St John *The Design and Construction of the British Library* British Library 1998

Wilson Colin St John *The Other Tradition of Modern Architecture* Academy Editions 1995

Wurman Richard Saul *Words of Louis Kahn* Rizzoli/Access 1986

Yoshida Tetsuro *The Japanese House and Garden* Pall Mall 1955

Index

Numbers in italics refer to the illustrations

Photographic Credits

1.1 photo by Vicens
1.2, 1.6, 1.7, 1.8, © The Glasgow School of Art
1.3 © ArTono/Shutterstock.com
1.9 © sandy young / Alamy
1.10 © VIEW Pictures Ltd / Alamy
1.11 © jeremy sutton-hibbert / Alamy
1.14 © Iain Masterton / Alamy
1.17 © moqub
1.18 © Arcaid Images / Alamy
1.19 © Jean-Pierre Dalbéra CC BY-SA 2.0
1.20, 1.21 © Claudio Divizia/Shutterstock.com
1.22 © Getty Images/Bridgeman Art Library
2.1, 2.2 Feilden Clegg Bradley Studios
2.13 © Foto Aviodrome Lelystad
2.17 © Architectuurstudio HH/Willem Diepraam
2.18 © Architectuurstudio HH/ Martin Schuurmaan
2.19 © Architectuurstudio HH/ Herman H. van Doorn
2.20 © Architectuurstudio HH
2.22 © Mcginnly CC BY-SA 3.0
2.23 photo GazMan7/Neil Jones
2.28, 2.29 © Foster + Partners
2.30, 2.31 © Dixon Jones
2.32 © GRANT ROONEY PREMIUM / Alamy
2.33, 2.34, 2.35, © VIEW Pictures Ltd / Alamy
2.36 © Geoffrey Taunton / Alamy
2.37 © VIEW Pictures Ltd / Alamy
2.38 © Dennis Gilbert/VIEW Pictures Ltd
2.39 © RIBA Library Photographs Collection
2.41 © Mike Peel CC BY-SA 4.0
2.42 © Chris Batson / Alamy
2.43 © David Baron CC BY-SA 2.0
2.44 © RIBA Library Photographs Collection
2.45 © AS London / Alamy
2.46 © The British Library Board
2.47 © Pawel Libera Images / Alamy
3.7 © Douglas Peebles Photography / Alamy
3.9 © Studio arch. Mario Botta . Photography Alo Zanetta
3.10 © Studio arch. Mario Botta
3.13 © Charles Correa
3.14 © Joseph St Anne/ Charles Correa
3.15 © Charles Correa
3.16, 3.17 © Jürgen Howaldt CC BY-SA 2.0 DE
3.18 Courtesy M.J.Long © RIBA Library Drawings & Archives Collection
3.19, 3.20 Courtesy M.J.Long © RIBA Library Photographs Collection
3.21 © The Aldo van Eyck Archive
3.22 © John Pardey
3.23 © VIEW Pictures Ltd / Alamy
3.24 © Frans Drewniac CC BY-SA 2.0
3.25 © VIEW Pictures Ltd / Alamy
3.26 © John Pardey
3.27 © VIEW Pictures Ltd / Alamy
3.28 © John Pardey
3.29 © Richard Weston
3.30 © John Pardey
3.31 © Richard Weston
3.32 © Margaret Richards
3.33, 3.36, 3.37 © 2013 Kimbell Art Museum, Fort Worth
3.38 © Binhe CC-BY-SA-3.0
3.39, 3.40, 3.41 Photo © Ivor Smith © FLC/ ADAGP, Paris and DACS, London 2014.
3.42 © FLC/ ADAGP, Paris and DACS, London 2014.
3.43 Photo © Ivor Smith/ © FLC/ ADAGP, Paris and DACS, London 2014.
3.44 Photo © Paul Raftery / Alamy © FLC/ ADAGP, Paris and DACS, London 2014.
3.45 Photo © Jacqueline Salmon/Artedia/VIEW/ © FLC/ ADAGP, Paris and DACS, London 2014.
3.46 Photo © Wiskerke / Alamy/© FLC/ ADAGP, Paris and DACS, London 2014.
4.1 © Jonathan Rieke
4.2 © Richard Weston
4.3, 4.4 © Jonathan Rieke
4.5 © Åke E:son Lindman
4.6 © Alvar Aalto Foundation
4.7 © John Pawson

4.8 © Åke E:son Lindman
4.9 © Morley Von Sternberg/E. & M. Jones
4.10 © E. & M. Jones
4.11, 4.12 © Edward Jones
4.13 © Morley Von Sternberg/E. & M. Jones
4.14 © E. & M. Jones
4.15 © Louisiana Museum of Modern Art
4.16 © Kim Hansen/Louisiana Museum of Modern Art
4.17 © Bjarke Ørsted/Louisiana Museum of Modern Art
4.18 © W Bagge/Louisiana Museum of Modern Art
4.20 © Egen Samling/Fotograf Broendum & Co/ Louisiana Museum of Modern Art
4.21 © LOOK Die Bildagentur der Fotografen GmbH / Alamy
4.22 © Andrew Whitehead / Alamy
4.23 © Kerry Hill Architects
4.27, 4.28, 4.29, 4.30 © Urban Splash
4.32, 4.33, 4.34. 4.35 © Savills
4.36 Courtesy M .J. Long © RIBA Library Drawings & Archives Collection
4.37, 4.38, 4.39, 4.40 Photo © Ivor Smith/ © FLC/ ADAGP, Paris and DACS, London 2014.
4.41, 4.43 © FLC/ ADAGP, Paris and DACS, London 2014.
4.45 Photo © Chris Hellier / Alamy© FLC/ ADAGP, Paris and DACS, London 2014.
4.46, 4.47, 4.48, 4.49, 4.50 © The Aldo van Eyck Archive
4.51, 4.52, 4.53, 4.54 © Keith Hunter
4.55, 4.56, 4.57 © Benson + Forsyth
5.10 © Beurs Van Berlage
5.12 First Floor Plan, Class of 1945 Library, Phillips Exeter Academy. Architectural drawing. Boston: Ann Beha, 2014. Courtesy of Phillips Exeter Academy.
5.16 © Hopkins Architects
5.17, 5.18 © Arcaid Images / Alamy
5.19 © Constance Barrett
5.20 © Hopkins Architects
5.25 © Dod Miller / Alamy
5.26 © Niall McDiarmid / Alamy
5.28, 5.29 © VIEW Pictures Ltd / Alamy
5.30, 5.31 © John McAslan and Partners
5.35 © tony french / Alamy
5.36 © Brendan Howard / Shutterstock.com
5.37 © VIEW Pictures Ltd / Alamy
5.38 © Gareth Hoskins Architects
5.40 © Hemis / Alamy
5.41 © f11photo / Shutterstock.com
5.44 © David Ball / Alamy
5.45 © Skdiz/ Shutterstock.com
5.46 © Sailorr/ Shutterstock.com
5.47 © Glaoadare CC-BY-SA-3.0
5.48 © Rogers Stirk Harbour + Partners
5.52, 5.53 © I sifa Image Service s.r.o. / Alamy
5.54 Digital image © 2014 The Museum of Modern Art/Scala Florence/© DACS 2014.
5.55, 5.56, 5.57 © FLC/ ADAGP, Paris and DACS, London 2014.
5.58 © Learoyd/Cullinan Studio
5.59 © Richard Learoyd/Cullinan Studio
5.61, 5.62 © Cullinan Studio
5.64 © Martin Charles/Cullinan Studio
5.67 © Atelier Peter Zumthor & Partner
5.70 Photo Fregoso & Basalto.© Fondazione Renzo Piano
5.71 © Fondazione Renzo Piano
5.72, 5.73 Photo Fregoso & Basalto.© Fondazione Renzo Piano
6.8, 6.13 © Alvar Aalto Foundation
6.15 © Lynn Morales / Alamy
6.16 © Brandon Bourdages / Shutterstock.com
6.19 United States Geological Survey
6.22 © RIBA Library Photographs Collection
6.23, 6.24 © The Glasgow School of Art
6.25, 6.26, 6.27 © Michael Moran/Rafael Moneo
6.28 © Rafael Moneo
7.1 © Alvar Aalto Foundation

7.2 © Elizabeth Waytkus
7.3 © Alvar Aalto Foundation
7.4, 7.5 © Jonathan Rieke
7.6 © Alvar Aalto Foundation
8.1 © Morley Von Sternberg/Stanton Williams
8.2, 8.3, 8.4, 8.5, 8.6, 8.7 © Hufton+Crow/Stanton Williams
8.9, 8.10, 8.11 © Morley Von Sternberg/Stanton Williams
8.12, 8.13, 8.14 © Stanton Williams
8.15, 8.16, 8.17, 8.18 © Morley Von Sternberg/Stanton Williams
9.5 © FLC/ ADAGP, Paris and DACS, London 2014.
9.7 Photo © Duncan Standridge © FLC/ ADAGP, Paris and DACS, London 2014.
9.8 © FLC/ ADAGP, Paris and DACS, London 2014.
9.9 Photo © Paul Raftery / Alamy © FLC/ ADAGP, Paris and DACS, London 2014.
9.10 © Arcaid Images / Alamy
9.11 © FP Collection
9.15, 9.16 © Arcaid Images / Alamy
9.17 Courtesy M.J.Long © RIBA Library Drawings & Archives Collection
9.25 © The Glasgow School of Art
9.26 © Jonathan Oldenbuck (CC-By-SA-3.0)
9.27 © Dan Farrar
9.28 © Jens Weber
9.29 © VIEW Pictures Ltd / Alamy
10.1, 10.3 © Aldo van Eyck Archive
10.7, 10.8 © Herman Hertzberger
10.9, 10.10 © Miralles Tagliabue EMBT
10.21 © The National Trust Photolibrary / Alamy
10.22 © Arcaid Images / Alamy
10.23 © The National Trust Photolibrary / Alamy
10.24, 10.25 © Dennis Gilbert/NTPL/VIEW
10.27, 10.28 Courtesy Peter Blundell Jones/© DACS 2014.
10.29, 10.30 Akademie der Künste/© DACS 2014
10.31 © Hemis / Alamy
10.32 Courtesy Peter Blundell Jones/© DACS 2014.
10.33 © imageBROKER / Alamy
10.34, 10.35, 10.36 © Charles Correa
11.7 © Studio arch. Mario Botta
11.12 © Igor Shapovalov CC by 3.0
11.13 Courtesy Richard Weston /© DACS 2014.
11.14, 11.15 © Georg Mayer
11.18 Photo Ivor Smith © FLC/ ADAGP, Paris and DACS, London 2014.
11.19 © GlowImages / Alamy
11.20 © Brendan Delany/Istockphoto
11.22 © Sam Dcruz/Shutterstock.com
11.23 Historic American Building Survey AA
11.28 © Artedia/VIEW
11.29 Artwork © Succession H. Matisse/ DACS 2014. Photography © JACA BOOK - BAMS PHOTO.
11.31 ©INTERFOTO / Alamy
11.32 © Gareth Byrne / Alamy
11.33 © age fotostock Spain, S.L. / Alamy
11.34 Digital image© 2014 The Museum of Modern Art/Scala Florence© DACS 2014.
11.37, 11.38, 11.39, 11.40, 11.42 ©Tadao Ando
11.41 © Pictorium / Alamy
11.49 © Hemis / Alamy
11.51, 11.52, 11.53, © Peter Blundell Jones
11.54 © FP Collection
12.39, 12.40 © Studio Egret West
12.41, 12.42 © Urban Splash
12.43 © Studio Egret West